Making Arrangements

Making Arrangements

Inheriting a Family
Funeral Home Leads to Trouble

A Novel
Brent Eliot Parker

SANTA FE

Sunstone books may be purchased for educational, business, or sales promotional use.
For information please write: Special Markets Department, Sunstone Press,
P.O. Box 2321, Santa Fe, New Mexico 87504-2321.

Book and Cover design › Vicki Ahl
Body typeface › Garamond
Printed on acid-free paper
∞
eBook 978-1-61139-223-4

Library of Congress Cataloging-in-Publication Data

Parker, Brent Eliot, 1980-
  Making Arrangements : Inheriting a Family Funeral Home Leads to Trouble : a novel
/ by Brent Eliot Parker.
     pages cm
  ISBN 978-0-86534-982-7 (softcover : alk. paper)
  1. Funeral homes--Fiction. 2. Family-owned business enterprises--Fiction. I. Title.
  PS3616.A74423M35 2013
  813'.6--dc23
                        2013043433

WWW.SUNSTONEPRESS.COM
SUNSTONE PRESS / POST OFFICE BOX 2321 / SANTA FE, NM 87504-2321 /USA
(505) 988-4418 / ORDERS ONLY (800) 243-5644 / FAX (505) 988-1025

For my dad, Brent, and all other funeral directors and funeral home employees who take care of other families during their most serious time of need.

Preface

The funeral industry has been an important part of my life. My father, grandfather, and great-grandfather were all morticians, and they all owned their own funeral homes. My great-grandfather, Emmons Johnson, started working in the funeral industry in 1929. My grandfather, Jim Johnson, founded J.E. Johnson Funeral Home in Charleston in 1960. My father, Brent Parker, started working at J.E. Johnson Funeral Home as a part-time and then full-time employee before establishing Cunningham-Parker and Johnson Funeral Home in 1979. That funeral home is still owned and managed by my mother Tonya, myself, and my brother Evan today.

For most of my life, I watched my grandfather and father work in a profession that few people really understood. The death of a loved one is often a difficult and traumatic experience. The important role of the funeral director is to provide emotional support. It's when that moment of loss and grief arrive that a funeral home and funeral director become an important component in the grief and healing process for families.

My father considered it a real privilege to have the opportunity to walk with families and friends in the midst of their sadness. My dad always made sure to stop, observe, and listen and share. To him, every person that came through the funeral home was more than just a person or an individual. Over time, they became a part of his extended family.

Funeral directors have maturity and empathy that is unmatched in many professions. Like doctors, teachers, and emergency services personnel, funeral directors have a sensitivity and tact and an ability to work with grieving and distressed clients. My father was the best at doing all of those tasks, but he was also an excellent businessman, with a business acumen and attention to detail that I have never encountered from anyone else in any line of work. He worked hard, often working every weekend and every holiday, to serve families in need. Watching him as a professional taught me a great deal about work ethic, professionalism, and what it means to be someone who makes a difference in the lives of people every day.

Yet as time passes, the funeral industry is changing. Many funeral directors, like my father, came from the "baby-boomer" generation and they are now retiring from the profession of funeral service. Unfortunately, there are not as many willing and certified morticians entering the profession, which has created tumult for the survival of the traditional "family owned" funeral home.

Over the last 15 years, many national and international corporations have stepped into the space created from retiring funeral directors and offered to buy funeral homes from families who find themselves with nobody interested or certified to run the businesses. What has ensued is many funeral homes in cities and towns across the United States being run by a company from a large city. The name and location of the funeral home remain, but the quality of individual attention and service to grieving families decreases while the price of services sharply increases. Moreover, veteran funeral home employees who are part of the fabric of the locally owned funeral home are suddenly replaced with a staff operated and managed by the corporation and not the original family owners.

When my father died from pancreatic cancer in 2008, our family was faced with a decision. Who would continue owning and operating Cunningham-Parker-and Johnson Funeral Home? The question and issue of ownership succession was a scary one, and even though our family remained owners and operators of the firm, many funeral home families struggle with an answer to that question each day.

That question was the impetus for writing *Making Arrangements*. I relate well to Colin Madsen, the protagonist in the story, because I dealt with many of the same issues Colin faces when my father died. Like Colin, the choices made in those months after my father died impacted the funeral home in the short-term as well as the long-term. Also, like Colin, I encountered and became re-acquainted with people that had known my father and knew of his excellent reputation as a funeral director.

In this novel, Colin Madsen is in his mid-thirties when his father, Luke, dies. He has inherited the family funeral home, but he has no interest in the business. When Colin meets Ava, his childhood neighbor and friend, they begin a romance that neither had expected. Having both weathered some of life's storms, Ava and Colin seem like an ideal match. But when Ava switches from the teaching profession to corporate sales in the mortuary business, this seemingly innocent move sets off a chain reaction of problems and tensions which threaten the relationship and their future together. Colin and Ava keep discovering new things about themselves, and about each other. They are determined to find what is most important to them in life and the story is an interesting journey to follow that quest.

I started writing this book in late 2008, so I could still remain close to my father, who I missed very much and still do. It wasn't until the Summer of 2013 that I was able to finish the novel and, in some way, complete my own healing of grief over his death five years earlier.

This book is about family, loyalty, and how business decisions often have lasting personal implications on a variety of people. More importantly, I hope you will learn a bit about the funeral profession and about the dedicated and compassionate men and women who work tirelessly to help families during their greatest time of need and the pressures that family-owned funeral homes face from corporate buyers.

1

Colin shoved open the morgue doors.

A burst of cool air rushed at him. The narrow room, with its white-washed walls, emanated a brightness that made Colin flinch. A slender shadow, undetectable from a long distance, came into focus. Colin squinted as the halogen lamp, arched overhead, cast enough illumination to define the features of the figure.

Luke Madsen hardly noticed the intrusion. Luke repositioned himself, hovering a mere inches away from the metal operating table. He adjusted the wide-brimmed, clear plastic helmet covering his face.

"Hey, Dad."

"Hey, buddy," Luke replied.

As Colin approached his father, Luke looked away and located a file folder near the burgundy sink ledge, adjacent to the operating table. Picking up the folder, Luke began scribbling notes on the parchment document.

Colin loosened the tie around his neck and held his graduation robe tightly against his waist. "Uh, Dad...I didn't see you at graduation. Were you there?"

Luke stopped writing and stayed motionless for a moment. He began writing again. "No, we were busy. I tried getting away but we got a couple of calls this morning. As you know, son, our business makes us the first ones to respond and the last ones to leave."

Before Colin could speak, Luke cut him off.

"But I am real proud of you: the salutatorian of the Concord-Carlisle High School Class of 1995."

"I really wish you could've been there Dad. My friends and teachers all liked my speech. They said it really was moving and inspirational for the seniors."

"I'm sure it was," Luke said, inserting the paper into a manila file folder.

Luke lifted the mask lid from his face stepped aside, and leaned back, totally regarding his son for a moment. He waived a finger at Colin. "You'll make a good funeral director yet. You are comfortable wearing a tie and you look good in one."

Colin blushed. "I'm not so sure about that."

Luke motioned for Colin to approach the table. "You remember Julia Thomas. She owned the Main Streets Market and Café in Concord. Her daughter Amy was in a few of your elementary school classes at Alcott School."

"Whew. Dad, that was a long time ago."

Colin bent forward looked at Julia. Dressed in a beige dress, her bright red hair shined like a warning flare. Her face was square with unblemished skin. She had thick, full lips that were pursed outward and a taut, curvy physique. Her eyes were light blue and buoyant the corners, revealing a fragile, congenial innocence. Julia appeared angelic, situated comfortably on the table.

"She's really pretty,"Colin said softly.

"She always was, even as she got older. It's a shame what happened. She was having some bad back pain about a year ago and the doctor's found her ate up with cancer. Started in the pancreas and moved to the liver."

Colin felt his stomach churn at the thought. "Dad, there's something else I wanted to talk to you about…"

"Amy was in yesterday with her dad making arrangements. She told me that she's always had a crush on you." Luke playfully elbowed Colin in the ribs a few times. "She's really pretty too, just like Julia. I will have to introduce you to her at the visitation tomorrow evening. By the way, did you tell Amos and Paula that you could work?"

"That's what I wanted to talk to you about, Dad."

"Oh," Luke replied. "Well, that's fine if you have something else to do. It will probably be a small visitation anyway, so we can get along fine without you, I think."

Colin tapped his foot as thoughts raced in his mind. He had rehearsed the speech several times, but now that the moment had arrived, all Colin could do was tap his foot nervously as he searched for the right words.

Luke walked back across the morgue table and opened a cabinet drawer, removing a small, stout glass jar along with a fluffy, flat white pad. Luke unscrewed the cap and slapped a powdery white chalk on his hands. Walking around the table again, Luke now stood prominently over Julia.

"I hope this powder is enough," Luke said. "Sometimes getting the hands just right is difficult no matter how much powder you use."

The morgue doors opened again. Amos and Paula filled the space. Amos, with his stooped shoulders and disheveled blue shirt and red tie, crossed his arms while Paula, looking like a tall drink of water poured into a power suit, clutched a file folder.

"Aye, Colin. Congratulations on your graduation. We're proud of ya."

"Yes we are," Paula added.

"Thanks guys," Colin replied somewhat sheepishly as he turned again to face Luke.

"I don't mean to interrupt," Amos continued, "but the Thomas family will be here in a little bit. They have some pictures and things they want us to arrange for them in the chapel before the visitation tomorrow and Owen called. He's on a date with some girl at Sorellina's in Boston and his credit card is inactive."

Luke nodded. "Call Sorellina's and give them the other credit card number. Paula can unlock the file cabinet in the arrangement office and get the card for you."

"And we just got a call," Paula added. "A John Freeman just died up at Emerson Hospital. I found his file. He was pre-arranged."

Luke cut a sharp glance at Colin. "Can you go to the hospital and pick him up?"

"I can't Dad. I got an offer for an internship at Pricewaterhouse Coopers in Boston. I'm going to take it. It lasts from May until August and then I will start school at Boston College in September. They want me to start tomorrow."

Colin was a bit surprised how quickly the words spilled from his mouth. Luke stopped powdering Julia's hands and stood upright.

Paula gasped slightly and Amos remained silent. Luke removed the helmet. The mint green lab jacket seemed to cling to Luke. His fair hair, sharp chin and brown eyes pierced the silence that gripped the room.

Luke took two deep breaths, crinkling his white dress shirt and purple tie, and leaned his slight frame against the morgue table.

Colin waited for his father to respond. He looked back at Paula, who was staring intently at the floor while a strangled smile crept across Amos's face. Luke held a stoic look at Colin for a few more moments, then spun around and faced the door.

"Thank you, Amos," he said dryly. Luke sliced the air with an index finger next at Paula. "Paula, call the hospital. As soon as I get cleaned up here I'll head up there."

As Amos and Paula disappeared and the morgue doors closed behind him, Colin was prepared to explain. "Dad, I'm sorry to be telling you this now, but I got the offer a few weeks ago and Mr. Burdette, my guidance counselor, thinks it will be a great opportunity for me."

Luke began removing the lab jacket. "When did you plan on telling me this?"

"I tried too, Dad. A few weeks ago. We were going to go to eat dinner at the Colonial Inn. Remember? I was going to tell you then, but you got two death calls and were gone for most of the night. I got busy with getting ready for graduation and I just forgot about it."

"That seems like a pretty big announcement to forget about."

Luke removed and hung up the lab jacket on a rusted metal hook that dangled from the wall just past the morgue table. He strode in short strides to the other side of the room and put the powder back in the cabinet and began washing his hands, avoiding eye contact with his son.

"PricewaterhouseCoopers is one of the premier accounting firms in the state. I can make some important contacts there and it will look really good on my resume when I start in the Accounting program at B.C."

Luke shook his hands over the small sink, removing any loose water droplets before grabbing a paper towel. "The state of Massachusetts requires 60 college credit hours before you can go to mortuary school. You can take plenty of accounting courses at B.C. and then come back and help us out. We could really use the accounting help here. Amos is usually too busy to fool with it and you know how I am with Math."

"I'm not sure this is what I want to do with my life," Colin said. "This is your business and your life."

Those words seemed to echo in the morgue. Colin stuffed his hands in his pockets and began shifting his weight from foot to foot. The morgue suddenly felt colder and smaller than usual. Luke took extra time drying his hands, crumpling the paper towel forcefully and slamming the soppy wad into the trashcan in the corner of the morgue. The thud of the wet ball hitting the bottom of the can made Colin flinch.

Luke walked back over to the body of Julia Thomas. He peered at her hands more closely. "Good. The powder set well."

Colin removed his hands and flung his arms into the air. "Dad, we can't resolve this if you just keep shifting the focus of the conversation."

"It sounds to me like you've already resolved it," Luke replied. His mouth formed a thin line.

"Well, I guess we're done then." Colin grabbed the knob and flung the door back in a fit of frustration that vibrated the wall. The whole room seemed to absorb it for a moment.

Colin had managed to make it into the hallway before he froze and craned his neck to the ceiling.

The door to the arrangement office across the hallway was open and he could hear a quiet conversation between Paula and Amos. "Be sure and tell Owen to write down the three numbers on the back of the card correctly or they won't be able to run it," Paula instructed. Colin imagined Amos nodding in his usual quiet and thoughtful way.

"Just a minute," Luke commanded from behind Colin.

Turning around, Colin faced his father. With hands on both hips, Luke slightly licked his dry lips. The motion made his deep-set brown eyes twinkle and the shimmer accentuated the dark hue. He rested both warm hands on Colin's shoulders.

"Ever since you were fifteen, you have assisted me and Amos and Paula in any way-getting cars lined up, helping me in the chapel and morgue, setting up flowers, directing people at the cemetery, helping to dress and casket bodies. When we've been busy, we couldn't have made it without you."

Colin let out a small breath as he studied his father. A forehead set with deep ridges and fleshy bags under both eyes is all Colin could focus on, choosing to remain silent. His father smelled clean, like dial soap.

"You need to remember that your great-grandfather was a funeral director, so was your grandfather. This funeral home is a part of the Madsen family legacy and you will always have a connection to this place."

Colin had those memories as a little boy, being with his father while he was working and watching him and Amos dress and casket bodies, quietly and reverently. Even at a young age, before Colin could explain the importance of that kind of work, he knew it was something very significant and essential.

"You understand what I'm saying son?" Luke asked.

Colin nodded, and then felt his stomach lilt with guilt. As Colin titled his head, he felt the smooth fingertips of his father slide under his chin, retrieving his downcast gaze.

"Son, I'm proud of you and I want you to do what makes you happy. If you want to pursue that internship before starting school in the fall, then I want you to go for it. Just remember to do your best and give it everything you have." Luke slapped Colin's shoulders twice. "Just remember, Madsen Funeral Home will always be here for you."

"I will Dad. I will remember."

Colin flashed a toothy smile and turned back into the hallway, relieved. Amos and Paula reappeared from the arrangement office, grinning satisfactorily when they saw him.

As Amos reached an arm around Colin and ushered him up the hallway, Luke called from behind them.

"Colin?"

"Yeah, Dad?"

"I love you, son. Don't forget that, either."

2

Colin closes his eyes and takes a deep breath. Standing in front of the Sleepy Hollow cemetery gate, Colin looked to the East, watching the early morning sun fracture the frozen sky into a kaleidoscope of color, with dark reds and fiery orange streaks of light making a temporary imprint above the cemetery ridge.

Stepping closer to the gate, he notices the flecks of faded paint and rust dangling from the rod-iron bars. Unlatching it, he steps on the narrow paved road and scanned the grounds. The small, sloped cemetery inside the fence has an aura of hallowed ground. Colin doesn't know if each grave holds the life of someone important, or someone who was special to someone else.

Seven erect tombs on the western side of the cemetery have inscriptions on the doors. The tomb doors were open, debris rising up covering the entryway to most of them.

He lets out a long sigh.

In proceeding towards Luke's grave, the air feels heavy on his lungs, forcing heavy breathing. Colin looks around, observing other broken gravestones, some extremely old and dilapidated. Those graves are speckled with a granular substance, making them difficult to interpret or read. The cemetery ground buckles slightly under his feet. Colin smells nothing, other than the cold, still, calm air. As he approaches the grave, his steps grow smaller.

Finally, the grave marker comes into focus. The flat, pewter headstone at the base of his grave is decorated with ornate marble lettering declaring this place to be the final resting place of Luke Madsen.

Dropping to his knees, Colin rests his trembling hands on the ground, while his soured stomach tumbles around, making him momentarily woozy. He reaches into his jacket pocket and removes the deed and "intent to sell" forms. He clutches them tightly in his hand, while staring at the name of his father on the headstone. Colin closes his eyes, trying to picture Luke at the funeral home and his reaction to it being sold.

In that moment, Colin recounts how Luke knew everyone. Colin could ask him anything about any family member in town and he could tell me who their parents are, who they are married to, what they do as an occupation, and if their parents are still living. Luke put the community first, and they loved him. The Madsen home would be filled at Christmas time with succulent, mouth-watering cakes, pies, and candies from many of the widowed women in town or the surviving children or grandchildren of the parents Luke helped bury over the years. They gushed about him, and Colin and his father, along with Owen could never go anyplace without Luke running into someone he knew.

Colin opens his eyes. Tears began trickling down his cheeks. Colin thinks about the house having a telephone in each room, including the bathroom. It would ring constantly, especially at night when a doctor or hospital or family member would place the death call. Luke missed plenty of holiday dinners, Sunday church services, and many anniversaries because he was busy comforting grieving families. Sometimes, Colin would talk about Luke and it was as if we were speaking about a mythical figure or someone part of an urban legend. He never understood why his Dad spent so much time there. He always said it mattered. Luke was always at work.

Colin brushes away the tears. "Dad, I wish you would just tell me what to do."

The words hung in the icy air. Colin extends a hand, and traces the letters of his name. Luke loved cemeteries because of the serenity and respect they commanded. He brought so many families to these places. Luke often told Colin as a child to not be fearful of cemeteries, for they keep our loved ones safe once they die.

If you trace the letters with your fingers, you will never forget their names and their importance in your life...

Colin mumbles the expression aloud as he outlines the letters on the gravestone. Colin bows his head and begins to pray silently, seeking some divine guidance to help him with the decision to sell or keep the Madsen Funeral Home as a locally owned and operated family funeral home.

As Colin prays, he hears something heavy collapsing behind him. Turning around, he notices a woman kneeling in front of a headstone, two rows behind him. Intrigued and curious, his eyes narrow on her. With low hanging bangs, flowing red hair and black-rimmed glasses, the woman stared ahead with an expression both wary and challenging.

Dressed in jeans and sneakers clad in a blue windbreaker, the woman appeared underdressed for the occasion and overdressed for the weather.

The woman weeps heavily. Colin watches her rest an open hand on the surface as she caresses it with the other hand.

Then, she falls back. Colin winces and waits for another sound. Instead, he hears a slight wind sliding through the cemetery. He stands up and takes long strides towards her. As Colin gets closer, he can see the woman stumble and pull herself upright.

Colin sees her ruddy eyes and tear-stained cheeks. The wind tosses her hair over her shoulder. The ascending sunlight spreads across her, creating a large shadow that hides parts of her frail physique.

The woman regards him for a moment, turns and walks away, not a word passing between them. When Colin turns back to face Luke's grave, something else occupies the vacated space in front of the headstone. Colin notices a man swivel back and forth in front of the headstone. The man steadies himself after several moments of listless movement, and then stops moving altogether.

Colin approaches, cautiously. From behind, the man had an elongated frame with a narrow waist. He wears a faded denim baseball cap pulled tightly over his head, only revealing the bottom lobes of his ears. Thick tufts of salt and pepper hair jut out from under the base of the hat and the scraggly arrangement of the air made his entire head seem larger than the rest of his body. The man wears a faded navy blue coat that had old and fresh dirt stains splattered throughout the surface of the coat and dark brown stains encircling the knees of his faded jeans.

As Colin steps closer, the man inhales and exhales a long, deep breath.

"I'll be out of your way in a minute," he said. The man went back to swaying back and forth, rummaging through a bag of tools, cleaners, and rags.

The statement hung in the air for a moment. Colin couldn't speak. Instead, the smell of fresh dirt and lemon-scented cleaning solution permeated his nostrils. Colin reaches into a pocket and pulled out a handkerchief and dabbed his running nose.

"Um, can I help you with something?" Colin asked.

The man stopped moving again. He stepped back, turned on the balls of his feet, and faced Colin. With narrow eyes and thin lips pressed tightly against his face, he flared his nostrils in response.

"I should ask you if I can help you with something."

Colin stepped back and furrowed his brow. *I am in no mood for a game of verbal jousting,* Colin thought to himself.

"This is my father's grave," Colin replied primly, assuming the man was in the wrong place.

"I know that, young Colin Madsen."

Colin blinked twice as the man looked back at him. Colin studied the man as his face softened and eyes widened. Colin could see his steely blue eyes searching him, trying to ascertain the next move.

Colin coughed. "How do you know my name?" He leaned in. "And who are you? I come here quite a bit and I've never seen you at this cemetery before."

The man nodded. "My name's James and I am one of the caretakers of the cemetery."

The man slowly lifted his arms. Colin wondered what he might do next.

Colin felt a moment of calm come over him while his cheeks burned with embarrassment. The air had grown still again.

"Each week, I come out and polish the tombstones. I start at the back and move my way to the front." He winked at Colin. "I start with your daddy's first."

"Why? There are so many headstones and graves here. Some in pretty bad shape. Why does my father get special treatment?"

"Because, your daddy was a good man," James replied. "You might not know this, but a lot of the people buried here came up here with your father." James scoured the cemetery and nodded in different directions. "The Holmes family is buried over there, Henry and Mabel Thaxton over there, the Baileys just near the fence."

"Wait," Colin interrupted. "I still don't understand."

"Your daddy helped so many families say goodbye to their loved ones," James said, pressing his lips against his face. "He was especially kind. So many people he helped comfort. Also those people I mentioned, your daddy was here when we buried them. He was here with their families to comfort them."

James stood back and looked Colin up and down. "Yep, you were too young to remember a lot of it, although you look just like you did in those pictures that he showed everybody. He sure was proud of you. Of course, you're older now. Anyhow, that's why you're here, ain't it, to spend some time with your daddy?"

James's comments froze Colin. The silence continued but Colin chose to end it.

"Yes, yes. I guess. But I still don't understand why you chose Dad's headstone first?"

"He's worth it."

For the first time since the discussion began James stepped aside and Colin looked down. The granite headstone was a rich shining black in the sunlight. The block letters carved across the front appeared polished and it gave them a look of royalty, as if a king resided there.

Colin didn't know what to say. Transfixed on the clean, shiny headstone, he forgot for a moment that James was still there.

Colin prepared to thank him for his kindness, but only managed an impish smile.

"Come with me," James said.

James walked away from Colin and headed to the middle of the cemetery, a mere 30 yards from Luke's grave. James dropped to his knees and began the same rhythmic swivel motion that Colin witnessed earlier.

They had come upon two shallow graves with flat rectangular headstones. The metal was chipped and the lettering identifying each plot had faded some. A small bug crawled over the chipped edge of the tombstone. Seeing it, James flicked it away.

James pointed down at the graves. "My mama and daddy are buried here," he said, his voice sounding knotted. "I lost them both at one time in a car accident. I thought I wouldn't make it through the funeral. When they put their caskets into the ground, I fell down, crying for hours. Your daddy stayed with me until I was ready to leave. I reckon we was here for about five hours or so after the funeral."

He looked down at the grave. "Your daddy didn't say much to me, but as an only child who had lost his parents, I knew I wasn't alone. He took care of me and I will always make sure, as long as I'm responsible for these grounds, to take care of him."

James rested his hands on his hips, while the earnestness in his eyes accentuated the deep grooves in his face. "Your daddy didn't work with dead people. He worked with living people."

A slicing wind cut through the cemetery again, rustling the wet, mashed grass. Colin lifted one foot and planted it firmly on the ground. James rolled the opaque bottle in his hand, the cleaning solution bubbling and rocking slowly. James leaned forward, nodded slowly at Colin, indicating the conversation was over.

As he walked away, Colin called out to him. "James?"

James fiddled with the belt on his pants and pulled them up. "Yeah?"

"I have a decision to make...a pretty big decision. It concerns the funeral home." Colin paused and made a sweeping gesture with one arm. "And some of what has happened here. I don't know when to finalize the decision. I mean, when it will be the right time to finalize it."

James turned to Colin, casting a longing glance across the cemetery before settling another look on Colin.

"Well, every decision in life is tough. Look to yourself. When the time comes, you'll know what to do. I promise you, you'll know what to do."

3

Colin woke to a chilly room. The visit to the cemetery, the conversation with James and the pending decision led to a fitful, restless night of sleep. Colin sat up, groaning as the previously relaxed muscles in his back tightened and became tense, compressing his ribs slightly together and siphoning off a small puff of air from his lungs. Looking around the room, Colin rubbed his swollen eyes with the knuckles of both hands. Sleep-smeared, he blinked hard twice and chuckled.

His father had been dead a year. Colin was alone on Christmas Eve in his boyhood home in the small town of Reading, Massachusetts. After being away for so long, he was now suffering from insomnia. He slipped into his clothes and went downstairs to make coffee. The old house seemed to welcome him with every familiar creak of the steps.

Colin sat down at the kitchen table with his coffee and picked up the deed to the the Madsen Funeral Home. He had left it there last night after he read it over once more trying to decide the future of the family funeral home. He set his mug down and began pacing across the floor. His problem this Christmas Eve morning was edging out any spirit of the season he might have felt. Outside the bare trees stood stark against the gray morning. When he heard a church bell tolling he put the deed down and began to reminisce. He needed a diversion from the problem that lay heavy on his heart.

The issue facing him was that he had to decide in the next thirty days whether or not to keep the business. If he decided to not pay the back taxes owed and relinquished it, the state would allow the building and the property to be purchased by someone else. He was troubled with the decision because although he didn't want to be a mortician, his father had been well respected and loved in the town. If Colin let the place go to the state, or someone else, he'd be left with the gnawing feeling that he was betraying his father's memory. Or perhaps more to the point, he would be betraying his father's legacy which had been earned by his kind and caring ways towards his patrons and neighbors.

A light blanket of snow covered the ground and a weak sun filtered through the gray clouds as Colin gazed forlornly out the wide bay window in the living room. Although the mean Yankee winter had not hit them yet, it was cold. Nonetheless he decided to walk to the business, so he put on his parka, slipped a scarf around his neck and stepped out into the brisk morning. He hadn't been gone so long that he didn't still know the neighbors. The neighbor to his right, old Mrs. Ogden, was leaving for church as he passed.

She called out to him, "Good morning, Colin, Merry Christmas."

He waved to her. "Good morning, Mrs. Ogden. Merry Christmas to you." He walked along the street he knew so well, passing many duplicate houses; white clapboard with black shutters sitting close to the street in the Colonial style. After he had covered a couple of blocks he arrived in the center of town. Deciding he was hungry he stopped into a familiar diner, the Old Town.

He fondly remembered that as a high school student it was a great place to hang out with your friends and make a cup of coffee last two hours. The diner wasn't busy yet. It was toasty warm inside and especially welcoming in the frosty morning. He immediately recognized one of the waitresses, Mrs. Kelly, who beamed when she spotted him.

"Why if it isn't young Colin ! How are ye, lad? Merry Christmas to you."

Colin sat down and took off his scarf. "Good morning and Merry Christmas to you, Mrs. Kelly."

"Are you back in town or what?"

"No, just here to settle some family business."

Always nosy, Mrs. Kelly said, "Something to do with the funeral parlor?"

"Yes it does, Mrs. Kelly. I have to decide whether to keep it or not."

"Oh Lord, ya dad was such a wonderful man. Lots of people in this town remember his caring ways. Bless him."

Colin ordered ham, eggs, toast, and coffee, chatting with the old lady as he ate. Done, he bid Mrs. Kelley goodbye and stepped out into the chilly morning air again.

He was feeling full and content as he continued through the quaint town center. It was decorated for Christmas, the epitome of festive. Wreaths and laurels hung everywhere while paper snowflakes covered storefront windows. The statues of Revolutionary War heroes and an old cannon in the square let the visitor know he was in New England. Just outside of the center he came to the Madsen Funeral Home. The building itself was pre-Civil War and had the gables and turrets to prove it. Colin let himself in the front door. It was quiet. But he knew the funeral home business did not take holidays off so he guessed someone was working.

He looked around. Colin's dad never wanted his business to be cutting edge or ultra-modern and he kept it small town rustic right down to the beams in the chapel ceiling. His footsteps echoed as he passed through the outer parlor to the office. Amos met him there. Amos was his father's longest employee and most loyal friend. The man's face lit up at the sight of Colin. "Colin my boy. We didn't even know you were home."

"How are you, Amos?"

"Fine, just fine. Trying to finish up downstairs for a showing tomorrow. Terrible thing, a man dying so close to Christmas Eve. Young man with a family too. They delivered him here earlier. I had to come down to let them in."

"Anybody else here?"

"No. No need to interrupt anyone else's Christmas. All that's needed is me," Amos said. "Let's go into the office. I have some coffee brewing."

Colin was over caffeinated but didn't want to decline. Coffee meant conversation and camaraderie and he needed that now. He sat and watched as Amos fetched the cups.

Amos was tall and whippet thin. He still had his hair, a mane of silver now. His long Yankee face wore every wrinkle as a milestone of his life. From sturdy New England stock he and his family traced their roots back to the early settlers. As he served the coffee he asked, "Are you here for the reason I'm thinking?"

"Amos, I'm afraid I am. I've never been so....so..."

"Confused?"

"Yeah you could say that. I never had any interest in the business and now it's as if my dad is telling me from the beyond the grave that this place is mine."

Amos sipped some coffee. "I can see how you are struggling, son, but it's a lonely decision. I'm glad you're back. This business belongs to you."

Amos motioned to a pile of mail on the desk. "I'm glad you want it because others want it. There's a letter there from Hamilton National. It's been here for a few months."

Colin repeated the name, "Hamilton National?"

"Aye. You know, the big national funeral home chain. You know what that's about."

"Yeah I can guess," Colin said with a twinge of sadness. "Do I need to ask you how you feel about it, Amos?"

"I don't think so. I'm like an old fixture. I've been here so long I can't picture myself anywhere else. Me and your dad started together at this place back in the day and earlier I thought it might be going. Sad thing. End of something. But I don't have to worry about it now that you've come home."

Colin waxed philosophical. "Yeah. It's the nature of things. I just have to try to honor Dad's legacy while still doing the right thing."

Amos shrugged. "I guess I wouldn't want the decision you had to make, no matter what my personal feelings about it are."

They sat in the quiet morning and listened to the big grandfather clock tick. Amos said, "Are you open for suggestions regarding a next step?"

"Sure."

"Well how about sticking around and watching things for a few days, get the feel of what's going on here. Then I think you'll feel better about your decision."

Colin smiled, relieved. "You know, Amos, I could always count on you to make a good call. I think I'll just do that."

Amos lifted his mug of coffee with a knowing wink and they toasted the idea.

4

Before the funeral concluded, Amos placed Colin near the rear doors of the chapel.

In his mind, Colin repeated the instructions: "When the minister's done, I'll ask the room to stand. The pallbearers will come in from the side family room and gather with me around the casket. The minister will lead us first, followed by the casket. You make sure nobody blocks the doorway. Paula will help the crowd go out the doors near the side of the chapel."

It seemed simple enough, though Colin knew Amos was using jargon and procedures that he didn't quite understand.

Colin tugged at his red tie and the large knot he had created. It felt like someone had tied a heavy rock around his neck and placed the stone right near his Adam's apple. Wearing a tie for him was an anomaly, especially because the president at Feeley and Driscoll in Boston preferred a casual dress policy for employees.

Colin took in the view of the cathedral chapel, beautifully appointed with off-white walls and padded bench seating. He imagined the chapel could seat around 150, depending on the number of people in each row. The goldenrod carpet was thick under his feet. The whole chapel felt warm and home-like, reminiscent of being in a living room.

Even the casket seemed like a centerpiece someone would stage in their living room. The casket was made of beautiful cherry veneer and gold trim accents. The detailed casket corners, high domed top and swinging solid wood bars made a beautiful impression.

The short, portly minister asked for the attendees to repeat with him *Amen,* which they did in unison. In the corridor outside the chapel, Paula motioned for Colin to enter the side doors. Colin entered as the canned music played softly overhead. The minister shuffled away from the podium before collecting himself near the casket. Amos emerged from the side, whispered something to the pallbearers and then asked the people rustling quietly in their seats to stand.

The pallbearers emerged from the side family room; an accordion of heights, sizes, shapes and ages. Amos and a waifish young man secured the casket from each end, turned it sideways, and pulled. The minister nearly missed his cue and slipped in front of the moving casket before he was squeezed against a chapel pew. Colin smirked, wondering what that would look like to the attendees.

As Amos and the men made their way to the rear of the chapel, Colin observed two of the pallbearers in a hushed exchange. One pallbearer was tall and broad-shouldered and he frowned, pulling one side of his lip back and tight against his face. The other pallbearer who was slightly more diminutive than the other one had a wide nose and sharp chin. He jerked his head back slightly and frowned, almost as if he were daring the other pallbearer to step out of line and come over to do something about it.

Paula entered the chapel and stood between pews, allowing the rows to leave the chapel one by one. Amos opened the rear doors. A stiff wind burst in the room from outside. Colin could see Amos looking at him; his gray eyes dark and poignant. Amos took a deep breath and then commanded softly, but firmly, "Gentlemen, lift straight up on the casket and hold your positions." They did as instructed, and the two end pallbearers were locked in a stare with each other that did not break as they lifted the casket.

"All right, gentlemen," Amos continued in a deep voice, "follow me and Reverend Newman here to the hearse and we'll load the casket."

The group moved slowly and methodically past Colin. For the first time, one of the pallbearers Colin had been watching caught him staring. He scrunched his face and gave Colin a pointed look. Colin glanced away quickly, but heard the other pallbearer say "Granny never liked you Chris, you fuckin' hilljack."

Chris jutted his chin. "You're such a prick, Eric."

The casket and men disappeared around the corner. The chapel emptied quickly and Paula returned, moving between the pews with determination. "Colin, grab the flowers by the podium and carry them to the hearse. Amos wants you to ride with him to the cemetery."

Her comment caught him by surprise. "He didn't mention that to me earlier."

Paula whipped her head around. "Amos wants you to experience an entire funeral. The casket isn't loaded into the hearse for posterity."

After Colin collected the flowers, he gathered his coat, gloves, and earmuffs and walked outside and around the funeral home. Despite the bitter cold, Colin liked winter, mainly because there is much less standing between the heavens and earth in winter. The dry air, frigid and clear, allowed Colin to breathe in the sky in its purest form. Colin looked up, wondering if he could see his father through the thin cloud cover. He missed him, and hoped his exercises as a pseudo employee would help make his decision easier.

Amos looked like a stuffed animal in his heavy trench coat and gloves as he motioned for Colin to come around the vehicle. He opened the hearse door without saying a word.

He removed his gloves and blew into his hands and slapped them together. "Going to be a cold trip to the cemetery today, lad."

After Amos started the engine, Colin reached toward the dashboard and turned on the heat. "Where are we going exactly? I don't know too many other cemeteries other than Sleepy Hollow, where Dad is buried."

Amos moved his seat back. "We're heading to South Burying Place, all the way near the back of the cemetery. I'm glad we've got some strong pallbearers because the hearse can only go in so far. We'll have to carry Mrs. Ellison the rest of the way."

Colin wanted to tell Amos about the exchange between the two pallbearers in the chapel, but wondered if it was his place to say anything.

The engine revved and then purred as Reverend Newman and the rest of the processional followed behind the hearse. "I take my time here, Colin. Every processional moves at its own pace and you can't always let the number of cars behind you determine the speed of it."

Colin interlaced his hands and crossed his feet. The hearse went onto Concord Turnpike for a short time and then turned onto Main Street. As the hearse began moving at a slightly faster pace, the buildings and people of Concord whisked by in streaks of colored blurs. What Colin liked most about Concord was something he never saw in Boston: quiet, tree-lined streets with big, old homes, classic town commons and enough attractions to please the most dedicated purveyor of small-town charm set against a Colonial backdrop.

Amos sat up in the seat, gripping the steering wheel a bit tighter. The hearse cabin was warm, and Cullen felt his eyes get a bit heavy.

A block and a half down Main Street, near Keyes Road, is the South Burying Place. Amos looked sideways at Colin. "You know much about South Burying Place?" Amos asked. "They also call it the Main Street Burying Ground."

Colin looked out the window as they passed the entrance to the cemetery. "I can remember Dad talking about coming here once in a while, but that's about it."

"It has three hundred graves; its oldest stone is dated back to sixteen hundred seven. It supposedly got the name South Burying Place because of a belief that a body set for burial should not be carried across a stream for fear its soul might be washed away."

Colin perked up a bit. "That would make for a great ghost story."

"Aye," Amos said. "But we don't tell that to the families we serve. It might make them a bit nervous, if you know what I mean." Amos winked at Colin.

The narrow paved path began to disappear in front of the hearse as they passed the entrance gate. "The cemetery is the resting place for thirteen veterans of the Revolutionary War. The headstones that mark the graves were destroyed by a hurricane in nineteen thirty-eight, then rebuilt sometime later."

Colin leaned against the door, studying Amos for a moment. "How do you know all this, Amos?"

Amos brought the hearse to a halt and put the vehicle in park. He let out a hearty laugh. "I didn't care for much for it, but Luke loved all of the history about cemeteries. When I think about him filling my mind with the details, it really brings back many good memories."

"You really miss him, don't you?" Colin asked.

Amos unbuckled his seatbelt and let out a sad sigh. "I do, Colin. Very much."

"I do too, Amos."

As both men stepped out of the hearse, Amos called to Colin. "I am going to organize the pallbearers and bring them to the rear of the coach. You get the door open and make sure everyone remains behind us."

"Uh, okay," Colin called back, unsure if Amos could hear him.

"Oh," Amos added. "Watch Reverend Newman. He likes to wander."

The sarcastic and slightly irritated way Amos said 'wander' made Colin grin. Colin did as instructed, and soon the pallbearers had reclaimed their earlier positions on both sides of the casket as Amos pulled it toward them. Chris and Eric kept giving one another furtive glances as they mumbled to each other, but Colin could not make out the words.

The men shuffled their feet as they carried the casket. The South Burying Place cemetery smelled of winter: wet leaves, snowflakes, and frozen tree bark. The trek to the cemetery was tedious. Revered Newman, walking with a slight list in his gait, was shivering. Amos looked back at Eric and Chris. "Lift up and hold the casket steady and try not to let the back of it dip towards the ground." They grunted and lifted the end of the casket higher.

The group climbed a steep embankment, walking as fast as Reverend Newman could lead. Several of the men where wheezing a bit and coughing from the exertion.

Reaching their destination, Amos stood at the end of a steel mesh grid, which covered the deep grave. "Set it down easy boys...that's it."

Chris nearly slipped on the green skirt surrounding the grave. "Shit," he sniped, drawing a disapproving glare from Eric. As the casket lay on the grid and the men stepped back to join their families, Eric attempted to punch Chris on the shoulder, missing as Chris dodged the gesture. Both men froze and stared at each other intently, before an over exaggerated cough by Amos broke them up.

Reverend Newman assumed his place at the head of the casket and began quoting scripture from the Bible. Colin stuffed his hands in his pockets. He recognized the words as the Old Testament, though he was unsure of the specific verse. Colin observed some of the family and close friends huddled together around the casket, sobbing quietly and offering loving embraces to one another. Eric and Chris stood on the outside of the group, away from each other, staring blankly out at the cemetery, as if nothing was happening.

Surrounding the committal, tree branches sagged under the weight of snow cover. Other branches appeared brittle in the frozen air, some snapping around them while Reverend Newman offered a word of prayer. To Colin, the trees seemed dead, but like everyone else, holding its breath for spring.

"Amen and amen," Reverend Newman said, smiling impishly at the family as he backed away from the grave. Amos stood beside Colin.

"Walk back with the family and make sure everyone gets back to their cars safely. We don't want any of Mrs. Ellison's family slipping and getting hurt."

Colin rustled his hands in his pockets and assessed the crowd: the older women wiping away tears from their frozen cheeks, their husbands remaining close and everyone trying to walk away from the grave gingerly, moving back down the cemetery slope.

As instructed, Colin lagged behind and scanned the group several times, ensuring nobody fell. By the time everyone reached the bottom of the hill, a small group had broken away from the larger group. At the center of the circle were Eric and Chris.

"Granny left me more money than you in her will!" Eric barked. "That's because I'm going to college and you'll just go back to Vermont and play video games all day."

"I don't care about the money. Besides, she loved us both, you ass!" Chris retorted. "You've been on me since I came here and I've had enough of your mouth!"

A middle-aged woman, who Colin presumed was their mother, stepped in to intervene, but Eric and Chris stepped closer to each other.

Baffled, Colin stood motionless for a moment, then tried to take action.

"Folks, we really need to get back to the cars. The service is over. It's really cold out here...we don't want anyone to get hurt."

Eric and Chris must have heard the word *hurt*, because Chris clenched a fist and reared back. "Oh, I'm going to do something about it all right. I'm going to do something about it right now!"

Eric flinched, but the fist landed squarely on the bridge of his nose. The loud snap that followed was reminiscent of the breaking branches heard near the grave.

A stream of blood sprayed into the air, followed by the screams and gasps from onlookers. Colin watched Eric reach forward and grab Chris by the hair and both men fell into the circle of onlookers and disappeared.

5

Colin collapsed into a chair in the family waiting room and rubbed his hands together.

Paula approached with a warm cup of coffee. Colin extended his arm and Paula gently placed the cup in his hand and wrapped his fingers around the mug.

"You don't want those to get frostbite," Paula said softly, as Amos entered the room.

Paula stood and rested her hands on both hips. "And?"

Amos rested his own cup of coffee on the edge of the desk as a wisp of damp hair hovered above an eyebrow. "I just got off the phone with Sandra Ellison, the mother of those two ill-mannered young men. Eric, the younger lad has a broken nose, but otherwise is fine. She wanted me to apologize to you both for her sons' behavior."

Colin watched Paula straighten her posture. "Serves him right. There is no sense to behave like that at a funeral. That is not the time or the place to argue. What's wrong with people?"

Colin pursed his lips and rested them against the rim of the cup as steam rose in wisps. The heat felt good on his chapped lips. After taking a sip, he settled back into the chair. "How often does that happen? I'm with Paula, that is a terrible moment to fight with someone."

Amos shrugged. "Families are certainly different today. Sometimes when the head of a family like a grandmother passes away, and she was the person that kept the family united, you see things start to fall apart."

Paula scoffed. "What were those two fighting about in the first place?"

"Money," Colin interjected, smacking his lips after taking a generous sip of warm coffee. "One of them said that granny left him more money or something like that." Colin stared at the coffee for a moment before taking another sip.

"Ridiculous," Paula replied. "Money isn't everything."

Amos chuckled. "Families are complicated things."

Colin saw Amos collecting loose slips of bright pink paper from the tray on the desk that said *Messages*.

Colin set the coffee cup aside, stood up and stretched. "My boss in Boston always says, 'Madsen, it's not always about money, but 99.9% of the time it is.'" He laughed at the cleverness of the statement, but looked up to find Paula glaring at him with arms crossed as Amos rustled the messages. Paula then waved away the comment.

"We need more accountants like we need more trial lawyers," she said, walking between Colin and Amos into the back hallway.

Amos stepped back and filled the doorway space. "Colin, I'm going back to the arrangement office to return some phone calls. We are quiet for now, but today is Thursday and that usually starts our week around here. Oh, I hope today didn't bother you too much. All families are unique and they handle loss differently. Your daddy taught me that much. Go home and relax. We'll see you tomorrow."

Colin felt a lump form in his throat. It was Thursday—New Year's Eve. One week had passed since returning to Concord and he wasn't any closer to deciding what to do with the funeral home than he was when he arrived.

Colin went to the closet and collected his overcoat and gloves which were still damp from the trip to the South Burying Place Cemetery.

He turned down the narrow hallway and called for Paula. She didn't answer. As Colin made his way back to the front room, he noticed two narrow ovals on the face of the telephone were illuminated. Colin surmised that Amos and Paula must be on the phone. Colin waited a moment and put on his coat and headed outside.

Even though he had been inside for just an hour or so, fresh snow was falling again in Concord. Colin breathed in the cold air, vapor clouding out when he exhaled. As Colin walked around the perimeter of Madsen Funeral Home, he examined some icicles along the edge of the building, noting the serenity of the image.

Large flakes of snow began to swirl from the sky as a strong wind howled and whipped down, testing the eaves of the building. Colin debated whether to keep walking since the weather appeared to be getting worse.

Ahead, a short, narrow alley divided the funeral home from the last house on the block; the Hewitt residence. The alley rarely experienced much traffic. The house, surrounded by a wire fence, stood at the corner edge of the block. The front porch faced Main Street while the rear of the house approached Thoreau Street. Other houses behind it seemed so diminutive they appeared insignificant.

Colin slipped on some black ice and flattened his palm against the back of the funeral home, steadying himself.

He looked around, hoping no one had seen his near fall. Rather than seeing people, Colin could see the outlines of the Hewitt home through the falling snow. As he got closer, he noticed the paint peeling off in spots, and the slats in the shutters on the upstairs window nearly broken out. The wind caused the shutters to tap against the house, hinges squeaking. Debris littered the front of the house, while a broken banister from the front porch was secured to the porch frame only by a rusted screw. Colin couldn't imagine Pete and Madeline Hewitt letting their home deteriorate in this manner.

Several cars whisked by behind Colin, and a couple of them honked. He ignored them as he approached the front porch. The house appeared deserted. Before stepping up the front porch steps, Colin walked around the house, awkwardly navigating the thin strip of yard sandwiched between the house and the fence. The solid crunch of his winter boots against the packed snow filled the space with a familiar sound. The sun, low in the sky, illuminated the upstairs rooms making the two windows facing Colin look like dim red eyes, while the back door appeared as a gaping maw.

By the time Colin returned to the front of the house, the sun had disappeared and the house became cloaked in shadows. He stepped onto the porch, searching for a doorbell. Unable to find it, he knocked on the door, at first softly but then with more vigor.

"Mr. Hewitt, Mrs. Hewitt, anybody home?"

All Colin heard was another low moaning sound as the wind lashed against the house. He took a step back and wiped his dripping nose with his glove.

"It's me, Colin Madsen."

Before Colin could say another word, a sharp pain coursed through the base of his neck. Instinctively, Colin reached for the back of his head to locate the source when another bolt of pain surged through his shoulders and back. Then, another burst near the neck. Colin lost his balance and fell.

6

When Colin awoke, the snow scraped his frostbitten nose. The pain had subsided, but he found himself on the ground, lying flat on his stomach.

He groaned and maneuvered his arms to push himself up. As he tried, a heavy boot pushed him back against the ground.

"I've called the police."

Colin didn't recognize the smoky voice. "I was just looking for Mr. and Mrs. Hewitt. They live here. I'm Colin Madsen. I own...er...my dad used to own...the funeral home up the street. I was just visiting." He found the more he talked, the more his spittle became mixed with the snow, numbing his lips and making them feel like an inflated balloon.

He heard the voice sigh; a moment of silence passed. Colin held his breath for a few seconds, collected his strength, then spun violently in a half-turn to face the voice.

His eyes settled on a shivering frame wearing snow-packed mitts and a ski mask. The rounded end of a baseball bat hovered inches from Colin's face. He flung his palms up, squinted and looked away.

"Please don't swing," Colin pleaded.

Dropping the bat, the figure bent down and extended a hand. Colin slowly looked up and saw the hand as well as an envelope tucked under an arm. He waited a moment before grabbing the outstretched hand. The figure pulled, bringing him up to one knee.

Colin looked up, making fists. "What in the hell do you think you're doing?"

"I would ask you the same thing."

The figure reached up and removed the mask. Ringlets of disheveled chestnut hair fell over the woman's wide green eyes like a protective visor.

"You are trespassing. Get up."

Colin did as instructed, and when he steadied himself, he noticed that he towered over the woman in front of him.

"Look, I didn't mean to cause any trouble. I was just looking for Pete and Madeline Hewitt. I'm Colin Madsen. I went to school with their daughter Ava and I'm back in town for a few weeks

The woman cut him off. "Madeline died three years ago and Pete's in a nursing home. As for Ava, you're looking at her."

Colin focused on her face. The last time he saw Ava they were at the Concord-Carlisle High School graduation twenty years earlier.

Ava grew up in the large white house right behind the funeral home. Colin first met her in homeroom. In fact, mandatory seat assignments meant that Ava and Colin would sit across from each other for the next four years. She seemed reserved, only talking to Colin occasionally in broad terms about basic subjects. However, Ava quickly developed a reputation as the girl who pushed the boundaries of acceptable behavior. Madeline, a grade school teacher, and Pete, a warehouse foreman, maintained strong discipline and steadfast religious beliefs and forced them on their only daughter. Colin remembered hearing stories in high school from Luke about Ava sneaking out of the house at night to meet a boy or to smoke cigarettes in the alley facing Thoreau Street. The Hewitt's despondency led to frequent consultations with Luke regarding her behavior. In fact, Colin could still see his dad and Pete Hewitt having long conversations over the fence in the parking lot behind the funeral home, presumably about Ava and other matters.

Because he was shy and socially awkward, Colin never pursued Ava, even though Madeline would see Colin outside of the funeral home periodically and encouraged him to call on Ava. As a classmate and neighbor, Colin knew Ava kept her emotions close, though occasionally her eyes would reveal a flash of emotion or simply go flat. The jocks and preps at school seemed drawn to her like moths to a flame. Guys in gym class who considered Ava a conquest, were attracted to her for being coy yet brazen. But that was two decades ago.

Colin was stymied for a moment. He blinked. She had a calm but unsettling gaze in her green eyes.

"Don't stand there gawking at me, Colin. Mrs. Kelly at the Old Town is telling everybody that you are back."

Colin lowered his hands as he felt his face blush.

"So this is how you greet people, by assaulting them with a baseball bat."

"I thought you were trespassing. I drove by and honked the horn at you, trying to get your attention. Then I saw you walking to the back of the house. I thought you were casing the place and looking for an easy way in."

Colin scoffed, while brushing the snow off his coat and pants. "I would never do that. For one, I'm not a burglar, and secondly, I loved your mom and dad. I could never do anything to harm them."

Ava's rigid posture softened. "I'm sorry about hitting you with the bat."

"Hitting me three times with the bat," Colin added. "Where is your mom and dad, anyway?"

"I had to put Daddy in the nursing home this past summer. Since then, the house has been broken into three times. I try to keep an eye on it as much as I can, but it's hard sometimes. I don't have the money to put in a security system, but Amos and Paula have been a big help in keeping an eye on things."

She stopped speaking and shook. "What are you doing at my parents' house anyway? I thought you lived away from the Reading/Concord area?"

"I...I do. In Boston. I'm just visiting Amos and Paula for a few days. I saw your mom and dad's house as I was leaving and it brought back some memories."

From a distance, Colin heard sirens approaching. He felt his stomach lurch. The fact that Ava was keeping his attention long enough for the police to arrive worried him, and he felt trapped somehow.

"You called the cops."

Ava looked back as another snow squall began. She twisted the top button on her coat as she removed the envelope from beneath her arm. Colin took a long look at the envelope and waited a moment. His fingers darted forward and snagged the envelope.

"Hey! That's mine!"

Colin waved the envelope in front of her. "Call off the police and you can have the envelope back."

Ava furrowed her brow, displaying a sour look on her face. As she contemplated a response, Colin repeated the stipulation. "Call off the police and I will give you this envelope back."

She reared back and crossed her arms. "That's a pointless demand, Colin, because the envelope is not for me. It's for Amos."

7

Ava stood away from Colin inside the funeral home family room.

"I wouldn't have let the police take you away."

"I'm sure the two cops that showed up were so glad that you wasted their time." Colin took a deep breath. He felt his temper cooling slightly in the warmth of the funeral home.

"Is Amos still here?" Ava asked, tossing the envelope on the couch. Colin noticed the pecan brown freckles that dotted her face and arms as she turned around.

"Yes. Well, he was earlier."

As if cued by command, Amos appeared in the doorway of the small office next to the family room. His thin physique was enhanced by his rumpled white shirt and wrinkled mauve tie.

His gray eyes sparked with excitement. "Ava. Ava Hewitt. So good to see you." Ava raced to Amos and embraced him as his gangly arms wrapped around her tightly. After a few long seconds, they pulled away, each regarding the other.

Colin ignored them, but noticed a small, square box wrapped in packing tape under the small chair on the opposite side of the desk. Colin squinted, looking for a label but it seemed unmarked. He did not remember the box under the chair earlier.

"You too, Amos. I'm sorry that it's so late on Christmas Eve, but I wanted you to have this."

"Won't you sit for a bit?" he asked.

"I can't really. You seem busy."

Amos took the envelope and placed it on the table. "Oh, don't worry about that. Paula just left and I was finishing up in the back. I've transferred the phones upstairs. Jenny is getting dinner ready and she can answer the phones for a few minutes. Please, have a seat."

Colin watched as Amos motioned to Ava to enter the family room.

Amos looked at Colin and curled his mouth. "Have you been out playing in the snow, lad?"

"Not exactly."

Amos glanced at Ava then back at Colin. Colin cocked his head to the side, peering at Ava. "We had a little incident at Madeline and Pete's house, didn't we Ava?"

Amos leaned in slightly toward Ava. She flashed an impish smile at Amos before frowning at Colin.

"I'm just glad you two ran into each other. I almost didn't hear you all come in. I heard a bunch of sirens back in the morgue and when I came up front, I heard the door open."

Amos had settled into a chair and Ava sat on the couch, folding her hands and placing them in her lap.

"Colin has come back to the funeral home," Amos said, speaking to Ava, and then turning to face Colin. "Paula and I are glad to have him around. He is a Madsen and this funeral home is his. We are looking forward to him getting reacquainted with everything. This place needs a Madsen running it."

Amos nodded quickly before leaning back in the chair. Ava glanced at Colin and arched an eyebrow.

"I thought he was just visiting," she said, smiling and nonchalant. "I didn't know he was coming back to take over the business."

"Well, that's not entirely true," Colin began to say.

"Yes indeed," Amos interrupted. "Luke would be so proud that his son is thinking about the business after all."

Colin stared at the floor. "We will have to see how everything works out. But for now, it's good to be home."

Amos winked at Colin. "Colin even went out with us today on a service." He leaned forward and tapped Ava on the knee. "That's always the first step...just jump right in and see how everything works. I've got to say, it felt good having a Madsen riding with me to the cemetery. I appreciate the company; Luke and I always had our best talks in those slow rides to the grave."

Colin kept his eyes on the floor before moving them to take in Ava and Amos.

"You two should be going. It's Christmas Eve. Go on and enjoy it. I'll finish up here and lock up. Jenny has a roast and mashed potatoes waiting for me upstairs." Amos paused and licked his lips. "It's my favorite. Got to stop with life sometimes and enjoy good food," he said with a hearty laugh.

Ava smiled at him. "I wondered if you and Jenny still lived upstairs."

Amos glanced up at the ceiling. "Aye. We do. It's easier to keep an eye on things from up there. We are like landlords. When we get a death call, I can be down here and ready in a few minutes. Plus, Luke was kind enough to let us live upstairs for free." Amos looked at Colin and grinned.

A wave of guilt passed over Colin. He had forgotten about that agreement and that Amos and his wife Jenny still lived upstairs. The apartment was small, just two bedrooms and a living room with a bathroom, but it would be comfortable for two people. The fact that Ava remembered the agreement before him left him unsettled.

Amos stood up and gave Ava another small embrace. He rubbed his hands together. "Good night Ava." He turned and nodded at Colin. "Good night, lad. Talk with you tomorrow, but only if anything is going on."

As Amos left the room, Ava stood up, cleared her throat and reached for the coat and gloves that were wadded up in a pile on an empty seat next to the wall.

"What's in the envelope?"

"None of your business." Her voice was tight.

"You can either tell me or I can see for myself."

Ava froze and then turned to face him. "No, that document is between me and Amos. You weren't around when we discussed it or when we signed it. Ask Amos and he can tell you."

"I'm asking you."

She sighed. "I'm not sure that I should tell you. It's a business transaction between the funeral home and me and I think Amos should be the one to discuss it with you."

"In case you didn't know, my name is on the building. I'm entitled to know what is going on here, especially if it concerns money changing hands from you to the funeral home."

Ava pulled the coat on as she approached Colin. "I think you and Amos need to talk about more than that. How can you let Amos believe that you are taking over the business when you are just here visiting for a few days? He's a good, kind man Colin and he deserves your honesty."

A lump formed in his throat. He thought about the papers inside of his folder that he needed to handle. Only twenty-nine days left for him to make his own business transaction.

"I will tell him later. I'm not even sure that I don't want to consider running the business. I just don't know yet."

Ava tossed her hair over her shoulder. It smelled sweet, like honeysuckle.

"So are you going to tell me what's in the envelope or not?" Colin asked.

She pointed at the envelope. "Go ahead. See for yourself."

Colin rolled his eyes and opened the envelope, jerking a thick packet of stapled papers from inside. His eyes began scanning the contents. The language was clearly written by an attorney, and with Amos's name and Madsen Funeral Home typed into several blanks. Colin turned the page and scanned further. He looked up at Ava, who had crossed her arms and rested her weight on one leg.

Colin furrowed his brow before dropping the papers to his side, focusing on Ava. "You donated your family house to the funeral home?"

8

Colin looked out the front door window of his childhood home at Haverhill Street. He kept thinking about what Ava told him as he left the funeral home and he wasn't satisfied with the explanation. Ava had lost her elementary school teaching job and was considering leaving Concord. Amos felt the funeral home needed the extra parking space so families wouldn't have to park around the building or several blocks away on Main Street. So Ava deeded her family's house to Madsen Funeral Home. Without knowing the results of the appraisal of the Hewitt house or the finances of the funeral home, Colin wouldn't know if the acceptance of the deed was a wise investment. And now that Ava knew Colin hadn't been completely honest with Amos or Paula about the reason for his return to Concord, he wondered how long he could hide his true intentions. What if she tells Amos and Paula the truth?

He wanted to be upstairs in bed under warm blankets and falling into a deep sleep, but instead, his head hurt. Colin wandered listlessly from the kitchen to the foyer. Without his father around, the house had an eerie silence. He looked onto Haverhill Street. It would be dawn soon, but outside in the dark the pine trees swayed softly under a thick sheet of bright white snow and the streetlights cast blurry shadows on the ground. The packed snow on the yards and roofs of the homes in the Reading neighborhood filled the night with a serene image.

Colin thought about the deed given to the funeral home and how a decision had to be made in twenty-nine days. Perhaps Ava was right—Colin should tell Amos about his real intentions for coming back to Concord and the funeral home. How would Amos react? What if Amos was disappointed in him? The thought made him shudder. Amos had been running the funeral home for over a year with little communication or guidance from anyone else. Now, Amos saw Colin as someone coming back to a place he belonged, except Colin didn't necessarily want to be involved in the funeral business right now, or maybe ever again.

"Coffee. I need some coffee." Colin made his way across the wooden floor, which stretched across the foyer and throughout the house with no carpet to hide it. His feet were cold, despite the thermal socks he wore. As he moved down the small hallway, Colin passed the bedroom. He thought about taking another look at the funeral home deed and making sure he understood all of the options completely. Instead, he turned his attention to the coffee pot next to the sink in the middle of the kitchen counter.

Colin looked at the mirror on the wall and regarded himself for a moment. He shivered. Colin had a somewhat muscular build, but was more lanky than solid and that always made him appear non-threatening. The light in the kitchen highlighted his angular cheekbones, amber eyes and black hair. Colin sighed and continued into the kitchen.

As Colin fumbled with the coffee pot, a metallic chirping noise came from the furnace. It had been running for most of the night, aside from a brief moment when Colin adjusted the thermostat. Still, Colin blew into his hands, trying to warm the tips of his fingers.

After several scoops of ground coffee had been put in the filter basket, Colin's cell phone rang. He went into the living room looking for the loud alarm ringtone, finding it vibrating on a table surrounded by mahogany chairs. Colin turned on a lamp as he scooped up the phone.

As he took a breath to speak, Amos cut him off.

"Colin, how are you, lad? I know I promised I wouldn't bother you on Christmas Eve, er...day now as the case may be. But I could use your help." Hearing his voice made the earlier guilt return.

Colin rubbed his eyes, trying to wipe away the headache.

"Sure, Amos. What's up?"

Amos paused. "You sound tired. Did I wake you?"

Colin held the phone away for a moment and stared at the screen clock. It read 5:47 a.m. "No, it's okay, Amos. I've been awake for a while."

"Good. Listen, Margie Stover died over on Newton Road, near Long Lake Park. We buried her husband, Paul, about six months ago. He was a nice fellow. Worked over at Emerson Hospital, although I can't remember what he did there." Amos stopped for a moment, exhaling deep breaths into the phone.

"His brother, Sam, was on the board of Middlesex Savings Bank for years. We buried him too."

Distracted with the details, Colin shifted the phone for a moment and leaned forward as Amos kept prattling on. Under the small television stand set by the wall, Colin squinted, focusing on the image inside the framed picture. As he looked closely, he saw himself and his brother Owen, standing on a beach with frothy, cascading waves crashing around them. Colin grinned. He remembered that picture. It was taken when they were in elementary school, a month after their mother Rebecca had left Owen and Colin at home for a few minutes to get some fingernail polish. She never came back. Luke took the boys to Clearwater Beach that summer for vacation in an attempt to restart the family dynamic without their mother. That trip was one of the few times that Colin could remember Luke voluntarily taking time away from the funeral home. In fact, his father must have taken the picture. Colin hadn't seen it in years. Colin now felt nothing but sadness. He missed his father so much. Since his death, Colin vowed to not remember how pale Luke looked after the heart attack that killed him. Instead, Colin tried to remember happier moments, like the one captured in the photograph.

"Colin? You still there?"

Colin sniffed and wiped a tear from the corner of his eye. "Yeah, yeah I'm here Amos. So his brother worked at the Middlesex Bank?"

"Whose brother?"

Colin settled back in the chair. "Paul's brother."

"Paul's brother died Colin, and so did Paul."

Colin let out a breath. "I know that Amos. Never mind."

Static filtered through the connection before Amos continued. "Margie is a rather stout woman and the paramedics are at the house and they are going to help me get her loaded onto the cot. Can you meet me at the funeral home and help me get her to the prep room and onto the table?"

Colin felt his muscles grow limp as the softness of the chair absorbed him and sleep crept in. "Sure. What time do you want me there?"

"In about an hour or so."

Colin yawned generously and his response was garbled. "An hour then. Okay. Fine. See you then."

"Oh, Colin," Amos quipped. "One more thing." Colin began to realize that a conversation with Amos always meant one more thing.

"Yeah?"

"I didn't call Paula. She has family visiting from Vermont. Whataya say you and I handle Margie this morning?"

He yawned again. "That's fine, Amos. We can handle it."

Colin heard a door click shut followed by the ignition of a car engine turn over. "Thank you, Colin. See you soon."

❀

Even without heavy snow, the early morning chill and gusty winds made Colin's body shiver and his bones ache. The gray clouds hung low and tight around Concord as he made his way to the funeral home.

Colin pulled his car slowly in front of the building. He could hear a low moaning sound, which was perhaps nothing more than the wind blowing against the building. In stepping from the street onto the sidewalk, the snow crunched under his boots, like cracking frozen puddles.

Colin walked around the side of the funeral home, down the sloped sidewalk to the parking lot, looking for Amos. The only car he saw was a beige Volkswagen Jetta turning onto Main Street. The car made an awkward loop in the middle of the deserted road. For a moment, Colin thought the car would swerve and head for Thoreau Street, but the driver swung the car hard back to the right before steadying it and speeding down Main Street.

He stared again at the vacant Hewitt home. Its decrepit edifice stood tall against the road and funeral home. It had once been a place of life and home. Now, it looked like it could fall at any second. Its wooden boards were sticking out in a lot of areas along the side. The red paint had all but flaked off, but there was one part near the base that was perfect; the only part of the house that had been unharmed by the weather and neglect.

A cold burst of wind made Colin shiver as he wondered how soon the home would be destroyed to make way for a new parking lot for the funeral home. What would Ava's parents think of her decision? What would they think of Amos's decision to readily accept the offer?

Colin walked up the narrow, snow-packed back steps. He didn't have a key to the funeral home yet and felt stupid for not asking for one. Luckily, as he reached the door he found it had been left ajar. As he stepped inside, warm air slapped against his cold face.

He stood in a narrow entryway between two visitation parlors. Colin waited for a moment, hoping to hear Amos, but instead there was silence. Colin flipped on the light switch. He peered into the first family room and regarded the gas log fireplace, solid oak bookcases, and the grandfather clock. The other parlor had dual stained glass windows, several small sofas and plush chairs.

At the end of the parlor hallway, Colin saw a light coming from the casket selection room. He walked in and an angular shadow jumped. It turned completely around slowly and shrieked.

"Colin Madsen! You scared me to death!"

Paula covered her chest with an open hand and exhaled a quick burst of air. "I didn't know you were here."

"I could say the same about you," he replied. "Why are you here anyway? It's Christmas Day."

Paula waved off the comment. "It's also Thursday, which is a workday." Paula spoke with little inflection in her voice.

"I thought you had family in from Vermont."

Paula turned around, bent over, and grabbed a white cloth. "Yes, they are in. My brother married a real witch unfortunately," she sneered. "And he and the witch have two teenage daughters who inherited their personalities from their mother."

"Unfortunate," Colin added.

Paula raised a finger. "Exactly. They have been staying with me for a couple of days. It's been two days too long." Paula walked away from Colin and stood in front of a solid mahogany hardwood casket. It had a high gloss finish. Paula began rubbing the cloth over the surface of the casket. "Anyways, one of the princesses wanted cereal for breakfast and my brother used all the milk yesterday to make this easy-bake chocolate cake that tasted like charcoal. So, I was going to the store to get some milk and when I passed by the funeral home, I saw Amos closing the garage bay door and getting into the Suburban. I figured I'd better come inside and see what's happening."

Colin stood alongside Paula and rested his hands against the velvet upholstered interior of the casket. Dressed in jeans and a maroon Boston College sweatshirt, Colin felt underdressed at first, but now was glad he would be able to move freely and comfortably in his attire.

"Amos told me that he was picking up Margie...uh...Stover and asked me to come and help him and he told me not to say anything to you about it."

Paula moved to a different part of the casket and began wiping in wider circles. "That's sweet of him, but Margie is a big woman. It'll take both of you to get her on the embalming table."

She cut Colin a quick glance. "Can you fluff up the interior of the casket?

Colin frowned. "*Fluff* it up?"

"Like this." She pushed Colin aside and took the edges of the interior fabric and draped them over the sides of the casket. She removed the casket pillow and plumped the crumpled fabric, mashing it until the pillow gained a shapely appearance. She laid it gently inside the casket and smoothed over the rest of the laced fabric surface interior with one hand.

"There. Just like that." Paula gave a sharp nod and winked at Colin. She stood back and regarded the selection room. Colin followed her eyes as they surveyed the room. There were a wide array of caskets with pullout drawers which were labeled with the names and styles of interior colors and fabrics. Prices and a description of the caskets were displayed on the individual casket lids. At the back of the room, there was a selection of men's and women's clothing available for families to choose from and purchase for the deceased if they desire.

Paula looked down at her watch. "Amos should be back soon. I'm not sure when the Stover's will be in to make arrangements, but at least I have the casket room ready for them." She walked past Colin again and turned off the lights. Colin found himself in the dark and raced after her.

She moved down the hallway, walking in light, quick steps. The carpet absorbed each step. From behind, Colin watched her walk with carefree confidence that was most noticeable in her quick, purposeful steps. Paula wore a petite, pinstriped pantsuit that fit her small frame well. Both pieces of the suit were lined and the long sleeves buttoned at the wrist and notched collar on her jacket were fine pressed.

They both reached the small office behind the front family room. Colin looked through the bay window in the family room and saw that a few white flakes of snow began peppering the sidewalk and street.

Paula pulled open the desk drawer, removed a pair of glasses and put them on. She picked up the phone receiver just as Colin began to speak. She cut him off. "There are few days off in the funeral business, Colin. Even when you think you have a day off, you are still working."

Colin nodded, although he still felt guilty that Paula was at the funeral home on Christmas. He turned around and visualized Ava and Amos sitting in the family room with him yesterday and Ava's insistence that he tell Amos and Paula about the real reason he returned to Concord and the funeral home. Maybe he could tell Paula first, gauge her reaction, and then they could both tell Amos together, provided that Paula agreed with Colin's reasoning.

"Six voice mail messages already." Paula pushed the glasses up her nose. Her face with rounded cheekbones and high trimmed brows came together. "It looks like word is spreading through the Stover clan and beyond about Margie."

Colin scanned the room looking for the envelope Ava left for Amos. He didn't see it. Colin thought about asking Paula, but she was frantically writing down information on a pink notepad and progressing through the voicemail messages.

Then, Colin plopped down in the chair in front of Paula. She pressed a button on the phone pad and tore off a sheet of pink paper. "Give this to Amos, will you? Sometimes he forgets to come up here and get his messages." Paula smiled.

Colin looked down at the note before folding the paper. The message read: *West Concord Pharmacy: prescriptions ready for pick up: Amos Boggs.*

"Is Amos sick?"

Paula ignored the question. "You should probably head back to the prep room and see if he's been able to get the cot carrying Margie unloaded from the Suburban and up the elevator from the garage. If not, you'll have to walk around back and help him."

She furtively scribbled more information onto the pink message page, tearing off a sheet as she deleted another message.

As Colin stood, the funeral home door opened.

Amos walked in. A gust of cold air rushed in behind him. Colin looked back at Paula who placed the phone receiver back on the base. Colin could see her clumps of makeup between her wrinkles.

"Do you need Colin to help you, Amos?

Amos slapped his hands together in an attempt to remove something that wasn't there. "No, no I don't."

Colin turned to face Amos. "Where's Margie?"

Amos chewed on his lip for a moment. "Margie Stover is at another funeral home."

9

"Margie is at Newsome's Funeral Home, to be more specific."

Amos stood in front of them, a little hunched over. The dark age spots on his neck and hands were more pronounced and his hat sat halfway on his head.

Paula stood up. "Why is Margie Stover at Newsome's?"

"Wait, Newsome's? You mean the other funeral home here in Concord?" Colin rubbed his chin. Colin remembered being at the funeral home after school or on a Saturday afternoon when Oliver Newsome and his son Will would come into the funeral home from time to time to see Luke. Colin remembered Luke fawning over Will somewhat, but not having much interest in Oliver. Colin tried recreating their images in his mind, but it had been too long since Colin had seen either of them.

"Yes, that is the same Newsome's, Colin," Amos replied, slightly annoyed.

Paula tossed her hands in the air. "What happened when you got to the hospital? Did the family change their minds?"

"Not exactly," Amos replied brusquely. "When I got to the house, Margie's sister Eliza was there along with Margie's two grandchildren. They must have been arguing before I got there because I heard shouting when I entered the house and then everyone got quiet when I explained the removal procedure. That's when the one grandson told me that Newsome's had already been there to pick up Margie."

Colin waited as a long moment passed throughout the room. "Is that common? I mean, can families change their mind, just like that?" Colin snapped his finger to emphasize the point.

"I'm afraid so," Amos said. He tugged at his brown suspenders, which held up his waist-high dark pants.

Paula collected the pink message slips and aggressively stuffed them into the wire holder on the desk by the phone. "They should've called and told us they'd changed their minds. Amazing."

Amos waived away the comment. "It's just a shame. I've known that family for years and Margie Stover loved your daddy, Colin. She brought in all kinds of cakes and pies and cookies all the time and always visited with him. Margie Stover is a good woman. We've buried so many people in her family."

"I wonder what's changed?" Paula asked.

Colin sat back down in the chair. "Well, based on what happened with the Ellison service, I bet the grandchildren had something to do with it."

Amos scratched his head as he moved further into the room. "You were with us on that service last week?"

Colin looked up at Amos. "How could I forget it."

"Remember, Amos," Paula said. "That was the bloody nose service."

"Broken nose service," Colin added.

Amos crinkled his mouth but the old skin hanging from his chin, which normally flapped around when he talked, didn't move. "That's right, that's right. Reverend Newman had that service." Amos closed his eyes, and touched his index finger to his forehead in meditation. "Too many services in a row, I guess." He looked around the family room and small office and checked his watch. "Why don't we close up and head home. We still have the rest of the day to enjoy."

"That means I have to go back home and back to my family," Paula said, a pained expression on her face. She gathered the messages from the wire holder and handed them to Amos.

Colin stood up. Seeing the messages, Colin remembered what Paula had told him. "Oh, Amos, West Concord Pharmacy called, they said your prescriptions are ready. Are you not feeling well?"

Amos flashed his easy, charming smile. "I just take a little old man medicine to keep on going, lad. Thank you for the reminder."

"I'll go turn off the lights in the parlor and casket rooms," Paula said as she turned away.

Amos read through the messages quickly. "Nothing that can't wait until tomorrow."

"Do you think the Stover family will change their minds again?" Colin asked.

Amos turned to face Colin. "I don't think so. Newsome's should be embalming and preparing the body for the funeral and burial right now. Once that happens, well, Margie is where she will stay."

Colin stepped back and the heel of his sneaker clipped the corner of a box. He bent down and looked under the open space beneath the chair. The same box that sat in the chair yesterday during Ava's visit had now been moved under the seat.

As Amos sauntered through the office, heading for the hallway, Colin called out to him.

"Amos, do you want me to do something with this box? Move it someplace?

In a few seconds, Amos returned. He turned around and lowered his eyes toward the floor, squinting. "No, leave that box there. Those are embalming supplies for Newsome Funeral Home."

10

Colin swallowed. The grandfather clock in the front family room, surrounded by the sofas, chimed loudly.

"Wait a second, Amos."

Amos had moved into the darker corridor leading down to the casket selection room and the viewing parlors. Colin leaned a hand onto the desk as Amos stopped his shuffling feet and reappeared.

"I don't understand. We just lost a client to a competitor this morning, and based on what you and Paula said, this is a client we've served for years."

"Family, Colin. Not client."

Colin winced. In the profession of accounting, people are clients. "Whatever. It just doesn't make any sense to me that we are giving supplies to a rival funeral home. In fact, that makes as a much sense as Ava Hewitt giving Madsen Funeral Home the deed to her parent's house."

Amos set his jaw and stared straight ahead for a moment. "I think you are mixing the two issues." He spoke in a self-contained, deliberate manner. "Will Newsome called me a week or so ago and asked if he could borrow some morgue supplies: embalming fluid, makeup, cotton cloths, and the like. They had been going through a busy spell and didn't have enough supplies to get them through it before their ordered supplies had arrived. So, I told them we could loan them the supplies and he could reimburse us later. As for Ava and the Hewitt home..."

Colin cocked his head. Amos displayed a faintly smiling, middle-distance squint of someone lost in thought.

"Yes. Tell me about Ava and the Hewitt home."

"I figured it was only a matter of time before she told you. As you can probably tell, their home sits right behind the funeral home against our parking lot. Since Madeline and Pete haven't been around to take care of it, the house became a target for vandalism. It's not good for people to come to the funeral home or to services to find the police in the parking lot."

"Didn't you think to contact Ava?"

"I did, several times. The police did too." Amos stepped into the office. "She promised to watch it more closely. The last time the house was vandalized, someone started a small fire inside the kitchen. The police think it was a homeless person trying to keep warm during the night. I think that was the end for her."

"Couldn't she sell it?" Colin asked.

"Ava had it appraised, but the location of the house, along with its condition didn't get good pricing. I think she just wanted rid of it and she came and asked me if she could deed the house to us."

A tightness formed in Colin's chest. *I am the son of Luke Madsen, the owner of the funeral home. Why didn't someone contact me about what to do with the house?* He disregarded the thought. His lack of presence around the funeral home answered the question.

"So, now the funeral home is the owner of an old, falling-apart, vandalized house." Colin's voice was tense, as if something were coiled and ready to spring. "Well, we don't have to worry about Ava doing anything with it because now *we* have to do something with it. It's our responsibility now, Amos."

Amos looked Colin in the eye. "I would like to tear it down this spring and then we can add extra parking. It will keep our families from having to park along the street and side streets, especially for our families that have mobility issues."

Colin let out a long, exaggerated breath and a dry chuckle. He rubbed the back of his neck. Blood roared behind his ears in time with a hammer pounding inside his head. He wanted to leave—perhaps leave the deed to the funeral home on the desk and go back to Boston and forget everything.

"I am sorry I didn't tell you," Amos said hesitantly. "The issue hasn't come up until recently and I know that you are going to be in charge around here and it was my responsibility to tell you."

Amos looked away and shifted his weight from one foot to the other. Colin felt his heart beat a little faster. He wanted to shake Amos, or scream, or just tell him the truth about the deed and the funeral home and what Colin wanted to do. A stab of guilt hit him. He had no right to be mad at Amos, especially since he and Paula had been running the funeral home by themselves for over a year without any guidance from Colin or anyone else.

"Well, I'm going to the back for a moment to close up the prep room and check on Paula. I'll see you tomorrow." As Amos spoke, he made no eye contact with Colin. His shoulders slumped forward and he walked dejectedly from the room. His guilt almost made Colin want to cry or throw up.

The hammering headache made Colin feel drowsy. He needed sleep. A sudden succession of shrill rings cut the silence. Colin jumped up, startled. He waited for Amos or Paula to answer it. Peering towards the phone, the light on the console continued flashing. Colin hesitantly picked it up.

Searching for the right greeting Colin mumbled, "Madsen Funeral Home?"

"Good, I'm glad you're still there," replied the exasperated voice on the other end. The typical non-rhotic Boston accent of the speaker was strong and clear.

"Amos?"

"No, sorry. This is Colin. Colin Madsen."

Silence passed over the line. Colin could hear the other person breathing quickly.

"Hey, Colin. Long time, no chat. It's Will Newsome."

Colin furrowed his brow and held the phone away from him for a moment. He grabbed a pencil and the pink message pad and wrote the name *Will Newsome* in the middle of the page.

"Is Amos, there?"

"Yes, yes, he is," Colin stammered. He circled the name Will Newsome on the message pad repeatedly. "He...we were getting ready to leave." Colin paused for a moment, unsure of how to proceed. Perhaps he should let Will do the talking and he would provide requested information.

"Never mind. Can you just tell Amos that Garrett and Brandy Stover are on their way over to the funeral home to see him."

"Right now?"

"Yes, right now."

"Who are Garrett and Brandy and why do they want to see Amos?"

Another silence came across the line. "They are the grandkids of Margie Stover."

Colin tore the message from the pad and crinkled the paper. "Funny you should mention Margie Stover, Will. Amos went to the hospital this morning to pick her up and came back without her. He was told that the family decided to use Newsome's instead." Colin launched the wadded paper at a trash can across the office, but the ball hit the front edge of the can.

Will smacked his lips. "Yeah, well, there are some problems with that now."

"Really? I'm listening."

"So, how are you, Colin? How have you been? I've not seen or heard from you since your dad's funeral."

Colin decided to play along, but only for a minute. "I'm good. I came back to Concord to work through some issues here at Madsen's."

"Good, good," Will replied, talking louder than before.

"How's Oliver?"

Will perked up. "He's great, thanks for asking. Dad retired about six months ago and moved with Mom to Florida. Vero Beach. I'm running the funeral home now."

Colin redirected the conversation. "Now, why are Garrett and Brandy Stover coming over here?"

Will sighed. "They asked if they could talk to someone at Madsen's before making arrangements with us. That's all they told me, Colin. I'm not sure why. I really need this call. We really need this call. December was a terrible month for us and Margie has plenty of money. And before you say anything, I've looked at the paperwork. She has *plenty* of money."

Colin leaned back into the chair. "I'm not sure I need to hear all of the details, Will. Amos and the grandkids will take care of it." Colin checked his watch. "When will they be here?"

"In about ten minutes. They left just a few minutes ago."

"What about the body? Do you still have it?"

"Yes, I do," Will replied. "Tell Amos to call me when they are through making arrangements and we can work out the transportation."

"All right, Will. I'll let Amos know." Colin looked at the box on the floor again. His headache hadn't subsided. "Oh, and you might want to come over and pick up the embalming supplies you are taking from our morgue," Colin added. "You might need them to help prepare Margie for her funeral."

Will huffed and hung up.

11

Amos and Colin waited in the front room. Colin stared at the brown box as Amos made some notes on the inside of a manila folder.

Colin looked up at the grandfather clock. "They should be here any minute."

"Indeed," Amos replied, not looking up. "Did Will say anything specific about why they were coming?"

"No. When I pressed him on it, he changed the subject."

Amos closed the folder. "That's usually a sign of bad news."

The door flung open and Garrett and Brandy Stover stepped up from the sidewalk and into the room.

Garrett moved to the middle of the room, wearing baggy jeans and a long sleeve tee-shirt, swaying deeply as he stepped. He was a sturdy guy, with a wide, scowling face, and shiny black hair in a bowl cut.

"Which one of you is Amos?" For a young man, his voice was surprisingly gruff and dry.

Amos rose, and tucked the folder under one arm. "I'm Amos Boggs, the funeral director in charge here at Madsen's."

He extended a hand and smiled at Garrett. Garrett looked Amos up and down, and ignored the open hand. His mouth was mouth tight. "You the undertaker?"

"I am. I will be meeting with you today to make some arrangements for your grandmother, Margie."

Garrett motioned behind him. "This is my sister Brandy."

Brandy timidly entered the room. The late morning sunlight beamed into the room for a moment as she held the door ajar, casting a long shadow in front of her. She smiled meekly at Amos and nodded.

They both turned and looked at Colin. "I'm Colin Madsen. I, uh, own the funeral home."

Garrett had deep-set brown eyes that sized Colin up. Those eyes were also puffy and red-rimmed. Brandy stared at Colin, expressionless.

Standing together, the two siblings could not be more different in appearance. Garrett was big; about 6'3", 200 pounds. Brandy was petite, dressed in a black leather jacket, black skinny jeans and black sneakers. Her long brown hair was swept back into a neat ponytail with wispy bangs brushed to the top of her forehead.

Amos gestured with his hand. "Let's go back to the arrangement office where we can get more comfortable and talk over a few things."

As Garrett and Brandy walked around Amos, he whispered to Colin. "Take that box of supplies for Newsome's back to the morgue. As soon as we get something worked out, we will call Will."

Colin stepped into the office and collected the box, which was heavier than he expected. He waited until the disjointed patter of feet had subsided. Colin walked down the narrow hallway and past the arrangement office. The door was closed, but a stream of light shone from under it. Colin heard Amos addressing Garrett and Brandy in the arrangement office, discussing services and prices.

At the end of the hallway, Colin set the box on the floor. The entrance to the preparation room had a number of signs warning that only licensed personnel were permitted beyond this point and to be aware of formaldehyde and other chemicals present behind the door.

Colin opened the door and set the box inside. The antiseptic smell of the prep room overwhelmed him. He reached inside and fumbled for the light switch. Despite trespassing many times as a kid, Colin never could remember how to turn on the lights. After running his hands along the wall, he grazed the knob and turned it.

The preparation room had two embalming stations, white tiled floors and walls, stainless steel fixtures, and an electric chain body hoist. The three dressing tables ran along the outside wall of the room and the cabinets that stored supplies were easily accessible to the dressing tables. Colin opened one of the cabinet doors and was greeted by a variety of embalming fluids and cosmetics supplied by Dodge.

In the hallway, Colin heard voices, quiet at first but growing louder. Outside, he heard Amos speaking.

"I do think that it's in your best interest to stay at Newsome's," Amos pronounced. "I think that you and Mr. Newsome need to discuss pricing and payments. We just cannot get in the middle of your disagreement."

As Colin approached, he saw Garrett throw up his arms. "I thought you all were about service and putting families first."

Amos stood more upright upon that remark. "We are."

"But you all made the decision to call Newsome's after calling us first," Colin interjected. "You can't keep changing your mind. You need to make a decision and stick with it."

Amos honed in on Colin. "I didn't see you, Colin. How long have you been standing there?"

"Long enough."

"Great, just great," Garrett said in a strained voice. "Now you are going to double team us and make fun of us."

"Not at all," Colin replied. "I had to dispatch my staff on Christmas Day to the hospital to take care of your grandmother, which is fine. But since Amos arrived at the hospital this morning, you two have been playing a game with us and Newsome's. This is not fair to you, us, the folks at Newsome's, and especially your grandmother."

One side of Garrett's lip curled up and over a canine tooth. "Hey, I don't like your tone, man."

Amos attempted to intervene. "Colin, I think it's best if-"

"Amos, how many members of the Stover family have we buried over the years?"

He let out a long breath. "Over five...going back several generations."

"We strive for service that is second to none for the families we serve, delivered in a meaningful, compassionate manner."

Garrett flared his nostrils. Brandy stood behind him, her face red as she appeared to shrink as the conversation progressed.

"But in order to provide that service, we have to have trust and open communication with the families we serve. And, you have to admit, that hasn't happened so far today."

Garrett pressed his lips tightly against his teeth and seethed. "This was all Brandy's idea to come over here. Newsome's is closer to maw maw's house anyways."

Brandy stood between Garrett and Colin and slugged Garrett in the chest with an open fist. "We are here because you spent maw maw's money on stupid things like that new truck and skis and a bunch of shit we didn't even need. Now we do not have enough cash to cover her funeral expenses."

Colin let that statement hang in the air for a moment. Colin watched as Garrett grabbed Brandy by the arms and pressed them to her sides. "Don't say that. It's none of their business."

Amos stood behind Colin and spoke softly. "That is the discussion we were having earlier. How the expenses are going to be paid for."

Brandy spoke again, tears welling in her eyes. "I'm so sorry about this," she said, seeming to speak to everyone and nobody at the same time. "I know that many of maw maw's family were buried here and that man over at Newsome's was pushy in trying to get us to plan the funeral but when we told him we didn't have much money, he basically asked us to leave."

"Brandy, shut up!" Garrett barked.

"It's true. Everything I've told them is true." Her voice trembled and tears began trickling down her cheeks.

Colin turned around to face Amos. Amos looked pallid and silent. Colin looked down at the floor, his eyes darting back and forth. He searched for a way to resolve the situation.

When Colin turned around again, he saw Brandy and Garrett whispering in hushed tones. Garrett stood on his toes, towering above Brandy. She was leaning into him, with folded arms, grimacing.

Colin cautiously approached them. This time, they ignored him.

"Listen, folks, I'm sorry for your loss. Amos tells me Margie was a wonderful woman." He paused and looked at Brandy who met his gaze. "And you are right, Brandy. Margie did have many of her family members here and Amos tells me she made the best desserts in Concord."

Brandy smiled faintly and Colin could almost feel Amos doing the same thing behind him.

Colin steepled his hands, drawing them to his chest. "I lost my father a year ago and I miss him every day. In fact, not one day goes by that I do not think about him." The headache Colin had been managing now made its way to his chest as his tongue felt thick in his mouth when talking about his father. "But you all need to think about what is in the best interests of your family and what is in the best interests of Margie. I don't think she would want to see you all fighting like this."

Again, Colin let the comment hang and the silence between them pool. Garrett stepped away from Brandy and looked sheepishly at Colin and Amos. He ran a hand through his hair.

"Fine. Whatever. That still doesn't solve the issue with coming up with enough money for the funeral."

Amos stood alongside Colin before speaking. "I think you need to leave Margie where she is at Newsome's. You don't want to be in a situation of having to move her across town. I think your maw maw deserves better than that."

As Brandy turned to face them, she crossed her arms and dropped her. Her leather jacket crinkled as she moved.

"I have an idea. We will provide you a casket for free," Colin announced.

Amos stiffened. "Colin..."

He turned to Amos. "It's okay."

"I don't necessarily think it's okay, lad."

Colin faced Garrett and Brandy again. "I will call Will and tell him that we will provide you a casket. That will absorb some of your expenses."

"Folks, folks," Amos interjected. "You still need to realize that you'll be responsible for purchasing a vault, the opening and closing of the grave, and any other charges that Newsome's has accrued so far concerning embalming and preparation."

Colin raised a finger. "But it's a start. I agree with Amos, in the interests of everyone, you do need to keep Margie at Newsome's. Does that work for you?"

Garrett and Brandy searched one another for a moment. "Okay. We agree."

"Great. I suggest that you head back over to Newsome's and meet with Will again and explore your options. Meanwhile, we will call him and tell him about our agreement and deliver the casket."

Colin looked at Brandy and Garrett for a moment before facing Amos. He had surprised everyone, including himself, with a firm decision to resolve the problem, which would also irritate Will Newsome in the process, although that wasn't the immediate goal.

Amos leaned into Colin and whispered curtly, "When they leave, we need to talk."

As everyone stood motionless for a moment, Colin stepped back, unfolded his hands and smiled. "The exit is right behind you folks. Let me show you out."

When Colin retuned back into the parlor hallway, Amos was gone. Standing in the main hallway, Colin took in the funeral home. It was 100,000 square feet of space decorated in rich, warm colors, probably selected by Paula. Ahead, Colin heard the rustling of papers in the arrangement office near the casket room and followed the noise.

Amos had several file folders on the desk. Several of the folders had been emptied and their contents strewn across the desk.

He kept searching through the paperwork from the folders and didn't face Colin. "I wish you had discussed with me your plans."

"Amos..."

"Drat! I can't find the financial report from the fourth quarter."

"Why do you need that now?"

Amos stopped moving and stared ahead, regarding nothing as he spoke. "Because, Colin, we do have to make some money here so that we are around to serve other families. We really can't afford to be giving away merchandise, even when it might be the right thing to do. I need to take into account how much that casket is going to cost us, longterm."

Colin leaned against the doorframe and crossed his arms. "Amos, you're right and I'm sorry. I should've spoken to you first. I was in the casket room earlier with Paula and I saw some of the less expensive caskets near the back of the room. When those two mentioned that money was going to be a problem, my mind went back to those caskets. I figured it would be fine to donate one to them."

"Their issues with merchandise and services for Margie Stover's funeral are something they need to work out at Newsome's. You were wrong to interfere and I imagine Will won't take kindly to your meddling."

"Isn't one of our goals as a funeral home to deliver service with dignity and respect, delivered without distinction of social, cultural, or economic background?"

"Aye." Amos finally faced Colin, his eyes shimmering under the overhead light. His lip trembled for a moment and he sniffed.

"Amos?"

"I'm sorry. You sounded so much like Luke there for a moment."

Colin grinned. "See, I did pay attention to what you and Dad talked about when I was down here as a kid."

Amos swallowed hard. "Yes, yes you did." His voice was soft. "And the decision you made with those grandkids is the same decision your father would've made had he been here." His eyes flickered at the end of that statement. "But you have to understand that we have expenses here that need attention: taxes, prep room supplies, casket bills, general maintenance and upkeep of the building. We have to be prudent with the money we collect. Now, we have a house behind our building that will need to be refurbished, sold or torn down. These are expenses that we have to be prepared to face as a business."

"If we need to closely watch our expenses, then why are we giving Will Newsome morgue supplies?"

Amos waved away the concern. "I give young Will supplies that are near the end of their shelf life. We have to dispose of them after a certain date and instead of throwing them out, I have been giving them to him. He knows the specifics of our arrangement. Besides, he's only asked for supplies twice."

Colin looked on as Amos dropped his gaze and searched the desk. "There it is." He lifted a manila folder from the desk and stuck it out at Colin. Colin slowly grabbed it.

"What's this?"

"The funeral home's financial report from the fourth quarter. I think you need to read it. If you are going to run things around here, I shouldn't be keeping these numbers hidden from you."

A moment of levity passed over Colin. "I am a trained accountant after all."

Amos remained stoic and reorganized the desk. "I'll call Will over at Newsome's and then close up. I'll see you tomorrow?"

Colin gave a curt nod. "Yep. See you tomorrow."

Colin opened the file folder as Amos patted him on the shoulder before leaving. He quickly scanned the various columns of numbers, which would seem overwhelming to most people, but was something he revelled in doing.

As he began processing the data, Colin looked up for a moment, finding his mouth slightly agape and his lips dry. He looked back down at the spread sheet.

Madsen Funeral Home had made money during the year. But the revenue generated was not enough to cover all of the expenses.

12

Colin walked home from the funeral parlor, his mind busy. He looked up at the sky and found the sun shining down through a break in the clouds. How appropriate. Christmas morning and a sign from God. But what does it mean? It seemed positive but about what? To sell the place. Or not to sell the place? The funeral home had been making a small profit, but not as much as Colin assumed.

By the time he got home, the midday sun was shining brightly. Since he hadn't slept much the previous night he was thinking about a nap before dinner. Thinking of some of the great meals he'd had at the Concord Inn, Colin considered going there to eat. It was a favorite of tourists and townies alike. It would be kind of lonely eating by himself on Christmas Day but he didn't mind. He had grown into adulthood independent and was able to be comfortable with his own company when need be.

He lay across the bed, threw a quilt over himself and sleep came quickly. When he awoke, it was partly cloudy and the long shadows of afternoon lay across his yard. He had to defrost his Jeep Liberty for the short drive over to the Concord Inn.

The Concord Inn was pretty busy and when Colin was seated he was a bit surprised that he didn't feel lonely amongst all the holiday patrons.

A cheery fire roared in the huge floor to ceiling fieldstone fireplace. He perused the menu and thought about ordering a martini. He remembered dinners he had here with his family and later, when it was time to make choices in life, with just his father.

As he waited he gazed about at the quaint room. It was Colonial in every way. Multi-paneled bay window. Wide pine floors. Pewter sconces with electric candles. The young college girl waitresses, cute in Pilgrim costume.

He was just about to order when he was distracted by a woman approaching his table. At first he didn't notice her, but as she got closer he recognized the striking brunette. It was Ava Hewitt, his childhood chum.

He stood when she reached him and an awkward silence passed between them. "Ava. I'm glad to see you. Please sit down."

She looked a little flustered. "I...called the funeral home and Amos said you were gone. I stopped by your house and your neighbor told me you might be here."

"I'm so glad you found me. I hope you'll have dinner with me. The prospect of being alone on the evening of Christmas was beginning to daunt me."

Ava met his gaze and gave a puzzled look. "I thought after what happened earlier at the funeral home with the envelope and Amos..."

"Don't worry about it. Please, join me."

She smiled, revealing a dazzling row of white. Loosening up a bit she said, "You always struck me as the strong independent macho type."

He grinned. "Me too. Until you find yourself alone at dinner. He wasn't faking his enthusiasm. She was a godsend. "Could I get you a drink?"

She nodded.

He signaled a waitress and ordered her a Scotch and water. Then he turned back to her. "What really happened with your teaching career, aside from what you said about it at the funeral home?"

"Mostly messing it up."

"I'm sure you were a good teacher. Tenacious, but good." Colin winked at her as she ran her fingers around the base of her glass.

"Yeah, but I found that it wasn't everything I expected." There was an awkward pause in conversation until she said, "I thought I was going to be the female Mr. Chips. You know. Everyone would love me as I broaden their horizons and introduce them to the mysteries of the universe."

He cocked his head. "And it didn't turn out that way?"

"Nope. Modern kids are mostly spoiled little brats. Even in an upscale town like this."

"I'm sorry, Ava. I think I know what you mean. It's got something to do with our culture. It was kinda different when we were growing up. We didn't dare back talk our parents or our teachers."

"Or the cop on the beat. But it isn't that way anymore."

"So now what's the plan?"

She sipped her scotch. "Don't really know. My father left me a decent inheritance and the house, but rather than invest it I foolishly spent it willy nilly. I'm getting to the point where I need a job."

As he was about to speak, an older gentlemen stopped at their table. "Excuse me, are you Luke Madsen's boy?"

Colin stood. "Yes I am. I'm afraid I don't remember you."

"Bub Daniels. Your dad, took care of my mother's funeral."

"I'm afraid I wasn't ever much involved."

"That's okay. Don't let me interrupt your dinner. I just wanted to tell you that my family will never forget the kindness your dad extended us at that" he paused, "bad time." Bub continued. "He was a fine man and a Christian gentleman."

"Well thanks, Mr. Daniels. That's so nice of you to say. You have a nice evening, and Merry Christmas ."

After he left, Ava said, "I bet you get that a lot."

"No. Nobody really knows who I am. I left so long ago. I guess he did though."

Turning back to her, he said, "I was kind of surprised to see you deed your house over to us so it could be turned into Madsen Funeral Home's new parking lot."

She twirled a finger through her hair. "Well, I had no interest in the place after my folks died, so I knew you people always needed a parking lot so I sold it to Amos."

Colin grinned. "Yeah, things have changed. I remember you and I playing in your yard. Remember I used to come through that hole in the fence?"

She smiled. "I do remember. A lifetime ago."

"Of course, some smacks to the back of the head with a baseball bat can also jog some memories."

She had a third drink while he was still nursing his second. He couldn't help gazing at her. Probably the most attractive woman in the room and she had no pretense about it in any way. After a sip of the new drink she asked. "So why are you really back?"

"I told you, I've got some decisions to make. Namely to sell the funeral home or not."

"What's your inclination?"

"I haven't formed one yet so I did promise Amos I would stick around a few days to watch the operation. He thought that might help me make up my mind."

Ava took a slow sip of her drink. "He thinks you're staying longer, Colin. You wouldn't let it go out of business would you? It still supports Amos and Paula and the families in Concord."

"No I wouldn't want to put them out but one of the things I have to consider is that if I sell out, then whoever buys it might very well do just that. So that's no guarantee. The only guarantee is if I retain ownership and keep running it."

"Is that possible?"

"I'm not sure about that either. I have a full time career in Boston to tend to."

Dinner came and they were occupied for a while. The plates of pecan crusted chicken, red-velvet potatoes and asparagus gave off pillars of steam. The scents made Colin ravenous and he began cutting into the tender meat immediately, pushing the food into his mouth. Ava ate slower, but ordered a fourth drink during dinner.

When they left, Colin said, "How did you get here?"

"My car," she said, reaching into her purse for her keys.

"Look, it would make me nervous to let you drive home."

She gave him a coquettish grin. "You're such a gentleman, Colin. But I'm a big girl. Driving with a few drinks in me is no problem."

He hesitated. "I still feel uncomfortable letting you drive...

"Okay, then drive me home. But you have to drive me back in the morning to get my car."

"Deal," he said smiling, feeling better. "Where are you staying?" he asked as they got into his car.

"I'm living with my sister Veronica over in Concord Village. I have a nice little suite of three rooms," she said.

As they walked through downtown Concord to the car, Ava cuddled into her fur coat. He said, "Nice fur."

"Yeah, one of my extravagances. I should have a sensible wool coat. This nice fur might be seeing the inside of a pawn shop soon."

Evening in Concord was festive. Most windows had Christmas lights and the downtown area was colorfully decorated by the Chamber of Commerce. By this time only a few late diners were on the streets. She gazed about. "I always loved this town. Bur right about now I'm probably going to find it too expensive to live in."

He slowly turned his head towards her. "Oh I'm sure you'll land on your feet. You've got a lot going for you."

She grinned. "Think so?"

"Yeah I do."

The drive was an easy one. Her sister lived off of Constitution Way, near Concord Village. The row of houses in the village featured inviting Pottery Barn colors. Ava motioned for him to drive ahead to the last house on the block. A shortage room off the main house greeted the car as it pulled up. Colin had forgotten how close Concord Village was to the train, shops, restaurants, and had easy access to Route 2.

They both got out of the car and Colin exchanged a hug with Ava and he was off.

He thought about her for the rest of the night, trying to recall their childhood days. The reputation she developed in high school and her trouble-making ways forced her parents to remove her from public school during her senior year. He had stayed at the local high school. They must have lost touch about then as life took them in different directions.

He couldn't change the past, but he still looked forward to seeing her again in the morning.

13

Colin was scheduled to be at the funeral home the next morning at nine to continue observing the operations. Again he enjoyed walking in the quiet of the morning observing the town come to life. Shopkeepers opening their stores. Commuters heading for the train depot, briefcases in hand. Delivery trucks making their rounds.

When he got there, Amos was busy on the phone. When he finally got free he advised Colin that a family member was going to have to talk to management about a problem this morning. In the meantime, Colin helped himself to the coffee and pastry on the sideboard in the galley kitchen near the back porch of the building.

Paula walked powerfully into the room and rested a coffee cup on the counter. "The woman coming in today is Mrs. Sampson, the wife of the young man who is in the chapel." When Colin leaned in to listen further, Paula paused. "Did Amos tell you any of this?"

Colin shook his head.

"Well, Amos had to do more than the usual work because the young man had been killed in a bad car accident. His face was not fit for viewing without substantial work and the bill for the visitation and funeral has increased. Amos recommended that you sit in on the conversation so that you would understand the problem and perhaps have some input."

Paula emptied her cup in the sink and left it there. She reared back. "I think I heard the front door. That has to be her. Come on."

She grabbed Colin by the wrist and led him up the hallway, through the office, and into the front family room.

When the young woman entered, Amos guided her gingerly past them and to the arrangement office. Colin followed. As they situated themselves around the room, Amos sat behind the desk and introduced Colin but the woman's distant stare barely acknowledged him.

Amos started the conversation. "I understand, Mrs. Sampson, that you are having some problem with your husband's life insurance."

The woman looked up at him, her eyes misty. "Well, I guess what the problem is, is that my husband didn't have the policy I thought he had."

Amos let her take her time. When she said nothing further, he said, "Do you mean you're having trouble collecting ? Can we help with the death certificate or anything?"

She again lapsed into silence. Amos waited patiently. Finally she said, "I guess the problem is that he had a policy but I didn't know how much it was. We'd talked about more insurance but with the kids and all there was always something else and...we never got around to getting more insurance."

As Amos reached for the Kleenex, Mrs. Sampson burst into tears and while she sobbed the two men waited patiently. Amos offered her more Kleenex. Finally she regained control.

Amos said, "Take your time, Mrs. Sampson. Please."

She turned her red eyes to Amos. "The problem is the policy won't cover even half of the funeral expenses. I'm a stay-at-home mom with three kids. I have no way of getting the money."

Amos's eyes almost clouded over. His sympathy was genuine. He said, "Well, if I understand you, you won't have the balance of our billing right away."

The young woman huddled deeper into her coat, as if she was trying to hide. "Sir, I don't know if I'll ever have it."

"Did you check with Social Security?" Colin asked.

She looked blankly at him. "The government has a minimum death benefit for everyone. It isn't much. Only a couple of hundred dollars," Amos said.

"Well that's more than I have now," she said.

Amos tapped his fingers on the desktop. He knew that this lady's story was common. He had dealt with it before. "Burial expense is one of the last things people consider in life. There are so many more pressing problems and expenses for a young family."

He reached across the desk and took the young woman's hands. "Mrs.

Sampson, we can offer you a payment plan. That is when you get a job or find some means of supporting yourself."

She didn't seem to hear him at first. Then she locked eyes with Amos and said, "You would do that?"

He smiled kindly and nodded.

When the woman left she seemed much relieved.

Colin said, "I think you handled that splendidly, Amos. It's what I would have done."

Amos sighed. "I'm afraid you're not familiar with the finances of the business yet, other than the spreadsheet I showed you. This is probably the worst time for us to have to carry several thousand dollars. And for a person who might not have any money for a long time-"

Colin interrupted, "What else could you have done?"

He sighed again. "Nothing really. Her husband's funeral is tomorrow. We can't very well cancel it." He paused a moment and then added, "Well, course, we actually could but that would mean storing his body. And that would be very unseemly. The man and his family deserve a funeral with dignity. We can't let the realities of life deter us."

"That's what I believe," Colin said.

"But again, Colin, as I said, it couldn't have come at a worse time as we have some significant expenses due."

"Which ones?"

"The insurance premium for one thing and the first payment to the contractor for the roof repairs that are needed. The roof is really old and if we hadn't done it last month, it might not bear this winter's load of snow. We couldn't have that."

"Of course not," Colin agreed.

Amos said, "Your father would have found a way and that's the same principle that I've been trying to operate on."

"And you're right, Amos."

Amos' sigh was more of resignation than relief. "I hope you understand what we are up against in a small town, especially one where we have built up a reputation for compassion. Not that that itself isn't a worthy goal but again there are the realities of business life. We can't take on too many of these problem cases and stay in business."

"I'm beginning to see that, Amos. It's kind of a delicate balance, isn't it?"

"Yeah, my boy, it sure is."

The rest of the day involved more mundane funeral parlor activities. Colin oversaw the delivery of supplies, which included embalming fluid, towels and other sundries.

As Colin headed home, his mind raced. He had absorbed at least some of the working environment of the business and when he got home he was weary. As he pulled in front of his house, the sunlight glaring off the snowy landscape accentuated the chill of the air, attacking his eyes and lungs, which erased his bleariness, but did not calm his thoughts.

After a frozen lasagna dinner Colin found himself at loose ends. His mind full of the events of the day he found he couldn't relax, so he picked up the phone and called Ava. She picked up on the third ring. "Hi. I was wondering if you'd like to have a drink with me somewhere."

She said, "Uh...oh yeah. I just have an errand to do with my sister, but I'd be available about eight-thirty. Would that be okay?"

"Sure, I'll pick you up at nine."

The Hawthorne Inn had a cheery fire in the fireplace. Colin loved this historic building and its eclectic furnishings. The Italianate-style building was surrounded by woodsy grounds that had been surveyed by Henry David Thoreau. The dining room featured Japanese ukiyo-e prints, a traditional Norman Rockwell painting and Haitian voodoo masks lined the walls. The whimsical lamps kept the room dim but cozy. Colin passed a Sheraton/Empire desk and a Persian helmet before finding a table in the dining room.

Colin ordered their drinks. "How did your day go?" she asked.

"Very interesting. I'm learning some things about the business that I didn't know before."

"Like what?"

"Well, some of the financial realties. We had a client come in today whose insurance doesn't cover half of the funeral expenses. She's a young woman with children and her husband's sudden death not only left her shocked but unable to support herself."

The drinks arrived. Ava hadn't dressed up for their casual date. She was wearing a white turtleneck sweater and fitted black slacks that clung to her curves. She wore only the lightest makeup which seemed to improve her looks. She had a fresh-faced bright-eyed look that heavy makeup disguises. He never realized just how beautiful she was. She said, "That's so sad. I guess we just don't plan for everything that we're going to confront in life."

"Amen to that," he said. He raised his glass. "Well, to brighter things. What shall we drink to?"

Her wide smile added to her allure. She raised her glass. "Here's to old times."

He smiled, clinked glasses with hers and took a sip.

Three drinks later he ordered some appetizers. As they munched on mozzarella sticks and sipped their drinks he said, "So what was your day like?"

"I had an interview in Boston. It's getting to be crunch time for me. I have to get a job."

"Oh? How did it go?"

"It's been years since I've applied for a job and I'm afraid I'm not up on things."

He cocked his head.

"Like, for instance, the number of women in the workplace outside of teaching?"

"Yeah," she replied, "the emancipated woman is out there and competing with men in the workplace. And all the traditional male jobs."

"What company and what kind of job did you apply for?'

"Account Executive. A fancy name for a salesperson."

"What kind of firm?" he asked.

She grinned. "Believe it or not a large national, excuse me, international service company that owns funeral homes. How's that for a coincidence?"

"Did anything in particular guide you to that job?"

"No. Mostly it was the one available. They did seem to like my qualifications, although I don't have a clue why. The Human Resources lady said that with my background I'm no doubt a people person." She paused and smiled. "Whatever that means. And she said that selling is a lot like teaching. You're teaching the customer what is best for them."

Colin sipped his drink. "Well that makes sense." He too grinned. "In a roundabout way."

As time passed, Colin found Ava warm, giving and even a bit perceptive. He wanted to make sure that while he was in town he would get to know her better.

14

A light snow had fallen during the night so when Colin arrived at the funeral home, he grabbed a shovel from the shed and began clearing the sidewalk. He went inside after an hour or so and got himself a cup of coffee. There seemed to be some activity as Amos and Paula were so busy on the phones he couldn't talk to them. He returned to his shoveling outside.

An hour later he again went back in, his face flushed from the cold December morning and his labors. He poured himself another cup of coffee just as Paula got off the phone. She wore her wire rim glasses and seemed efficient. She approached the kitchen area and said, "Morning, Colin."

Colin motioned with his cup, "What's going on? Seems busy this morning."

"Oh, uh, problems. We don't have a limo for the Jones funeral in the morning. The transmission in ours is in bad shape."

Just then Amos came in. He had heard their conversation. "When Luke was alive his limo company would respect a commitment. But the limo business has changed and the limo guys will dump a commitment for a better profit."

"How's that, Amos?" Colin asked.

"Joey Barnaby at Top Hat Limo down the street backed out of his commitment to the Jones funeral in the morning."

Colin cocked his head. "Joey Barnaby, the high school football sensation?"

"The one and only. Except he's not such a sensation. Word around town is that he's in business with some shady people. People who finance his limos. He's all about making money these days, not keeping promises to old friends."

"What's the solution?" Colin asked innocently, taking a sip of coffee.

"None, really, " Amos muttered, scratching his head. "Yankee ingenuity I guess."

Colin thought about the problem for a moment. "Can we use private cars?"

"It's possible," the old man said, "but I hate to do it. These people are grieving and they want to be together on the ride to the church and cemetery."

"How many of them are there?"

Amos considered it, and then said, "At least six, so far."

"Oh I see," Colin said. "You could end up needing two cars."

Paula added, "I hate to even contemplate that though in the end it may be necessary. We'd still be short a driver unless you volunteered."

"Oh, I'd volunteer. No problem."

"Still," Amos said, scratching his head, "I would really hate to have to do that. Like I said, they want to be together. I'm sure they'd feel, I dunno, funny to be squashed in some private car with the driver privy to their private conversation and grief."

Colin said, "But the limo driver, doesn't he hear ... ?"

Amos interrupted. "No, there's a privacy shield in the limo. They put it up and it's private in back."

Colin shook his head. "Shows you how much I know," he muttered and went back to sipping coffee.

Amos said, "Thanks for shoveling. I was worried that when we got around to it the walkway would already be iced over."

"No problem. I wish I could be more helpful with this limo thing."

"Well I've got things to do. Could you get on the phone and try to get us a limo for tomorrow? Paula can give you some numbers to call."

"Sure. I'll be happy to try."

Colin sat down at a side table with the Yellow Pages and a phone and started dialing. He was earnestly engaged for over an hour before he hung up frustrated.

Paula glanced over at him from her desk. "The limo companies are busy with holiday parties and such," she said knowingly.

"Yeah and most of them are on their answering service. Can't get anybody to talk to." Finally he connected with an actual person. "Hi, this is Madsen Funeral Home. We need a stretch limo for tomorrow morning for five hours or so." Colin listened carefully and then said, "Can I get back to you?"

Colin walked over to Amos. "Got a company over in Lexington. They say if they gave us the car it would have to be at a premium."

Amos said, "We don't have much choice."

"Wait, it gets worse. Not only would we have to pay the premium but they don't have a driver. I offered to drive myself. He said he would have to get with his insurance carrier and see if they could put me on the policy for just tomorrow."

"We have to get the limo. Are they going to let you know?"

"They said they would."

Colin waited until after lunch and time was getting short. He finally got his answer. It could be done but altogether it was going to cost over eight hundred dollars.

When Colin relayed this info to Amos, the old man said, "That cuts into the profit margin pretty deep, but I vote for it."

Colin got back to the limo company and made arrangements to do the paperwork before the close of business so that he could pick up the car early in the morning in time for the funeral.

When Colin returned later, Amos said, "I'm going to have to go over the procedures with you since you're now going to be one of the drivers. I know you've seen it a lot but it's different when you're on the operational end."

Amos carefully went over the procedures. The funeral procession cars had to be parked in a certain way in the parking lot. With little room to maneuver, Amos would park the hearse on the street next to the funeral home, followed by the limousine, and have the minister park behind them both. Colin would need to identify which cars belong to family. The first family car would be aligned close to the sidewalk facing the building. Each family car after the first one would follow the same parking alignment, until all family cars were arranged tightly together. Funeral attendees not going to the cemetery would have to find their own parking around the funeral home.

"Now," he said, "one of our biggest problems on our way to the cemetery is that sometimes lots of people, although seeing a funeral procession, still have no problem cutting in, cutting us off and other rude driving habits. So just take your time and watch my movements with the hearse. You'll be fine."

By the end of Amos's talk Colin felt reasonably confident.

In the morning he got up early and drove over to Lexington to pick up the limo. His first problem was getting out of the limo company's driveway. The garage doors attached to the rusted metal building were small and nestled close to the entry lane in the parking lot. After talking with the company owner, who chewed fervently on an unlit cigar as he gave instructions on how much space the limo needed to turn and break, Colin felt ready to take the limo back to the funeral home. Although he was aware of the extra length needed to turn the vehicle from the parking lot onto the street, Colin still ran over the curbing as he made his way onto the street. There was an embarrassing thump and he hoped the owner hadn't seen it. He quickly sped off.

By the time he reached Madsen's Funeral Home in Concord he was a bit more familiar with the big car though he had yet to figure out things like heating, defogging, the intercom system, and how to operate the privacy partition. He sat in the car for another fifteen minutes to figure it out. He realized that part of the driver's job was to open the doors and assist the passengers in and out.

Amos guided him into the spot behind the hearse, then they got busy affixing the funeral flags to each vehicle as they aligned them in order.

The first stop would be the church. It was a nine o'clock funeral mass at St. Bartholomew's over in Lincoln. When they got to the church, Colin would have to fill in as one of the pallbearers as they were one short.

Amos took him aside. "Colin, as we set the coffin at the foot of the altar, could you go outside and try to guide in one of the cars that got cut off and lost?"

Colin nodded.

"And we can't start without them," Amos added. "They are the mother and aunt. They're old people so you'll have to be patient. I have to set up things here. Do you feel confident enough to guide them here?"

"I think so."

Colin went outside. It was a cold morning, with slate gray clouds. He pulled up the collar on his full-length cashmere topcoat. He had a piece of paper with the people's cell phone number. He called. A elderly person's shaky voice answered. "Hi, this is Colin from Madsen's. I guess you folks got cut off. Where are you now?"

"I don't know," the voice said, now even more shaky and nervous.

"Don't worry. You're not going to be late. We are going to wait for you. Can you describe where you are?"

The lady said, "Let me see. There's a CVS and a Burger King at a big intersection."

Colin hadn't been around the area for a number of years and he didn't know every new Burger King or CVS. He said, "Anything else?"

There was a pause. "Oh dear, I'm so lost. I don't know where I am."

"Relax Mrs. Jones. We'll get you here."

After some trial and error Colin figured out where they were and painstakingly, in halts and starts guided them to the church. It was twenty minutes later when they finally pulled up and parked across the street. He hurried over, assisted the women out of the car and as they clung to his arms he escorted them into the church and their pew in the front.

After the mass they returned to the vehicles and started out for the cemetery. Colin was concentrating on keeping his distance from the hearse when he heard a noise from the back. The privacy partition was up but he was sure that he'd heard something. They had just pulled into the cemetery. When he put the partition down he could see that the deceased's aunt had fainted. He pulled off onto a cemetery side road. He hurried to the rear compartment. The woman's head was slumped onto her relative's shoulder and the people in the back were upset. Colin hurriedly phoned Amos ahead in the hearse now pulling up to the burial site. "Amos, I have a person whose fainted here. What do I do?"

Amos said. "I forgot to mention that kind of thing, but I do remember I slipped a tube of smelling salts into your coat jacket. I forgot to tell you. Pass it once or twice under her nose. If that doesn't work. Don't panic. I'll call a doctor. Where are you anyway?"

"One street back. On the left."

Colin found the smelling salts and passed it under the lady's nose. She moved slightly. When he did it twice more, she sat up. "How do you feel ma'am?"

The lady caught a deep breath and in a short while felt well enough to carry on.

◈

After the funeral they were all gathered in the front office. Amos let out a long sigh and turned to Colin. "Well, what do you think?"

Colin too let out a long sigh. "To tell you the truth when you look at it all as an outsider or a funeral participant it all looks so smooth and organized. It isn't until you're on the inside, that you realize how many things can go wrong."

Amos smiled. "Amen to that."

15

Colin had volunteered to go over to Concord Auto Repair that afternoon and discuss the future of their hearse. It had broken down again and the question to be considered was whether or not it was feasible to install a rebuilt transmission or buy a new limousine. The answer hinged on what condition the rest of the vehicle was in. In either case it was going to be a financial hardship for Madsen Funeral Home. Colin had an appointment with the shop for twelve noon and he wasn't looking forward to it. He and Amos were going to have to sit down and figure out some creative financing. True, finance and accounting was his field but most of the clients he worked with were high up on the business totem pole and did not have the problems a struggling small town business did in a bad economy. They had reserves. Madsen's did not.

While business had not slackened, it being a recession-proof business, accounts receivables had increased for their funeral home and they were feeling the cash flow crunch.

About a quarter to twelve Colin was slipping on his overshoes and preparing to go to the repair shop when the phone rang. His face brightened. *Maybe that's Ava calling about our date Saturday night.* But it was a male voice, fast talking and confident. Colin recognized him immediately let out a long sigh. "Owen. Hey brother how's it going?"

"Hey man, I just found out where you were. Had to do some checking at the business. How's things at the old digs?"

"So, so, Owen. Things are a bit tough right now."

"Have you made any decisions?"

"No. I'm kind of immersing myself in the business to try to find out what to do. I—"

His kid brother cut him off. "Hey, Colin, I need to talk to you. I was thinking about this afternoon."

"Well, I have to go over to the repair shop and talk about the limo, but I should be free by one. Is that okay?"

"Yeah, sure. Where?" Colin had to smile at Owen's brisk manner. Some would call it rude, but hey, that was his kid brother.

"Do you remember the Old Town Diner in the town center?" Colin asked.

"Heck yeah. Old Mrs. Murphy. See you there at one."

Owen had not waited for an answer but in his assumptive way just expected Colin to be there.

After meeting with the mechanic, Colin headed for the Old Town Diner. He arrived fifteen minutes early and parked. He was in a gloomy mood. The news about the limousine was all bad and he would have preferred a call from Ava rather than Owen. He had a suspicion as to what Owen wanted to talk about.

As Colin entered the Old Town Café he heard Owen's voice before he spotted him. He didn't announce himself right away but spent a moment watching his younger brother shmooze Mrs. Murphy. From behind, Colin immediately recognized Owen. He's was around five feet ten, but seemed taller because he always stood with his chest stuck out and his back straight. Owen swept his short, curly brown hair to the side but his flirtatious behavior was not impressing Mrs. Murphy.

As Colin walked up Mrs. Murphy eyed him. "Why hello, Colin. Ye brother here has the gift I'll tell you."

Colin grinned. "What gift is that, Mrs. Murphy?"

"The gift of the Blarney Stone. He can charm a monkey away from his bananas."

Owen, wearing a wide grin, said, "Hey brother, let's sit."

Mrs. Murphy asked, "Coffee for ye, before ye order?'

Owen said, "Right, Mrs. Murphy. You've not only got outstanding looks but a good memory."

The older woman rolled her eyes but anyone could see she enjoyed the flattery.

As is his way, Owen skipped the pleasantries and got right to the point. Colin had always thought Owen could use some maturing and some values, but evidently nothing had changed with the brash young man who only loved one thing more than his partying lifestyle—his passion for money.

Colin stopped him, running his eyes over the preppy sports jacket, the up to date haircut. "What, no, 'how are you'?" Colin asked. "No, 'how's life treating you'? I haven't seen you since Dad died. What's new in your life?"

Owen Madsen was a strange mix of cocky and shy. A bit distant. It was disorienting to people who didn't know him. Colin knew that if Owen was not interested in what was being discussed, he would just look away and talk about something else entirely. Owen lit a cigarette and took a long, slow drag. "It's all good. You know, Colin. I need to talk to you about the business." He exhaled and watched the smoke rise towards the ceiling.

Colin lowered his eyes and sipped his coffee. He had an idea what was on his money hungry kid brother's mind. Colin's dad had arranged his affairs so that Colin was to have a sixty percent share of the business while Owen was to have forty.

Luke Madsen and Owen's grandfather Cyrus had originally owned the business. When Cyrus died, Luke became the sole owner. Owen had made his views of the ownership arrangement known from the beginning. With little interest in his father's legacy, Owen was for selling out.

So when Owen immediately came right out with it, Colin wasn't surprised. Owen laid his cards down. "I'm for selling. I've got some plans that require higher finances than I have at the moment."

Colin said, "Hold on, Owen, there are other considerations."

"Like what?"

"Like the future for Amos and Paula. Like Dad's legacy in this town."

Mrs. Murphy arrived with a hamburger and a refill for the coffees. "Thank you, darling," Owen said condescendingly. Mrs. Murphy darted her eyes at Colin, then back at Owen, huffed and scurried away.

Owen didn't miss a beat in munching down his hamburger. Between bites he said, "Come off it, Colin. You never liked the business either. You went off on your own."

"That's true but you must know that selling out wouldn't be Dad's idea. He would turn it over to Amos before he did that."

"But Amos can't afford it."

"How do you know that?"

"Look, he's probably still driving that fifteen-year-old Buick and living in the apartment upstairs."

Colin, using a more measured tone was trying to discuss the pros and cons, but Owen was having none of it. "Look, Colin. I just want my end. Can you buy me out?"

Colin sipped some coffee. "I'm not sure. Actually, I'm not sure that I want to if I could. I have some plans and considerations of my own. I'm here trying to make that decision. I've been working at the business trying to do just that."

Owen abruptly got up and said, "Catch the check, will you. I have to be somewhere. I'll be in touch."

Mrs. Murphy came back to the table. "Are you fellows going to—" she stopped as she saw Owen leave. "Going to want any dessert?"

"No thanks, Mrs. Murphy, but the lunch was wonderful as usual."

Colin went home rather than back to Madsen's. He had a lot on his mind and he knew he couldn't think it out at the funeral home.

At home he plopped himself down in his favorite chair in the family room and tried to sort things out. But his heart wasn't in it. He wanted to think about something else. And Ava had been on his mind very much lately. He found himself looking forward to some more dates, perhaps on the weekends. He would have liked to see her more but she was in training during the week for her new account executive job.

It was almost three-thirty and he had made no decisions, either about the limo, the sale of the business, or buying out Owen. He called Amos and told him that he would be by in the morning to help out with the Johnson funeral and to discuss the limousine with him.

He more or less drank coffee and waited until six when Ava would be home. He knew she was tired every night and had studying to do but he wanted to see her tonight. He wasn't sure why. He just very much wanted to see her. He was hoping she'd break her weekday routine.

She didn't answer her phone at six. He looked outside. It had been snowing since early afternoon. *Maybe she'd been delayed on her commute.*

By the time he spoke to her it was after eight and his hopes for seeing her were waning. Although she was glad to hear from him, he could hear how tired she was. He said, "I was hoping we could get together tonight. Maybe a drink or a cup of coffee."

"Gee, I'm sorry, Colin. I've got my sales manager here from work. We're going to go over some of the stuff we're both having trouble with."

When Colin hung up he was surprised at his reaction. Jealousy. He wondered if the "someone" from work was a male or female. He stopped short, realizing he had no exclusive arrangement with her. As far as he knew they were only seeing one another on a casual basis. There was nothing serious about it.

He was surprised when Ava called him about eleven while he was getting ready to go to bed. She said, "I hope it's not too late."

"Of course not, I'm always happy to hear from you," he said, brightening.

"Yeah, I had some stuff that I was having trouble with and my co-worker's here to go over it with me. She's staying the night. We had no idea it got so late." There it was. It was a *she* that she was with. It was amazing how good that made him feel.

Ava said, "I'm afraid I'm going to have to cancel our date for Saturday night."

The comment hung in the air as Colin thought about it.

"Yeah, they decided to squeeze our group in for the out of town training, and they are flying us out Saturday morning."

"Oh, I know you mentioned out of town training, but I had forgotten about it. Where are you going?"

"Boca Raton, Florida."

Colin hoped he wasn't sounding like a love struck schoolboy when he asked, "Oh? For how long?"

"It's going to be a couple of days. Possibly longer if we don't get all the training in."

Trying to disguise his disappointment with a casual attitude he said, "Oh well, I guess you gotta do what you gotta do."

After he said it he wondered how it sounded. Cliché? Corny? "Well, will I be able to see you before you leave?"

"I don't know, Colin. I have to pack. I have to make arrangements. You know, my dog, stuff like that."

Again feigning nonchalance he said, "Okay then. I guess I'll be seeing you on the Internet. At least for the next few days or so."

"Yeah, I guess so. Well goodnight. Bye for now."

He felt like a kid disappointed at his birthday present. Also he was not used to these kinds of feelings. Of course, he'd had relationships with women, but not many. He had kept his nose to the grindstone, feeling there would always be time for romance someday. Except of course, he didn't know when it would hit him. Was it hitting him now?

16

Ava had been gone for two days and Colin was in the dumps. While the reason for it was obvious he hadn't had anything like these feelings in the recent past. He realized how upset he had been when he thought that it was possible that Ava had been studying with a male colleague. He shook his head. *Jealousy is a sign of weakness but at my age it's downright immature. I'm no schoolboy.* Still the feelings didn't go away. His analysis was reasonable but his emotions evidently weren't.

Colin had now been back in Concord and back at Madsen's for one week and by mid-weekend he was in a genuine funk. Not usually impulsive he broke the mold and called Ava in Florida. When she came on the phone he almost hung up, but he didn't. Trying to sound casual he said, "Ya know, I was thinking. It's cold, I'm lonely, and I have some free time. I thought about who I would like to spend it with."

"And?"

"And here I am."

Ava's laugh was deep and throaty and made him miss her more. "But Colin, I'm training. I'm not even available during the day."

"Nights would be fine. How about it? I could be there tomorrow afternoon. We can start the new year together."

"Well then in that case if you don't mind I'd love for you to come down here."

Colin didn't give her time to change her mind. Besides, he wanted to savor the feeling that she would be happy to be with him. They were both adults. Surely she didn't expect some kind of separate rooms or living arrangements. Did she?

He put the idea out of his head and started packing.

❧

He had some time to think on the plane. He wanted to think about long range plans that included Ava but all he could do was concentrate on the chance to be intimate with her. He had to admit he would be happy to see her no matter what the arrangements. He wasn't going to lose her if by chance she was prudish about things and insisted on separate rooms. This made him realize the strength of his feelings for her.

By the time the plane landed with a chirp of rubber, a thump and the roar of reverse thrusting engines, he was as excited as a teenager. *Let's face it,* he said to himself. *I've never felt like this before.*

He took a cab to her hotel, the Wyndham. As he passed the late afternoon beaches, Colin felt like he had sneaked away to a tropical hideaway. Outside the front of the hotel, he noted the old-world Spanish architecture and saw past the doorman into the inner courtyard, replete with fountains and a garden lounge. The hotel was oceanside and for any New Englander, the warm Florida sunshine was a blessing.

She said she had advised the hotel management that he was coming and to let him into her room. The room itself featured an open floor plan, a separate sitting room with a 32" flat screen television, complete with a sleeper sofa, wet bar, microwave, and mini-fridge.

He laid his suitcase on the bed, and ran his hands across the high-quality linens and extremely comfortable bedding. Not wanting to be presumptuous and unpack he went out to the balcony. It was a soft, sunny Florida afternoon. The fronds on the sturdy palms just off the balcony whispered in the gentle breeze. The Atlantic stretched away to infinity, sparkling like a sea of diamonds in the afternoon sun. After basking in its warmth for a while he went downstairs and ordered himself lunch in the hotel's outdoor patio restaurant.

He had a BLT with iced tea and lingered over the tea while he basked in the sun. It was now mid-afternoon and he found himself longing to see her. She said she would be back about six.

After returning to room he stretched out across the top of the bed fully dressed, keeping himself busy checking out the hotel brochures for a nice place to have dinner.

The next thing he knew her soft lips on his cheek awakened him. She was grinning. "You looked so peaceful I didn't want to wake you. Welcome to Florida."

He sat up a bit embarrassed. It wasn't his best 'man of the world' image but he was so happy to see her it was cast aside. "Oh, hi. I guess I was enticed by the warm sunshine and a big lunch. I guess I just succumbed to the place. Put a Yankee in the sun during winter and he is seduced." He swept her into his arms. At first, Ava stiffened and then relaxed. "It's so nice to see you."

"You too. I see you've been reading brochures. Come up with anything?"

"This one, the Palm Room at the Atlantico Hotel looks nice," he said, pointing to it in the brochure. "Do you know it?"

"No. The company's not cheap but that's a bit upscale for us trainees."

"Well it's not for me. Would you like to go there?"

"I'm so happy to see you, I think I'd be happy to go anywhere."

This was rather blunt and unforeseen. He had been worrying if the feelings he was having were pretty much confined to himself. It seems she missed him and it sent a thrill through him. A thrill the likes of which he hadn't felt for a long time.

She changed in the bathroom but with the door open a crack. He saw a flash of pink as she passed the door a couple of times.

Dinner was great. The food was wonderful but they hardly noticed so busy were they catching up and just enjoying each other's company. Afterwards they walked along the hotel's beach, barefoot, his sports jacket slung over his shoulder while her poly-blend maxi beach dress flapped against and away from her in the breeze. The air was crisp and a solitary seagull walked by. The sea ebbed and flowed and in the distance the waves looked like white horses, galloping in unison. Crowning all of this were half crushed seashells of different sizes rocking against some mini bays formed in the sand.

They were ankle deep in the surf. Both were quiet. Then Ava said, "Did you ever think...I, uh."

"What?" he asked, expectantly.

"Oh, just a silly little observation of mine that you could make about lots of things in nature."

"What's that?" He was curious, never having discussed anything serious with her.

"Just that this surf we are walking in this tide. Well, it's eternal. It will never stop. At least as long as the earth is here."

He had to ponder that as they walked along the silky water caressing their ankles. "You know, you're right. It will be coming ashore on this beach forever." They walked along in silence. "I never knew you were so deep," he said with a widening grin.

"I'm not really. But every once in a while I stop and think about these kinds of things. Puts you in touch with your own mortality."

Back at her hotel room he said, "How about a nightcap? I saw some interesting things on the menu." They had not discussed anything like sleeping arrangements and he wasn't thinking about it either. He was thinking of making the evening last as long as possible as he usually did back home. But this was different. The night might not end with him leaving tonight. In fact, he had no idea where he would go.

They ordered a couple of exotic drinks with an appetizer and when it all arrived they had it out on the balcony. There was a full moon and it cast a long line of silver on the nearby ocean.

When he caught her nodding off he said, "I didn't mean to keep you up. I know you're a working girl these days."

She grinned. "Well then," she said, taking his hand, "why don't you get me to bed so I can be fresh in the morning."

They fell into bed like lovers who had no doubts. Colin slowly removed the dress from her body. Ava displayed a wondrous gaze of playful curiosity as she smiled at Colin. Her uniform hair spilled down between her shoulders in bladed formation where the shortest strands barely tickled the skin of her collar bone. Colin moved his mouth and lips over her soft neck and narrow shoulders. Ava ran her equally lithe arms and hands under Colin's shirt as she removed it. Colin continued to kiss her neck and shoulders, then moved down to her midsection. Ava began to pant heavily as Colin loosened his belt and removed his pants. He slid a hand underneath Ava, moving his other hand to her inner thigh, touching her crotch. Ava grabbed Colin by the neck and kissed him forcefully, causing him to moan in delight as he thrust his erection against her.

Colin stopped and looked at Ava again. Her skin tone was light, lending her to porcelain glamour. Ava settled her eyes on Colin and seductively bit her lip and nodded. Colin bent down and kissed her again, this time their tongues exploring each other. Colin positioned himself above Ava as she caressed his chest and back. Colin groaned as he slid inside her, moving slowly then more forcefully, with passion.

Ava was as eager as him and soon they were both on the verge of orgasm. The night was full of sleepy, slightly boozy, but passionate sex. Twice they parted panting for breath and slightly sweaty. He didn't remember when they fell asleep, just that he was awakened by the sound of the shower. Ava came out of the bathroom with a towel turbaned around her head. Other than that she was naked. The way she padded around the room with such uninhibited ease set his loins to stirring. She grinned as she hurriedly dressed. "Sorry, babe, but I'm already late. You're not here a day and you're corrupting me already."

He grinned back, stretched out and enjoyed watching her get dressed. For a while he was going to forget his troubles, the cold Yankee winter and everything else. Except Ava.

17

The next morning Ava was off to her training early. She left him a note on the dresser. "Hope you're not too bored today. Just find time to miss me. Ha ha. Find something fun to do. It's the weekend and I can't wait to get this day over with. Best, Ava."

The message wasn't steamy but with just enough implied intimacy to let him know she was happy.

Colin had a late breakfast on the sunshine bright patio, another balmy Florida day ahead of him. He lingered over his coffee and rather than think about how to busy himself considered someplace nice to take Ava for the weekend. Colin scoured the brochures in the hotel lobby and considered every Florida destination from Disney World to the Keys. He decided on a one-night trip to the Keys and he made arrangements from the hotel room.

He told her about his plans that night at dinner. "Have you ever been to the Keys?" he asked. Then, caught up short, he added, "I suppose I should have asked before I made arrangements to eat at Louie's Backyard."

She smiled at him over the rim of her cocktail glass. "Sounds wonderful. Anyplace will be fine." She reached across the table and took his hand, stroking it softly. "Colin, I just enjoy being with you."

He grinned, thrilled inside. It almost made him feel like a kid again. Of the women he had known in his life no one had made him feel this way.

They went to the bar at the Wyndham to have a nightcap and dance. He thought that she felt wonderful in his arms as they swayed to the music in the soft tropical night.

In the morning they set out for the Florida Keys, which started about fifteen miles south of Miami. An irascible Florida sky left them guessing as to the weather. Right now it was sunny with a slight breeze coming off the ocean.

Colin had rented a Ford Mustang convertible. He'd never driven a convertible and in some ways it made him feel like a kid again. Nothing at all like riding in a sedan or a hearse, driving in the convertible gave them both a wonderfully spirited feeling of freedom and adventure. As they started down the long trail of isles and islands that curved off to the south southwest, he said, "From the brochures I found myself interested in Key West and Hemingway's old haunts and hangouts."

She agreed. "Always one of my favorite authors. But I never knew he was associated with Key West. I knew about Cuba and Spain."

"Yeah. They say his old room in the hotel is haunted."

She smiled. "Please, no ghost stories. I'm just getting myself attuned to the mortuary business."

That piqued his interest. "How's that going?"

"Well they do make a case for franchising. Some of the benefits over the old ways can hardly be denied."

"Like what?"

"Well, just having the power and prestige of a giant corporation behind you," she explained. "You don't have the problems the mom and pop places have. Your staffing, supplies and payroll issues are always taken care of by the company."

Colin agreed with a solemn nod. At the moment he really wasn't in the mood to talk business. He just wanted to be able to keep a lively conversation going. They drove along US Route 1 and passed giant shell and lobster statues and gorgeous mansions next to tiny shacks. A hilarious amount of fishing line tangled in the electrical wires on the bridges made Colin snicker.

As they drove further along taking in the diverse scenery of the Keys, Ava asked, "What are those tall trees with the red leaves? They couldn't be...?"

"Yeah, they are. They're royal poinsettia, a bit larger than what you're probably used to. Look like giant poinsettia plants don't they? And those coming up? The ones beyond the coconut palms? Those are hibiscus and the bushy ones are bougainvillea."

During a period of quiet when they both gazed up at the circling gulls, they found they didn't need to talk to be comfortable. All they needed was the sea, the salty air and the softness of the afternoon. Like old friends the silences between them weren't awkward. They would occasionally exchange happy glances and at those times no words were necessary. Or desired. Ava's favorite music on CD was enough to put them in a different world.

Marathon seemed like a comfortable place to stop for the day. As they passed the sign, Ava commented, "Marathon. Odd name for a town, don't you think?"

Colin smiled. "Your tour guide at your service. Seems that when they were building the famous Key West railroad line back in the thirties, the workers felt like they were in a marathon to complete it on schedule. Thus, Marathon."

She grinned. "Thank you, sir. Should I tip you for your information?"

He grinned back. "A kiss will do." She leaned over and pecked him on the lips.

They continued to learn things about each other. At lunch she learned that he was allergic to certain seafood so he had to stick with the tried and true hamburger while she was able to experiment with conch. Both were in love with the music of the nineties.

Noticing all the diving shops around, after lunch he asked her, "Do you have any interest in diving?"

"I've tried some snorkeling," she replied. "I'd love to do some more if you don't mind. You like tank diving I suppose?"

"Just a little. I like snorkel diving too. You don't have to worry about any technical stuff like your breathing gear and the gauges and all."

She smiled. "Okay, let's do it. Snorkeling it is."

Though he had seen her nude, he marveled at her figure in a one-piece black bathing suit. She was spectacular. Catching him staring, she said, "You like?"

"Very much."

❧

They spent the rest of the afternoon paddling about, in awe of the abundant sea life. Again he served as a guide and instructor, especially when it came to pointing out some interesting sea life. Everything from squid to barracuda. After they had had enough snorkeling they retreated to their blanket under a swaying coconut palm and had iced tea and a snack. He sipped tea as she stretched out on the blanket and slipped her sunglasses on.

When she got up a bit later they sipped more iced tea and watched the surf contentedly. The wind had picked up and the combers were white capped. He said, "I don't think I'll ever look at the surf the same again."

Sitting up in a lotus position she gazed at him. "Why?"

"Oh that thing you said back at the hotel about the surf. How it was forever."

She lay back, smiling. "One of my more profound moments. Really deep for me."

"Why? Do you consider yourself a more carefree type spirit?" he asked.

"Yeah. As I get older though I find myself thinking about things I had never thought of before."

"Like?"

"Like the surf. And eternity. And the mysteries of life. You know, stuff like that."

"I know what you mean. Getting older has that effect on us."

"My mother told me before she became ill that if I don't get cracking I'm never going to give her a grandchild," Ava quipped.

Colin became serious. "Listen to her. You're lucky to still have one of your parents."

She touched his arm. "I know. I know what you mean."

Before the afternoon was over the ocean lured them in. They plunged in together, frolicking like a couple of seals and emerged slick and wet and laughing.

After dinner they sat on the porch of their small hotel in lounge chairs and watched the water. The small hotel had no air conditioning but the constant sea breeze was enough to cool them off after their heated lovemaking.

By early afternoon the next day they arrived in Key West. After lunch at a seaside place they set out to explore the area. Following a tourist guide map they visited the Hemingway haunts listed on the brochure.

Nestled against the heart of Old Key West, the Hemingway home was surrounded by turquoise water. Colin and Ava wandered through the lush grounds and enjoyed the whimsy of the more than forty cats that lived on the property. Ava especially enjoyed the variety of flowers in the gardens.

Nursing a soda at the outdoor benches near the Hemingway home, Colin said, "I understand that this is where he wrote *For Whom the Bell Tolls*."

"And the *Snows of Kilimanjaro*," she said grinning. "I read the brochure too."

Colin was thoroughly enjoying her company. "I bet you didn't know that another literary giant is associated with this place."

She sipped her iced tea. "Oh oh. Got me. Who?"

"Tennessee Williams started *A Streetcar Named Desire* here."

They roamed the town hand in hand taking in the diverse sights, sounds and atmosphere, finding it had much in common with an artists' retreat back in Massachusetts; Provincetown on Cape Cod.

She said, "Did you ever notice how vibrant artistic people make a place? Places like this and P Town are not just for tourists to gawk at the locals. They are really inspirational places."

"I agree. Makes you want to pick up a paint brush."

That's when he found out that she was an accomplished piano player. He knew she had to interrupt their play time when they were kids to go home and practice but he didn't know she had stuck with it and was now quite good.

By the time they headed back to the hotel, exhausted but happy, Colin wondered if he was in love.

They awoke to the blinding glare of sunlight slanting in through the bedroom blinds. Tiny dust motes danced in the bright beam. Ava was in Colin's arms. Their lovemaking had been tender and poignant and reflected the longing both had been feeling.

As she fixed breakfast he was eyeing some of the stuff she had collected that now littered the bedroom and an adjacent small extra room. He picked up the framed picture, held it at arm's length and called to Ava, "Who's this?"

She peeked in at what he was holding and said, "If I'm lucky it's Robert Lincoln just after he joined the Union Army."

"Yes I remember, his mother didn't want him to go."

"But she lost out. Most men of the day wanted to get into the war even though they knew after the first few months how horrific it was.

"Today I am going to drive down to one of the smaller Keys and take a look at another Robert Lincoln. I want to compare the autographs. If they are authentic they will be worth a lot."

"Sounds interesting," Colin opined. "Uhhh. Can I go along?"

"I'm counting on it. I don't know my way around the Keys."

"So you just need a guide?"

She grinned at him. "I'm always learning about you. Another thing I've learned."

"What's that?"

"How sensitive you are."

That embarrassed him a little. Sensitive guys weren't considered macho. But then she said, "For such a macho guy."

Colin laughed. "What time should we start?"

"I say right now. We're going to have to stay again in Key West. It's a long way. We have to cross the panhandle using the Tamiami Trail to the east coast and then farther down the Keys."

They traveled under a canopy of hardwood hammocks with bright splashes of tropical flowers. Every once in a while they had to dodge green tree frogs leaping across the road. Ava said, "I heard they have black panthers here in South Florida."

"Not much chance of seeing one."

She took out a notebook and wrote something down. He cocked his head and said, "What's that?"

"Just some observations about you."

"What did you just write down?"

"Under sensitive I have now written cynical."

He chuckled. "Well if we don't see one I want you to erase that."

By lunchtime they were near the Miccosukee Indian Reservation where they stopped at a modest restaurant. Both had steak, fries and iced coffee. A sign outside the restaurant window advertised alligator wrestling at the Indian reservation.

"That's something I'd like to see," said Colin.

Ava rolled her eyes and took out the notebook again.

"What?" he said grinning.

"Sadistic," she said.

They started south on the chain of islands known as the Keys. At Islamorada they rested a while and then it was back in the car.

Colin said, "I looked at the map and about seventy miles before Key West, which is at the very end of the Keys as you know, is Fort Jefferson."

"Oh, the infamous 'America's Devil Island'."

"Yeah, that's the place they held Doctor Samuel Mudd, the doctor who patched up John Wilkes Booth during his escape across Maryland."

"Impressive, you're right up there on history, aren't you," Ava quipped.

Fort Jefferson was indeed fascinating for them. They saw the cell where Doctor Mudd was imprisoned and heard the story of how he helped save a lot of inmates from a malaria plague during his stay.

Ava explained the antique business to Colin as they drove, with sparkling green blue water on both sides of the roadway. She said, "Down here it's a little different than in New England although antiques can be found all over the country. But down here there's an emphasis on Spanish treasure retrieved from ships that were sunk in storms or in warfare. This guy I'm going to see now has quite a few items. The one I'm interested in is a sixteenth century doubloon."

"What will it be worth?"

She said, "If I were a dealer, a lot if I can get it at a good price."

Because of the time they'd spent dallying at Fort Jefferson they arrived in Key West after dark. They booked into a Main Street hotel and had dinner in one of Hemingway's favorite haunts. There was memorabilia all over the place. Pictures of Hemingway in fishing boats and on African safaris. Big posters of all his books. As she ate, Ava gazed around. "Boy, would I like to get my hands on one of those pieces."

"Why don't you ask the owner?"

"Maybe I will. You never know. That last picture of Hemingway seems to be crowding the door." She went up and took a look. It was autographed.

Returning to her seat, she asked the waiter to see if the owner would come to their table.

The restaurateur came over with a worried look on his face. "Something wrong with the food, folks?"

"Oh no. Your seafood is wonderful."

The frown disappeared from his face.

Ava said, "I was just wondering. That picture of Hemingway, the one nearest the door. It kind of overcrowds your wall there and doesn't look right."

The man looked at it. "Never gave it a thought."

She said, "Well, I collect things like that and I was wondering if you would like to sell it." She smiled. "I'll tell everyone back home where I got it and to be sure to pay you a visit."

The man returned her smile. "Why thanks. Uh…I dunno. You're right, it is kind of squeezed in there isn't it." He rubbed his modest chin beard and asked, "What would you pay for it?"

"Well it's near the door so I'm afraid it has some weather damage, but I'd go fifty dollars for it."

The man stroked his chin again. Then he said, "Sure. It's yours."

Ava was beaming when they left the restaurant. "Wow, I made a killing."

"Think so?"

"Know so. I've seen these on the Internet for five hundred."

Colin said, "Let me have your notebook."

"Why?"

"Just let me have it."

When she reluctantly handed it to him he turned to a fresh page and murmured "Ava" as he wrote her name, and a comment, down.

"What did you write?" She reached for the book but he held it away and out of her reach. She finally grabbed it and read aloud. "Crooked."

"Crooked?" she yelped. "That's not crooked that's just shrewd Yankee negotiating skill."

They went to bed early and fell asleep quickly. It had been another long day.

In the morning Ava got directions using her GPS to the dealer's house. When he took out the picture of Lincoln she looked at it for a long time. She seemed disappointed.

The man said, "What? It's just as I described to you and it's on the 'net."

Still frowning Ava said, "I'm not sure if that's Robert Lincoln's signature. Have you had it authenticated?"

"No. But I have it on good authority it's genuine."

"I don't know now."

While she was negotiating Colin looked around the shop. He found a seventeenth century cutlass with an English wordsmith's name engraved on it. He knew the wordsmith was famous. He asked the dealer how much.

The man said, "I've turned down three hundred."

"Oh," Colin said, a bit surprised at the high price.

When Ava joined him at the door, the dealer now looked chagrined.

"So you folks aren't interested in anything?"

Ava stopped just before opening the door. "OK, look. If you give us the picture and the sword for three hundred we'll take them both."

He lapsed into deep thought. "Okay. But only because things have been slow lately."

In the car Ava cackled like a witch stirring the brew. "What a score. What a day I'm having!"

Outside Colin took the notebook and began writing.

She smirked. "What are you writing now? Deceitful? Sneaky? Tricky?"

He said, "No. Very clever."

Ava smiled and took hold of his arm. They went to find a place to have lunch, a drink and a mini celebration. She was very pleased with her purchases.

It was a fun trip and by the time they got back to the hotel the couple felt like they had never been just acquaintances. Now they knew so much about each other. It was an unspoken thing, but both felt it. Both realized that the first day together in Florida they weren't learning about each other so much as trying to impress each other. Neither felt the need for that any longer. Not at all.

18

Colin had ignored his phone messages, which was a mistake. He would have liked to fly home with Ava and her group but after listening to several messages from Paula and Amos, including a threat from Paula to contact Owen, Colin was forced to take the early morning flight to Boston. While he was a little disappointed to be parting from Ava he did look forward to the alone time to think.

By the time the flight landed in Boston he had come to some conclusions. One was that he was definitely smitten by Ava and the other was that he needed to make some decisions if he was going to have his life in order. He wanted to be with Ava badly, but he wanted the fate of Madsen Funeral Home settled first.

Colin knew he should have shown Ava the deed to the funeral home. The timing and location of the trip was the perfect time for full disclosure about Madsen's and what Colin had to do. He had brought the deed with him to Florida, but could not muster the courage to tell her that the funeral home had to belong to someone by mid-February, or it would end up belonging to nobody but the state of Massachusetts. Now the deed stayed close to him inside his jacket.

Wearing a jacket felt odd, considering the warm, humid climate of South Florida. Despite begin gone for only a few days, his body had not adjusted to the temperature change. It was cold in Boston and the air smelled like snow. The gray morning was spitting an occasional snowflake but he hadn't seen any weather reports. Colin decided to skip going home and go directly to the funeral home. It was still early in the day and he wanted to talk to Amos some more about the finances of the funeral home from last year.

When he pulled into the funeral home parking lot, the Hewitt house had yellow tape wrapped around the fence, along with several **NO TRES-PASSING** signs affixed to various windows throughout the structure. Despite lackluster profits and several important expenses, Colin surmised that Amos must be preparing to move ahead with the demolition of the home.

As Colin walked up the side of the building, a huge burst of air blew up from the street, whipping his jacket open. He grabbed the lapels and pulled it tightly against him.

When Colin opened the door, he found Paula scurrying from the chapel to the front office carrying two small pots of flowers, while Owen vacuumed the carpet in the front family room.

Owen sensed movement behind him and turned off the vacuum. He spun on the balls of feet and threw his arms open. "Well, the prodigal son, or should I say, boss returns!"

Paula set the plants down in the chair and rested her fists against her hips. "Nice of you to join us." She gave Colin a look over and pinched his arm. He jerked it back. "You need to wear more sunscreen. You burn easily, just like Luke did."

"Paula, I know you and Amos have been trying to get a hold of me."

"Save it, Colin," she said tersely. "And don't worry, Amos and I have been busy and we picked up the slack in your absence."

Colin stepped closer to her when Owen impeded his movement with a forearm. "Word of advice brother, call someone the next time you decide to leave town."

Paula moved in front of them and waived a finger at Owen. "And don't you be so smug either, Owen Madsen. You are the last person we wanted to call, but we were out of options when we couldn't find Colin."

Owen turned and watched her head into the chapel. "Boy, I've missed her. Nobody exudes grouchy quite like Paula."

Colin locked eyes with Owen. "What *are* you doing here? Why aren't you back playing tennis at some country club on Nantucket Island? Or having brunch with someone famous who feigns interest in you but really hates your guts?"

Owen lowered his head and tapped Colin on the chest. "Let's see... you go MIA for a few days, you don't tell anyone you're leaving and you don't answer your phone. Then, I get a phone call from Amos asking if I've seen or heard from you. When I say no, he gets worried. I drive in from the coast to talk to Amos and find out there is a funeral going on." Owen rolled his shoulders. "Working on Sundays doesn't suit me. Anyways, I wait until the service is over, Amos takes the family to the cemetery and Paula and I strategize how to find you. She needed some help cleaning up after the service and I pitched into help, and then *voila*, you came through the front door."

Colin rolled his eyes. "Don't try to make yourself seem so altruistic. You came down here so you could stick your nose into everyone's business, then lecture me about leaving."

"Actually, Colin, I have been thinking that maybe you and I need to run the funeral home—together."

Colin felt the air go out of him. "What?"

"When we were at lunch the other day, it got me thinking." He leaned closer to Colin and lowered his voice to a whisper. "Clearly, you need some money to keep this place going and I always have the potential to make money."

Colin crossed his arms. "I know better than this. You do not do anything unless it benefits you. I was stupid to invite you to lunch last week in the first place."

Owen displayed a disarming smile, revealing a mouth full of pearly white teeth. "Is that any way to respond to a business proposal?"

Colin looked around the funeral home, grasping for a comeback that seemed just out of reach. He thought about the deed to the funeral home and the fact that in 45 days, he was no closer to making a decision than he was before. Perhaps that was why Owen really drove to Concord. As a real estate manager, he had connections with brokers, mortgage companies and banks throughout the state. Perhaps Owen had received a tip about Madsen's situation? The thought made his cheeks fill with blood. Colin suddenly felt extremely warm and stepped back and removed his coat.

As he walked across the room to the coat rack, Owen called out, "So you are just going to ignore me and leave."

Colin heard a rustling and crinkling of paper inside a pocket as he hung the coat. He leaned back and examined the coat, realizing it was the same coat that he wore to the funeral home nearly two weeks ago when he met with Amos and Ava. He bit his lip and smoothed over the pocket slowly, creating another crinkle.

Colin turned around to find Owen leaning against the doorframe into the front office. "So, are you going to answer me or not?"

Colin shook his head. "No, Owen, I'm not going to run the funeral home with you. Dad deeded the business to me in his will, and that is how everything will remain. You have a forty percent interest in the funeral home. If I need you for anything further, then I will let you know."

Owen pressed his lips tightly against his face. "So, that gives you the right to just leave town when you want to?"

Colin stepped closer to his brother and looked deep into his eyes. "I'm not saying what I did was right, but I am here to apologize. I do not need your help with anything."

Owen squinted then resettled a hard look on Colin. "You did get sunburned. You are not a big fan of the sun. Where did you go?"

"Florida, as if that's any of your business."

"With who? Are you planning on starting another version of Madsen's down south?" Owen belted out a full-throated, deep laugh.

Colin felt a lump form in his throat. "If you must know. I was with Ava."

"Ava" Owen ran a hand through his hair as his eyes darted back and forth. "Ava Hewitt?"

Colin swallowed. "Yes."

"No shit. Wow...my brother who would rather bury his head in a spreadsheet than talk to a woman went on a date with one...*to Florida!*"

"That's the problem," Paula added, reentering the family room. "You are not thinking clearly when you are thinking about something other than business."

Owen dropped his jaw. "Was it a nookie call, Colin? You went with Ava for some nookie? Oh, this is getting better and better. I'm so glad I drove down today."

"I'm not," Paula said, furrowing her brow. "Amos and I cleaned up plenty of your messes. I appreciate you coming down here and vacuuming the family room Owen, but now that Colin is here, you can leave."

Owen made a face as Colin interrupted. "Speaking of leaving, I need to talk to Amos. I need to apologize and explain." Colin thought that now would be the right time to tell him the truth about the deed and the deadline. "Which cemetery did he go to?"

Colin headed for the front door as he awaited her answer.

"Go home, Colin," Paula commanded. "Amos said he doesn't want to talk to you."

❀

Colin became depressed. He felt guilty for arguing with Owen in the middle of the funeral home. That discussion should have taken place between the two of them in private, but Owen always knew how to push and push Colin until he lashed out. In fact, Colin bolted out the door irritated and slightly hurt. Colin couldn't imagine why Amos wouldn't want to talk to him, but maybe Owen was right; Colin leaving with Ava after being back at the funeral home for just slightly more than two weeks had unsettled Amos and Paula.

He picked up his cell phone and called Ava. After a few seconds of static, the phone went to voice mail. Colin took a deep breath and planned on telling Ava what happened at the funeral home earlier, but instead he left an obligatory message asking her to call him soon.

After getting a cup of coffee in his own kitchen, Colin laid down on his bed and closed his eyes. He awoke to the sounds of wind whipping the outside shudders of the house. Colin pulled himself up and looked at the alarm clock next to his bed. The time read 9:19 a.m.

Disoriented, Colin leaped out of bed and looked for some warm clothes. He planned on going down to the funeral home to speak with Amos, even if he had to go upstairs and visit Amos in his apartment.

When Colin arrived at the funeral home, he was surprised to see two Concord Police cars parked out front. He hurried inside to find two police officers and a plainclothes detective milling about the office. The plainclothes man was talking to Amos. Colin decided to wait patiently and hope it wasn't something major. Paula flitted by and looked grim.

When Amos spotted Colin he interrupted the police detective and motioned him to come forward. Colin's eyes were full of questions so Amos started talking. "We had a robbery here last night. They got into the safe in the business office."

Colin's mouth formed a silent O. He had not expected anything like this. "How did they get into the safe? Did they take anything from the prep room across the hall?"

"No." Amos scratched his head and looked sheepish. "The darndest thing. Somebody must have had the combination."

This rendered Colin silent. The police detective stepped in and Amos introduced them. Motioning to Colin, he said, "Colin here is one of the owners of the business. Colin, this is Sergeant Phibbs of the Robbery Division." The man, dressed in a dark topcoat, blue shirt and striped tie looked more like he should be planting potatoes than investigating robberies.

Colin stuck his hand out. "Nice to meet you. Though not under these circumstances."

"I know what you mean. Too bad they got so much. Mr. Boggs here says that the business rarely has so much cash in the safe."

Since Colin did a double take, Amos said, "Old man Hubbard's funeral. Everybody in town knows that the old man always dealt in cash. Never wrote a check in his life. His daughter brought in twelve thousand dollars cash yesterday afternoon and I got too busy to go to the bank so I put it in the safe for the night. Came in this morning and found the safe open."

Sergeant Phibbs turned to Colin. "It's been snowing. No footprints and no signs of forced entry." He paused a moment. "I understand from talking with Ms. Matthews that you have been on vacation?"

"Yeah. In Florida."

Colin wasn't used to police procedure and techniques and although he didn't realize it at the time he had just produced a solid alibi.

Phibbs said, "I was just going over the possibilities that this was an inside job and who had the combination of the safe."

Colin turned to Amos. "Who did, Amos?"

The old man shuffled uncomfortably. "Actually nobody but me and my wife. I don't even think you have it, Colin. You haven't been a part of the business for too long and there would have been no reason to give it to you."

The detective said, "Oftentimes in cases like this someone who is pretty well trusted is able to see the safe being opened and memorized the combination, or it was written somewhere and he found it."

Amos was quick to add, "Like I said, Detective, I don't see how that could have happened."

Colin followed Phibbs and his detail as they walked through the funeral home as the forensics team went over the premises for fingerprints or DNA. As he was leaving Phibbs said, "I hate to say this, Mr. Boggs but unless fingerprints other than yours or DNA other than yours shows up there isn't much chance that we are going to catch this thief. But we'll do our best. I'll be in touch."

When he and his team left, Amos and Colin plopped down in office chairs in the front office looking stunned. After an awkward silence, Colin said, "I agree it has to be an inside job, Amos, but even more peculiar is that whoever did it not only had the combination to our safe but also knew about the Hubbard funeral and the old man's proclivities. It must be someone local."

"That cop said it was an inside job."

"I agree with that assessment."

"Me too," Amos said, as he poured them both some coffee. "Somebody here somehow got the combination. Like I told the police I don't have it written down anywhere. So how?"

Amos again looked sheepish as he sipped coffee. "I...I hate to tell ya this, Colin, but this couldn't have happened at a worse time with the payments for the limo repairs and all."

Colin didn't ask, just raised a brow. The old man went on. "Fred Hopkins dropped off our income tax return for this year and we owe a significant balance because we didn't pay off last year. We managed to get the payroll taxes in but not the business taxes." Amos inserted a blue folder between them.

"But don't we have insurance to cover the burglary?"

Amos shook his head. "Insurance was one of the casualties when we had to tighten our belts last year after your dad died."

Colin shook his head. He didn't notice those details on the spreadsheet. "Let's get back to yesterday afternoon. Was there anyone in the office at all during the day?"

Amos's face scrunched up in thought. "Nope. Don't remember anybody. Paula and I were busy with the Hubbard funeral."

"Well, I'm going home. Call me if you think of anything. Or you want to talk." Colin hoped that Amos would take that the right way. He hated to see the old man so troubled by this.

Colin went home. He could see that Amos was deeply embarrassed and upset about the robbery and the way it happened. Of course, Colin nor anyone else who knew him could cast any suspicion on Amos. Yet the old man could take no comfort from Colin's confidence in him. Amos still seemed guilty as well as worried about the bills and Madsen's future.

With no food at home, Colin found that he was hungry, and he doubted if there was anything edible in the fridge. He was right, there wasn't. So he walked down to the Old Town Café. He was in the mood for something New England. So he ordered corn chowder and a toasted BLT on rye. Mrs. Murphy was her cheery self until she put on her serious face and asked, "I hear there was trouble at Madsen's last night."

Colin knew that it must be all over town by now. Small towns were like that. He said, "Yeah, we had a burglary, Mrs. Murphy."

The old woman's face turned stiff. Not one for idle gossip, Colin felt sure that her distress was genuine. She also wasn't the type who would relish other people's problems. "Saints preserve us. What's becoming of people today? I swear it's a different world," she mumbled. "I'm sorry for your troubles, lad. Let me get your lunch," she said, as she shuffled off to get his order.

Ava wouldn't be back home till very late tonight so Colin had nobody to talk to. When he got home he opened up the tax return and began to study it. He had asked Amos for last year's return as well.

Colin compared the sales spreadsheet with the tax return. He was surprised at the drop in sales this year. Luke had always been the sparkplug of the business and so many people loved and trusted him. Now that he was gone that aspect of the business was gone too. There were a lot of new faces in town. People who had come to the area to work in the thriving 128 Industrial and Research belt. These people didn't know Luke of course, so they may or may not become customers. So he suspected there was more of a need for marketing techniques that Luke hadn't used.

Fresh from vacation Colin would rather just be with Ava and not fret about these problems.

He sat on the living room couch in front of the fireplace with a snifter of brandy, a comforting thing on a cold winter afternoon. It was getting dark when the phone rang in the middle of his dozing off.

It was Amos. His voice was hesitant. "Colin, you said to call you if I thought of anything. I had to think about it before I even called."

"What is it, Amos?"

"Well...Someone did come by yesterday afternoon. Will Newsome."

"Will? What did he want, more supplies from the morgue?"

"Yes."

Colin groaned.

"Will is having a hard time in business. He came by to borrow towels and embalming fluid yesterday before the funeral. I hate to turn him down."

"So he was here yesterday afternoon."

Amos nodded.

"Did you open the safe in front of him?"

"I honestly don't remember. But I'm inclined to think no. Like I said I was so busy with the Hubbard funeral. Mr. Hubbard had lots of kin and it seemed they were all here for the afternoon showing."

Colin thanked Amos for the call and his thinking was going in a different direction. He didn't want to tell this to the police. If he told the police that someone else committed the crime, that was in fact an accusation against a competitor and someone whose family had deep roots in the community. He didn't even want to believe that it was possible that Will did that. Maybe he would take it upon himself to do some snooping. He wanted to say goodnight to Ava but when he called at a time when he guessed she would be home he got no answer. Maybe her flight was late. So he went to bed and dreamed about burglaries in the night.

19

Amos was upset. He asked for a meeting with Colin in the morning. When he phoned Colin and asked him to come over, the angst was evident in his voice. To say that Colin was not looking forward to the meeting would be the understatement of the decade. When Colin arrived at ten the next morning, he was carrying several paper cups of coffee and a dozen mixed donuts for the staff. He had a sense everyone needed a little morale boost.

After handing out the coffee and donuts Amos turned to Colin. The old man's brow was furrowed with worry and he seemed more nervous than Colin had ever remembered seeing him. When he collapsed himself into a chair in the front family room, it seemed that he had something to say that he dreaded. "I hate to give you news like this but I don't see how we're going to make payroll let alone keep the lights on."

Paula crossed her arms across her chest. "Twelve thousand dollars for this business can't be swallowed up in the cash flow."

Colin took a deep breath and said, "How much would you say we need to get by?"

"Well," the old man said, scratching his mane of silver, "we were in tough shape before the money was taken. I'd say we need at least fifteen thousand by the end of the month or we'll have to close the doors. And that assumes that business for the next month is normal. As you know there is no 'normal' really in this business. We have competition from Newsome's and I have to tell you that they have been advertising quite a bit in the newspaper and on the radio in recent months. We should be too. We can't expect to get by on your dad's reputation alone. Not in these tough economic times with the competition we're now facing."

This was like a splash of cold water in Colin's face. While it wasn't really a shock it somehow wasn't entirely in his hands and he wasn't thinking about it. This twelve thousand-dollar loss was the proverbial straw that broke the camel's back.

Colin, in an uncharacteristic way wanted to get away from the business and all of its problems. So again, in an uncharacteristic way, he muttered to Paula, "I have to go figure this out, folks. I'll let you know what I come up with."

Without checking the old man's reaction he was out the door.

Colin was about to do yet another thing that he didn't usually do. Although it was only noon he sought out the bar in the Concord House Hotel. The crowd, such as it was at the small town hotel, was filtering in and the tinkle of dinnerware announced that it was the lunch hour. He sat at the bar and the pretty barmaid asked for his order.

"Jack and Ginger please, lots of ice."

As he nursed the drink, he confirmed what he already knew. He'd have to come up with the money personally. *Although, my brother Owen might be able to help.* He fished out his cell and dialed Owen at work. When the receptionist answered, she said, "I'm sorry, sir, Mr. Madsen doesn't work here any longer."

Doing a mental double take, Colin tried the home number. A sleepy sounding Owen answered. "Hey man, what's up? Decide to sell the place did you?"

Colin let the remark roll off him and explained the problem and the business need for a loan.

Owen was at first astounded that he was being asked for a loan. "Now you change your mind and you want Mr. forty percent here to be a real partner in the firm. Well, you're too late Colin. I'm between jobs. I don't have it. What little I have from my severance package I'm going to use to go to Marco Island and hit the links. My game is rusty." Then he was a bit more conciliatory. "I wouldn't be able to come up with enough to help anyway."

With that, after a few remarks about Owen's job prospects, Colin wished him well and told him to have fun on the golf course.

He couldn't think of anyone else who had any connection with the family or the business who could make them a loan. He concluded, *Well, I gotta hit my 401k as diminished as it is in this bad economy.* Not to mention the penalties he would have to pay for early withdrawal.

He ordered a BLT on wheat, and a cup of coffee for lunch. He enjoyed a comfortable lunch and relaxed a bit. He realized that he had been pretty much sheltered most of his life from these kinds of problems, never having to face business crises like his father had. After lunch he would make the phone calls to get the 401k withdrawal from his company. He found that he would have to come in and sign some paperwork, so he started down Route 2 for Boston.

Colin liked traveling Route 2, both for the peaceful, hypnotic quality that a two-lane road provided but also because it was the main alternative to the Massachusetts Turnpike Toll Highway. Route 2 eventually ended for Colin at Boston Common in Boston. It took the rest of the afternoon to sign papers and get a check for $15,000.00.

It was almost dark when he got back to Concord and he was feeling needy for the comfort of Ava's arms. When he called her phone he got her voice mail. Maybe it was too early. He was that anxious. When she didn't pick up at seven he called her sister on her private line which Ava had given to Colin. "Hi. It's Colin. How are you? I've been calling Ava's phone but I only get the voice mail. Do you know if she's out somewhere?"

"Oh yeah, Colin. She mentioned that she wouldn't have time to call you. Her company called and they needed one of the trainees to go down to Georgia and help out at one of the units down there that was having staffing problems. I'm sure she planned to call you when she got there."

"Oh I see." He felt a bit juvenile with the disappointment that he knew was in his voice so he cheerily said, "Oh no problem. I'll just wait to hear from her."

He slumped in his old lounge chair and stared at the blank TV screen. Absentmindedly he turned on the TV and settled in to wait for her call. When he snapped awake just before midnight he felt a bit chilly in the empty old house. He checked his phone messages. None. Wearily he trudged upstairs to the warmth and comfort of his bed. It had been a bad day overall.

In the morning he dropped by and gave Amos the check. The old man looked relieved. "I know this is rough, Colin, but we still have to sit down one day soon and plot out a business plan for this funeral home. We're on such a thin string that almost anything can sink us. We need some reserves. We need—"

Colin politely interrupted him. "Amos, I know everything you're saying is true but we'll have to talk later. I have things to do."

"Oh sure, Colin. I gotcha."

This was not entirely true. Colin was in a funk from the double bar-reled hits he had taken. There was still no call from Ava and that somehow bothered him. He knew they were tighter than ever and this shouldn't be a problem. Yet it bothered him.

With the need to think beyond his current melancholy he decided on a ride over to Lake Walden. It was a favorite boyhood haunt where he swam and fished and canoed every summer. He felt a need to go back, and drove through town and across Route 2 to the famed spot immortalized by Henry David Thoreau. He of the unique progressive philosophy known as Transcen-dentalism and the super deep mind. Colin had often visited his cabin in the woods by the lake, now a historic landmark, when he was a kid.

He soon found himself sitting in the parking lot and staring at the lake shimmering in the midday sun. It was true. Things did look smaller than when you were younger. Yet it was the same old lake where he had grown up.

Although he wasn't in the mood to talk about it, he knew that Amos was right. This loan was a stop gap at best. They did have to make plans if Madsen's Funeral Home was going to have any future. Then his mind wan-dered back to the twelve thousand dollar loss. It was definitely an inside job, but every instinct he had told him it was not Amos or Paula. The connection to Will Newsome haunted him. It was true he was having money problems. It was also true that he was there that afternoon ostensibly to borrow more sup-plies. But how could he prove that let alone get the money back? Colin knew that getting the money back would go a long way to insuring that Madsen's would survive.

When he got a check for the money the way the formula worked out Colin had an extra thousand dollars in his pocket. Out of nowhere he decided to invest it.

He went back to the Concord Hotel, had a late lunch and checked over the phone books at the telephone stand. One of the few remaining anywhere. He found a detective agency. It looked like a small ad for a small agency which was exactly what he wanted.

An hour later he was at a turn of the century brick building down-town. As he climbed the stairs to the second floor he wondered what this detective would be like. He walked down a short musty hall housing offices and stopped at one with the name Augustus Shaw. He went in. The office appeared to be empty. Then a door, evidently to the bathroom, opened. Shaw was an older guy. At one time he must have been muscular because he was still tight with a slight paunch. Colin introduced himself. Shaw's eyebrows moved almost imperceptibly at the name Madsen. He said, "Call me Gus. Augustus sounds like some old Roman senator."

Colin smiled. He liked him already.

When Colin sat in the visitor's chair Shaw asked, "Madsen. That's a familiar name. Are you connected with Madsen's Funeral Home?"

"Yeah. It was my father's. I'm taking part in running it for a while."

"I thought so. You know your dad was good to my family when my uncle passed. Nice guy."

"Thanks."

"What can I do for you, Mr. Madsen?"

"Colin, please. Well, as you might know we were robbed the day before last. They took twelve thousand out of the safe. Only the Manager and his wife have the combination."

"Yeah, I read about it in the paper. Have any suspects in mind?"

"Yes I do." Colin went on to give him the history of the business and the name of the only suspect they had. He added, "I only have a limited amount of money to try to find if my suspicions are true. At the rate you just gave me, that only gives me about a week to investigate."

Gus Shaw leaned back in his chair having taken in all the information Colin gave him. "Let's concentrate on what we have for now. Don't worry about the week. I know it's all you have to spend on this. Give me two or three days and I'll be in touch. Or even sooner if I hit pay dirt."

Somehow it was a relief to be doing something about the robbery rather than just lamenting their bad luck. This was a matter of honor if Will had something to do with this. After all, Will had been a friend and Madsen's had helped him out as much as they could. Towels and embalming fluid are not cheap these days. And what might have been trivial in the old days was now quite expensive. Not to mention the price of private detectives...now there's an expense he was sure his father never had to face.

20

Gus Shaw knocked on the door at the Hubbard residence. A middle-aged woman came to the door. Shaw asked, "Are you Mrs. Hubbard?"

"Yes. Can I help you?"

"My name is Shaw. We spoke on the phone. Mrs. Hubbard, I'm investigating a robbery at the Madsen Funeral Home. I wonder if I could ask you a couple of questions that might help me."

"Certainly, please come in. I just made coffee. Will you have some?"

"Sure. Thanks."

When Shaw was sitting in the dining room and looked around he thought he might have well been in a turn of the century home. The old Victorian appeared as dusty and from another era as a Henry James novel. With a cup of coffee in front of him he said, "The reason I'm here ma'am is that the money that was stolen from Madsen's was the entire total you folks paid the funeral home for burial services for your father."

"Oh dear," Mrs. Hubbard said, putting down her own coffee cup.

"Yeah, so I was wondering if you could answer a few questions. Does your family use cash to pay most of your bills?"

"Why yes. My father was very old-fashioned. We couldn't get him to open a checking account. It took a major effort to get him to open a savings account. He worried about 1929 all over again. He insisted on paying in cash. He said it was good enough for his father."

"I see. Can you tell me where the twelve thousand dollars to pay Madsen's came from?"

"Well let me see. He keeps a good amount in a safe in the house. I believe it's been in the safe since the old Pilgrim Savings and Loan closed years ago."

"I see. Who paid the funeral home?"

"I did."

"Do you remember what the money consisted of? I mean how many stacks? What denominations?"

"Oh yes, Papa always used one hundred dollar bills for big bills. There were twelve packets of ten one hundred dollar bills."

Shaw couldn't think of anything else and so he thanked Mrs. Hubbard for her help and left.

Back in his office he sat pondering. *The old Pilgrim Savings and Loan closed down over forty years ago. Used to be on Main Street. They had those distinctive money packets they gave you for your Christmas Club.*

He made a call to the Federal Reserve and asked a few questions, listening carefully to the answers.

When his part time secretary Joanne Collins came in about eleven he greeted her and said, "Joanne, listen, I need you to play detective for me."

She nodded, a gleam in her eye.

"At exactly two o'clock call the Newsome Funeral Home and ask to speak to Mr. Will Newsome. Tell him your relative just died and you wanted to discuss arrangements. Act confused. Keep him on the phone."

"Sure, Gus. Do I get a bonus?"

"My undying gratitude."

She grinned.

At a quarter of two wearing a dark suit, a somber face and a false mustache Gus sat in front of Will Newsome' desk and began discussing funeral arrangements with him. He took his time, sneaking glances everywhere via his peripherals. When Joanne called at exactly two and distracted Will, Gus got up to stretch his legs and accidentally kicked over the wastepaper basket beside the desk. Will looked up but Gus motioned him quickly as he himself picked up the small pile of trash. At the bottom of the pile he saw what he was looking for and quickly secreted it in his hand.

A few minutes after the phone call Gus begged off and said he would be back the next day.

Back in his office he sat at his desk when Joanne brought him in his afternoon coffee. He said, "You did good, Joanne."

He held up a money band with an imprint on it. "Do you remember these? Heck no you're way too young. The old Pilgrim Savings closed long before your time."

"Forty years ago? I wasn't even born," she said with a wry grin.

He left about three-thirty and said to Joanne, "See you tomorrow, Ace."

She smiled.

⬥

A half-hour later he was at Madsen's and talking to Colin and Amos. He began by saying, "I'm almost a hundred percent sure your suspicions are correct about Will Newsome. Look what I found in his wastepaper basket." He laid the paper money wrappers on the desk. "Is this what your payment was wrapped in?"

Amos blurted, "Hey that's right. I remember commenting on the old Pilgrim Savings."

"Also there's a good chance that the money has distinct serial numbers of forty years ago. A certain run that will be traceable."

Amos and Colin exchanged glances. Gus said, "I have a plan. Here it is, that is if you go along with it."

⬥

Next morning Gus was back at Newsome's. This time without the mustache. He got a querulous look from Will Newsome. Gus said, "My name is Gus Shaw, Mr. Newsome and I'm a private investigator hired by Colin Madsen."

Will blanched. He took a noticeable gulp. "What is this? I..."

"Look, Mr. Newsome, I can save you a lot of trouble and even some jail time. Just hear me out."

Will shut up.

Gus went on. "We have evidence that it was you that took twelve thousand dollars from the Madsen safe."

"Hey, wait a—"

Gus cut him off. "Please spare me the denials. I said we have evidence. Including fingerprints. True, without a good suspect the fingerprints on the envelope holding the money would be useless. But we do have a good suspect now. We can even trace the serial numbers of the hundred dollar bills if you try to spend them."

Will lapsed silent, his eyes boring into Gus. "You have nothing...I—"

Gus interrupted again. "If we can't convict you immediately we can and we will keep you from spending that money."

Will dropped his face into his hands at his desk.

Gus let a long anxious silence pass. Then he said, "But I have a way out for you. As the only other funeral home in Concord, you've been associated with the Madsen's for years. They are willing to let bygones be bygones if you return the money."

Will's brows raised.

Gus cocked his head. "That's right. No criminal prosecution if you give the money back."

"How can I be sure?"

"We thought of that." Gus reached into his inside suit jacket pocket and took out an envelope. "I've got a check from Madsen's for twelve thousand made out to you with the notation on the memo column that says repayment of loan. You'll also notice that Mr. Madsen countersigned the check, in effect cashing it for you."

Will looked dumbfounded.

"This is your out if the Madsen's were to go back on their word and try to prosecute you." Another long silence. "If you know anything about Amos Boggs you know that he is a man of his word. But." He let the word linger. "In case you have doubts I can give you a photocopy of both sides of this check which will show you simply got paid back by the Madsen's and Colin signed the check over to you."

"But why?"

"Maybe Madsen's was trying to collect the insurance money. Whatever it was, it leaves you pretty much in the clear."

Will was thinking hard.

Gus interrupted his thoughts. "This is grand theft, Mr. Newsome. You could get over fifteen years of Federal time."

His voice shaking, Will said, "There's no need for that. I'll get you the money."

"That's the sensible thing to do."

❈

An hour later Gus was smiling as he handed the money to Colin. "Guess it pays to know who your friends are."

Colin and Amos were speechless. In a much better mood now, Colin hurried home to call Ava.

21

Colin was especially glad to see Ava who had been away much longer than expected. While waiting anxiously for her at the bottom of an escalator at the Logan Airport air terminal he caught sight of her lush hair bouncing above the sea of passengers flowing down the stairs as she tried to spot him. As soon as she was clear of the crowd she flew into his arms and they clung to each other until it was getting embarrassing. With a blush in his cheeks Colin said, "What do you feel like doing, a drink to unwind with dinner or go straight home?"

She opted for dinner, planning to drop her luggage off whenever they could.

As they drove from the airport she let out a long sigh. "That was the most intense training of my life. No sooner did we get one problem under control when another popped up. I know the company didn't plan it that way it just happened, and although it was pointed out that this string of events doesn't happen every day, it could."

Colin got the impression that she liked the excitement of it.

He thought, *You're preaching to the choir, babe,* but he didn't want to dwell on business or business problems.

They agreed on drinks at the Yankee Inn, located between the Lenox and Pittsfield Town Centers. As Colin and Ava headed into the main lodge, they could see the snow-covered Berkshire Hills behind the Inn, which was crusted over with snow and ice.

Colin asked for a table in the dining room, next to the real wood fireplace at the back.

Ava sighed over the first martini. "Oh that's so good. I can feel it down to my toes."

"So you had a rough week, huh?"

"I'll say. How're things here?"

"Much the same with a few new wrinkles." Her brow raised. He recounted the burglary episode and its conclusion.

She reacted rather sadly, lowering her eyes. "It's such a shame when people, business professionals, do things like that. People of our generation seem so desperate to make it in business that they'll do anything."

"Sometimes it seems that way doesn't it," he said as he sipped his own martini. "The worst part is that while it may have saved his business it would have no doubt put us out of business."

After dinner they went back to his house and he got the fireplace in the back living room going. He brought out a bottle of chardonnay and they cozied down in front of the fire. The bottle was half-empty when they succumbed to their longing and made slow passionate love until exhaustion overtook them. He didn't want to disturb her so he got a quilt from the hall closet and covered her while he settled down in his favorite recliner.

In the morning, while he was getting breakfast ready, she got a call on her cell phone. He was putting the finishing touches on breakfast when he heard snatches of her conversation. The gist of it was something bad happened somewhere with the business and she was required. He was tense when she got off the phone. "You're not going to believe this," she said. He remained silent. She launched into it and was obviously animated and agitated. "They have more problems. This time out in St. Louis."

"And?"

"I have to be there tonight."

"Meaning of course you have to travel today."

"Yes."

It was obvious both were upset by the turn of events. She lamented, "Now that I did such a good job in Atlanta now I'm their go to girl for problems, evidently."

"How old is this company?"

"Well it's a new franchise as you probably know, but they're in the critical stages of development. You know, the point where they either burst onto the scene or fizzle. We've got the outlets we just don't have them all operating properly. You know, everything isn't working the way it's supposed to according to the training manual."

"Do you think they're putting the right personal touch into it that the business requires?"

"Oh believe me they know the importance of that. They know they're competing with the mom and pops that have not only been around a long time but for many generations. They're trying in their own corporate way to emulate the warmth and personal attention that the mom and pops give."

Seeing the disappointment in his eyes she took his hands. "I'm sorry. I promise I'll make it up to you as soon as I get back."

Trying to be a good sport he didn't pout but rather feigned his agreement with some enthusiasm.

But when she left some odd feelings began to percolate. Feelings he was in no way used to or familiar with. He realized that she was on a new job and had to do what her bosses wanted. Still he had a lingering and nagging doubt. Were they at the state in their relationships where she would (or should) do anything for him? Drop anything, maybe especially career wise, for his benefit? But wasn't that chauvinistic thinking? Was he a chauvinist at heart? As a career bachelor and one who never had any relationships as close as this one with Ava he was thoroughly confused. If he had to dash off to put out a business fire wouldn't he expect her to understand? Even if it involved disappointment? He knew most idealists felt that romance should always come before business. But what was it that every college kid learned in Voltaire's *Candide*? That everything must be viewed *in the best of all possible worlds,* a theme that runs throughout. It's easy to say that personal relationships and romance *should* come before business but let's face it he told himself, that's hardly practical. At least in the *real* world.

He realized that he wished she would say to her boss: *No damnit. I just got home. I want to spend some time with my man.*

Now he had to argue with himself. How practical is that? Especially at this stage of their relationship. After all, he hadn't given her a ring. He hadn't made any plans with her. Heck, he hadn't even told her he loved her yet, though he was pretty sure he did. But even that was a problem. Did he love her? How did one know?

He got pretty disgusted with himself with these juvenile questions. A grown man should have a better grip on his feelings than this.

Colin was feeling a strong need to talk to someone. This brought on another puzzle. In his thirty-five years as a bachelor, he of course had made friends. But were any of them close enough to discuss his most personal feelings with?

With nothing else to take up his time he decided to have drinks and dinner at the Yankee Inn. He hoped that sitting alone at dinner, he didn't look like the unhappy wretch he actually was feeling like.

But after dinner when he was preparing to leave, an attractive woman stopped at his table. She was probably his age or even a little older. Her long blonde hair, at least, made her look younger. But all in all she was very attractive. He was expecting the question 'are you with Madsen, etc, etc. I knew your father.'

But she didn't indicate that she knew him at all. Instead she said, "I work here as a hostess. I couldn't help notice that you had dinner alone. I was just hoping that you weren't stood up. I...I know what a crummy feeling that is. Whatever the reasons."

As surprised as he was he said, "Oh....ooh no. I wasn't stood up. Nothing like that."

She smiled, and it was genuine. "I'm so glad. Just thought I'd ask. I'm bold but usually not that bold. Anyway. Have a nice night."

"Uh...you too."

He was so rattled he stuck around for a night cap to think things out, knowing he wasn't in a good enough shape to drive.

Now that might be a sign. If that wasn't a pick up attempt I don't know what it was. The important thing, though, is that I didn't take her up on it or tried to pursue it in any way, even if it only meant making a new friend. That's got to mean something.

If ever a scenario called for Colin to seek out at least some innocent and platonic friendship, this was it. But he had no interest. Maybe he had just come to some major conclusions about himself. Ava's next step might prove that out. Or not.

22

By the end of the third week of January, the hard New England winter had subsided somewhat. There was a fresh, cool snap in the air.

Colin and Ava's relationship was changing too. They seemed more and more in tune on many levels. They both had discussed their favorite outdoor activities. Both recalled some of them from their childhood together. Like riding bikes, swinging at baseballs at the local batting cage, roller blading.

But there were also drawbacks. Ava had graduated from her training course and it seemed that she had such a high aptitude for the profession that she was quickly promoted to an assistant manager position in running the district which spanned from the rocky coast of Maine to the canyons of Arizona. This kept her out of town at least two weeks of the month, much to Colin's chagrin.

On the business level, Colin had made some major decisions. First, as a result of the debacle involving Will Newsome the funeral home was almost fifteen thousand dollars richer because of Colin's injection of his 401K money from his company. His leave of absence would be up in a few weeks and he was back to work in Boston with the distinct knowledge that he had to save enough money to keep in reserve for Madsen emergencies. Plus, he still had not decided that he wanted to keep the funeral home. If Colin decided to sell or walk away from the business, he would not need to save any money for funeral home emergencies.

In light of the damaged safe debacle, one of the first decisions Colin made was to forbid Amos or Paula to share morgue supplies with Will Newsome. The other decision he made was to offer to buy ten percent of his brother, Owen's forty percent. Owen was only too happy to accept. This gave Colin more controlling interest in the company, which confirmed two things: One, he might stay at his job in Boston and continue to own Madsen, or two, he could decide eventually to move back to Concord to run Madsen. Bottom line: he was committed to Madsen's future. He saw it as continuing his father's legacy. He didn't really feel that he owed it to his father, rather he felt that the Madsen name was important in Concord and didn't want to be the one to see its demise.

But of course with most of the fifteen thousand gone it was back to a kind of 'put out the local fires as they occur' mentality, which was even more difficult because he had the job in Boston to keep him busy. He knew that sometime in the near future the building was going to need some major repairs involving the roof and the sub structure, neither an inexpensive proposition.

During the days Ava was in town they had sometimes spent a couple of nights at his place on Haverhill Street and sometimes at her new condo in Concord on the weekends.

Colin had little or no interest in one of her favorite pastimes, antiquing, but he went along with it simply for the joy of spending the day with her. But what happened was the more he went the more interested he became in some of the auctions they attended in New Hampshire, Maine and upstate New York.

One such find was a Civil War Navy Colt that was gathering dust in the far corner of some New Hampshire barn. Colin was so fascinated with it that he bought it on sight setting him back several hundred dollars. And then, putting the cart before the horse he began researching the piece, which he found fascinating. It belonged to a Chief Petty Officer in the Union Navy, one Daniel McCane based on a ship, the *USS Mt. Washington* which hunted Confederate blockade runners off Hatteras. He traced the gun back to the development of the weapon, making Colt one of the country's first tycoons. He then tried to retrace its history in the McCane family when Chief McCane came home from the war.

Ava on the other hand was more into Louis XIV, Queen Anne, old spindles and other items uniquely interesting to the feminine psyche. But together they had a great time scouring the barns and attics of New England.

They had a great time, but a new set of circumstances emerged. Ava had been so adept at her job she remained constantly busy, and many of their plans and conversations were interrupted or cancelled because of business matters. This put even more pressure on her and more time away from home.

They were at dinner at 80 Thoreau Restaurant during their weekend stay at her condo when it came up. He could tell that she tried to turn the whole thing into a celebration (which it should have been) but knew he would be upset.

He asked, "How much do you love this job?"

Her answer was immediate. "Love it. Can't you tell?"

After an awkward silence she said, "I know you're not happy about it and neither am I, but I would waste everything I've put into this job if I didn't take another promotion."

"So those are your options?"

She leveled her gaze at him. "Yes, they are. I could refuse. But that would relegate me to the backwaters of the company and others would quickly take the job and move on up."

"Is that what it's all about? Moving on up?"

She looked at him. "Isn't that what taking a job in corporate America is all about, moving on up?"

He lowered his head. He said, "I guess that was a pretty dumb question. We're all trying to do what we like or do best when it comes to making a living."

That required no response from her and so there was a new silence, only the tinkling of her utensils, her head low.

She finally came up with, "My district isn't that big, maybe we can arrange for you to visit me some weekends and for me to visit you on others."

He didn't want to put a damper on her good news so he readily agreed to her suggestion having no idea how it was going to work. Or what the travel and hotel costs would do to his budget now constrained with the demands of Madsen's added to it.

He made a good effort at making the rest of the evening appear to be a celebration with all kinds of wisecracks about her becoming a captain of industry.

❧

The first time they were called upon to test this plan was when Ava was required to spend a considerable amount of time in New York City. The plan was for Colin to fly down on Friday night and stay over until Sunday night.

While they had a great time, having dinner at the Russian Tea Room and enjoying winter in Central Park complete with a buggy ride, inflation had taken its toll on the Big Apple. And if Colin didn't have a reserve on his credit card he would have run out of cash by Saturday afternoon.

While they were lying in bed enjoying a room service brunch Ava said, "I hope this weekend isn't breaking the bank."

Colin would never admit the hit his wallet was taking. He simply shrugged it off. After all, no man wanted to appear to his lady love that he couldn't afford to show her a good time. But the practicality of it required that he take a small loan from his credit union to get through to pay day. Thank God there were no major upheavals or problems at Madsen's. That day Colin understood how close to the vest he was playing it.

The first time their arrangement took her back to Concord he couldn't afford any side trips but they had fun skiing and fireside dinners at local Inns. He hoped she didn't get the impression that was all he could afford—though as it happened it was.

The other aspect of all this was that even the short time they had spent in Manhattan she had run into several men while they were out and about town. They were rather warm greetings as some were business associates and it was hard to admit that deep down he didn't like it. She was too beautiful to be out and around such glamorous places like Manhattan. It seemed as though it wasn't until they were out in the big corporate world that he saw just how alluring she was. Or was he by now so much in love that he was reverting to high school jealousy?

At some point in every relationship both parties feel certain of the other's personality and character. One afternoon they had been hiking the mushy trail around Lake Walden. The temperature had warmed into the 50s and the thaw had left the trails muddy. They passed the remains of Henry David Thoreau's cabin. A discussion about Thoreau ensued. Ava said, "Did you appreciate Thoreau when you studied him in high school?"

"Well, I knew every high school kid in America was reading about him but I wasn't particularly impressed."

Ava shrugged. "If I were to pick up a book to read on a long flight I wouldn't pick Walden."

"And why do you think that is?"

She shrugged. "I guess I'm a long way from the pure bred Yankee girl of old."

With a grin, Colin said, "Which is to say you're no longer dull, conservative and stubborn headed."

Taking up the challenge she said, "Which is to say I ever was?" She tossed her hair and locked eyes with him. "I'll dare you."

"And the dare is?"

"We swim out to the middle of the lake and back." He nodded. Until Ava said, "Naked."

That lost Colin at least half of his bravado. But he couldn't turn down the challenge.

It was already feeling like a bad idea when they began to strip. At the water's edge they plunged in and stroked for the middle of the lake. He was feeling daring by this point, however, glad to show her he was not a stuffed shirt.

They were almost to the shore when a group of hikers appeared on the trail opposite where they were to come ashore. The hiker's called, "Do you need some help? Hang on...that water's freezing...we will get you some help."

"We're fine!" they shouted back, secretly mortified.

Colin and Ava just treaded water. Ava shouted, "We had a bet going on here. We're coming in."

Someone on shore said, "Yeah, probably a good idea."

A few minutes later, ashore and scrambling into their clothes, Colin said, "Quick thinking. No flies on you."

"I might have lost my conservative ways but not my shrewd sense of malarkey."

As simple as the exercise was it taught Colin that he didn't know *everything* about his lady love. *I wonder what else I don't know about her?* It made him a bit more uncomfortable about her than he had ever been...and yet a bit more intrigued as well.

23

Colin was noticing some more changes, though subtle, in Ava. She talked a lot about the people in her office and some of them were men though she never suggested there was anything but business between them. But the subjects that they talked about left Colin feeling a bit ambivalent. It wasn't really that they were personal subjects but rather they were deep and that somehow seemed to take something from their relationship.

They were having dinner at the Concord Inn Saturday evening after a full day of antiquing. Colin had suggested it but the main draw was a big auction near the estate at Ventfort Hall in Lennox.

Ava was lingering over her first cocktail of the evening.

He said, "Did you have a good time today?"

"Yeah, it was great. I loved the place. And it's such a pretty part of Western Massachusetts."

"And all the history," Colin added. "I never realized how much history there was up there."

She smiled.

"That's why I think that writing table I bought has an interesting history. And though the seller only hinted at it I'm looking forward to researching the piece. I have a feeling it's important. After all, he linked it to a man named Davis who is associated with the spiritualist movement."

Colin looked a little blank.

Ava explained. "You know, before I got into the funeral business I didn't give much thought to the afterlife. Oh, I'm a good Baptist but I still never thought much about that sort of thing. But now, sometimes I do."

"Are you talking about psychics or ghosts?"

"Well, both, actually. Houdini was a showman and his wife kept his image alive but most people feel that was a commercial venture."

"You mean the fact that she is supposed to have communicated with him?"

Ava smiled and sipped her cocktail.

"This man Davis is supposed to have communicated with the dead in a very real way," she said.

"You mean thumping on walls and strange noises?"

"Well, something like that. This guy at work has done a real survey of it and there's places in Massachusetts like Salem that are the center of the movement. Of course, everyone is interested in what happens to us after death but few have done any real research up until the late nineteenth century and this man Davis."

Ava made eye contact with Colin. "You grew up in this business. Did you ever talk to your father about what happens to the spirit after death?"

"Yeah, but my father was a pretty straight-laced kind of guy who was faithful to his religion and he always looked at it in religious terms. Back in his day there were mostly Protestants in town but lately there has been an influx of other religions, mostly Catholic and some Jewish and even Islam. But no, he never talked about anything but the soul's ascendancy. Even if he buried the worst murderer in town he kept his rhetoric pretty much the same, sending that bad person off with God's blessing and grace as much as the good man that truly deserved God's grace."

Ava listened carefully, then she said, "Well, there are some remarkable stories out of the Poughkeepsie area about spiritualism and supposedly some real proof that contact with the other side has been made. I mean real contact not the showmanship of Mrs. Houdini. If I ever had the time I'd like to research it but as it is I'm up to my neck in the corporate side of things."

Colin sipped his drink and looked at Ava. His eyes were full of questions and she was curious. She asked, "What?"

"What do you think of the funeral home business?" he asked.

She thought for a moment. "Well to me, being trained as I was, it is a business just like any other business. Our challenge in corporate is to compete with the old-fashioned establishments." She blinked a second. "Like Madsen's. You know it's all balance sheets, spreadsheets and ninety-nine percent marketing using the amazing new advantages of the Internet and other social media outlets."

The couple had never discussed anything like this and suddenly it gave Colin a funny feeling. Like he wasn't sitting down with his girlfriend but with a competitor who would, if she had the chance, bury his business. He didn't actually believe this but the nature of the conversation had gone from the spiritual to the corporate and everyone knew that corporate America had already wiped out most of the mom and pop operations in every business from gas stations to convenience stores to restaurants. It gave him an odd feeling talking to Ava about these things. It wasn't like he was talking to a friend anymore.

She seemed to sense the bit of distance between them and went back to the original conversation.

"Each religion has its own theory about the afterlife I guess, but most everyone agrees that there is one. Nobody, at least no thinking person, believes that we go into the ground and eventually return to dust." She thought some more and then said, "No wait, that isn't true. Part of the Catholic burial service says something like, 'from dust to dust...' Of course, that's only the physical body. The spirit has a definite destination, either a good place or a bad place or even somewhere in between."

Colin sipped his drink. "I can see you've given these things a lot of thought. I have to admit I just followed my father's way and that was bringing comfort to the loved ones no matter what religion and he always kept it as a matter of compassion."

Ava perked up when she continued talking about her friends at work. "This guy at work has done some studying on the whole idea of reincarnation."

Colin said, "That idea gives a lot of comfort to some people. Of course it brings out the ego in many, too. Most people who believe they lived other lives think they must have been an important person. He was Napoleon or she was Cleopatra. Nobody seems to have been a simple farmer or a humble blacksmith."

Ava smiled. "I guess that's part of the appeal of reincarnation. The idea that we could have been someone important. There is a new field of hypnotherapy that has made great leaps and bounds in this field."

Colin raised an eyebrow. "This guy at work knows about this too?" He didn't realize that there was a tinge of jealousy in his tone.

"Well, yeah. The way he explains it, the therapist can put you so far under, so deeply asleep that he can actually move you back in time and find out what you were doing in the past. He has to be careful to stop you at the right place. In other words you might have been a Roman centurion in one life and then a common merchant in another. Depends on where he stops your memory and what you can recall."

She saw the doubt in Colin's eyes and remarked, "No, it's not considered quackery. At least not anymore. People today are much more willing to believe in things like this."

Colin said, "I suppose that in the modern world where things are changing so rapidly there is a natural movement to believe in all kinds of progressive ideas."

She quickly replied, "Well believe it or not, this guy went under hypnotherapy for his own personal reasons and it turns out that he was once an Iroquois Indian living in the Hudson River Valley. He partook in the French and Indian Wars and later fought with the British against the American colonials."

Colin, looking doubtful, said, "And he really believes this?"

"Oh yes. Very seriously. He claims that if you can trace your ancestry back far enough you will find clues to confirm this."

"I see it on TV all the time, outfits that trace ancestry and come up with all kinds of interesting facts about yourself."

"The Internet," she said, "has brought out the fact of how interested in themselves people are these days."

"Everyone wants to shine in some way, I guess," Colin said.

Dinner arrived and they got off the subject for a while.

Colin stopped eating a moment and gazed at Ava. "Do you think that these people who go to hypnotherapists are trying to find out something that makes them more interesting or special?"

She looked at him. "Of course. But you still can't necessarily discount the legitimacy of it."

He grinned. "You can if you believe it's a lot of hokum."

She seemed a bit defensive about his comment and it showed.

Colin suspected that he might just be reacting to this man at work whom she found so fascinating.

By the time dinner was over Colin was left feeling more distant from her than when they started dinner and the conversation. He couldn't figure if it was the subject matter that strayed so far from his own personal convictions and the way he was brought up in the funeral business, or if he was just jealous of this fascinating man at work.

Ava had an early meeting in the morning so she was going back to Boston that night and Colin was planning to be at Madsen's in the morning. He was thinking about going home to Boston with her but for some reason decided against it. He was no longer in a good mood and was afraid that he might provoke something unpleasant between them, and so he spent the night at home alone in Concord. Their parting had been affected by the conversation and both felt it.

24

Ava and Colin still enjoyed their many interests in common not to mention their ongoing romantic liaison, but Colin, one day, came to a startling conclusion. It was one he either never thought of before or one that he had kept buried in his subconscious. He and Ava were competitors in the mortuary business. In fact, part of her job was to knock people like him, people who represented years of faithful service to the community, out of business. And with their deep pockets and modern use of cutting edge technology they had the ability to do it. Sure, there would always be the faithful older folks in the town but what about the hordes of newcomers who had come from all over the country to work in the technology and medical fields in Massachusetts? These people had no connections or tradition with any mortuary. And the corporations could outcompete almost any family-owned firm. Not only that, as for the ability to compete Ava had proven to be no shrinking violet. Maybe her emergence in the corporate world had emboldened her.

Colin realized that must have been the reason that Amos had been distant with him lately. Even during the investigation into the missing money from the safe, Amos didn't make eye contact with Colin much, nor say really anything else to him that did not involve the investigation. Amos liked Ava, but perhaps the fact that her new profession threatened the survival of Madsen's had driven a wedge between him and Colin.

Colin drove from his house down to the funeral home a little faster than normal. Amos had not called him in a couple of days and Colin didn't checked the obituaries in *The Concord Journal* to see if Madsen's had been busy recently.

He found Paula on the telephone when he walked into the funeral home. She peered at Colin over the top of her glasses and motioned for him to come in.

"Stanfield, correct?" Paula wrote down the name in all capital letters as Colin sat down on the edge of the seat in front of her.

"Randy Stanfield. Okay. Please tell the family it will be a few minutes. We just had a funeral processional head to the cemetery and when he gets back, we will be on our way."

Paula delicately placed the receiver back in the cradle and ignored Colin for a moment.

"I can go make a removal if you need me to," he said.

She sat up and tugged at the corners of her mouth with a thumb and forefinger. "You can, but you will need to ask Amos first. I checked the file, he prearranged Mr. Stanfield, so he might want to make the removal himself."

"Where is Amos now? I really need to talk to him. He's been kind of cold towards me since I came back from Florida."

Paula scoffed. "He has every right to be, Colin. You took off out of here and didn't tell anyone. Plus, we were busy and needed the extra help. I think he might be questioning your commitment to running the funeral home, and quite honestly, so am I."

Colin watched as Paula removed her glasses and looked away. "I'm sorry. I shouldn't have said that to you."

Colin held up a hand. "No need to apologize. You were correct to say what you did. I did take off and I owe Amos an apology. I just haven't found the right time."

Those words resounded in his mind as Paula met his gaze. *And I haven't found the right time to tell either of you about the deed and the deadline.*

"Where is Amos?"

She folded her hands on the desk. "He went to Sleepy Hollow to bury a little baby that was only a few months old." Her eyes glistened as she spoke. "Poor little Addison. Amos is always at his best with some of the saddest funerals."

"That's where Dad is buried." Colin bolted out of the chair toward the front door. "Thanks Paula." As he stepped down onto the sidewalk, he balanced himself on the swinging door and looked back at her.

"Paula, I'm sorry for going to Florida with Ava and not telling you."

She pursed her lips and then nodded.

Colin pulled up to the front of the cemetery gate and killed the engine. It moaned and hissed as the heater turned off and the interior of the car got cold quickly.

He noticed the hearse pulled off the side of the drive a few feet ahead of him along with a few other cars of various sizes and colors. Colin got out of the car and approached the driver's side door, but saw that the car was unoccupied. Overhead, gray clouds blotted out the sun.

Colin slid between the slightly ajar cemetery gates. The cold northerly wind blew bitterly, chilling Colin as he entered. He stopped walking and listened. To the right, the chipped white headstones dotted the landscape. Colin always felt like a trespasser on hallowed ground when he came to the cemetery.

A small group of people marched across the cemetery grounds, huddled together. The men in the group, dressed in dark suits with heavy wool coats, cradled their female partners as the wind intensified.

Colin searched the cemetery and could not find Amos. He noticed the group coming from the right quadrant of the cemetery and Colin moved in that direction.

When Colin passed the ambling group and their hushed conversations and quiet sobs, silence prevailed. Colin saw Amos standing near the edge of the cemetery line, his head bowed.

"Amos."

He looked up for a moment, then back down at the small casket. "This is such a sad, sad moment. Funerals for little ones always are the hardest."

Colin felt his lip tremble as he stood alongside Amos and looked down at the small casket nestled tightly inside the open grave. The beautiful whitewashed wooden casket sat next to small vault with a soft white-gray marbleized exterior and a smooth high-gloss finish.

"Why are you here, lad? Don't you and Ava have someplace else to visit?"

Colin stuffed his hands into his pockets. "I came to say I'm sorry. I'm sorry I took off like that and didn't tell anybody. I notice you've been acting differently toward me lately and I think that has something to do with it."

Amos sighed and turned to look at Colin. "Yes, that is part of it, but not all of it. As fond as I am of Ava, and I am fond of her, you realize that she is working for our competition and not just another funeral home, but a corporate company that swallows up family-owned funeral homes and then eliminates the local staff."

Colin didn't make it a point to talk about this odd anomaly in their relationship but Ava often brought up her job, not in relation to Madsen's but to other such operations. She seemed proud of her company's ability to compete hard. She told him that a lot of these mom and pops were not being taken over by the family (exactly as in his case) and so all the corporates had to do was wait them out. She never seemed to realize that she was talking to Colin, a man steeped in old-fashioned values and traditions. It always seemed like she was talking about someone else. And of course she always was.

"I know. Honestly, the more I think about it, the more it doesn't settle well with me either."

Amos looked back down at the little casket. "And things are even more complicated because we now own her parent's house and we need to tear it down."

"Can't we have the deed reversed?"

Amos removed his hat and then resettled it onto his head. "We can, but we would need to get lawyers involved and that costs money. Right now, we need to really watch every penny."

"I know that too. I studied the spreadsheet and tax returns you gave me."

The wind picked up in intensity. A bush devoid of vegetation rattled against an unmarked tombstone in front of them.

"For the time being Madsen's had been holding its own with the influx of cash you provided, which should remove a couple of influences that could be a hindrance to future plans, like being able to tear down the Hewitt home and remove the debris."

The cemetery silence returned, but the silence did nothing to quell an unnerving feeling inside of Colin.

"Amos, there is something else I need to tell you." Colin let out a long breath and the steam from his lips puffed into thin wisps. He shifted his weight back and forth between both feet.

"All right lad...out with it."

Colin felt his cheeks fill with blood and they stung as the frigid air met them. "I am not sure that I really want to take over the funeral home."

Colin looked away and winced, awaiting a response. Even though Colin did not articulate the thought in the same way he had rehearsed the speech in his head, he felt slightly relieved at having said something.

When he turned slowly to face Amos, Amos knelt down. He removed a handkerchief from a pocket and wiped the casket with it. Amos placed a hand on the ground and pushed himself back up, although he faltered a bit and Colin leaned in to steady him.

"James will be here in a few minutes to close the grave for baby Addison. This is just so sad."

Once Amos steadied himself, Colin loosened his grip. "Aren't you going to say anything?"

Amos coughed. "What do you want me to say?"

"A scolding rant that would make me feel bad."

He made a face. "I assume you already feel bad about this. I knew that when you came back to Madsen's a few weeks ago that there might be a chance you would leave again. I wanted you to be around and see the profession for yourself, just as your daddy did and just as I do now. It's not a business for everyone."

Amos faced Colin again and placed his mitted gloves on Colin's shoulders. Amos leveled a serious look at Colin. "And you should not feel guilty for realizing this is not for you. You are still a young man with so much ahead of you. You're an excellent accountant with a good career in Boston. You've accomplished a lot and you should be proud of that."

"But the funeral home is part of my life, Amos. I've realized that over the last couple of weeks. You and Paula have been great and I am learning why Madsen's means so much to so many people." Not sharing his views sooner coupled with the calm response from Amos made Colin roil with guilt. His stomach clenched tightly.

"I'm not saying that I've made up my mind on what to do, but I just wanted you to know there is a possibility that I might not be involved with the funeral home. A chance I might do something else."

Amos pressed his lips tightly together. "What you're learning young Colin is that this business is built on a bridge of trust, openness and honest communication that creates lasting relationships with not just the family we serve, but with each other and the community in which we serve. No matter what you ultimately decide, you will be a better businessman and a better person from having experienced these ideals firsthand."

"But, Amos, I'm not sure…"

Amos stepped away from Colin. "If you'll excuse me, I need to find James so we can lay Addison to rest."

⬥

Colin sped to Logan airport from the cemetery. He had forgotten about his promise to pick Ava up at the airport that evening following one of her many visits to her district headquarters. Thankfully, the calendar in his phone pinged repeatedly until Colin checked the screen and turned off the alarm.

He pulled into the passenger drop off/pickup lanes at the airport. He and Ava were quiet while he negotiated the tricky new construction and got through the Sumner Tunnel. They were headed north and west to Concord before they began a conversation. Colin had a long face and Ava immediately recognized it. "Okay. Spill it. What's the matter?"

"I told Amos that I might not keep the funeral home."

Ava's hand shot to her mouth. "Oh my goodness. That's a bad one. What was his reaction?"

Staring straight ahead, Colin said, "It certainly wasn't bad…and Amos was being Amos—offering hope and being optimistic."

"That sounds right."

"I'm taking it real bad. The guilt is killing me. We have been busy recently and my trip with you to Florida left them shorthanded. The fact that I didn't tell them I was leaving or check in with them while I was gone really rattled him and Paula. They are tough but my actions have them floored. When I leave…er…if I leave, they are going to be shorthanded. I feel like they have been accustom to having an extra person to help out with removals and funerals and then that will be gone."

Ava said, "Maybe I can help."

For the first time he glanced over at her.

She said, "I know a couple of retired morticians in my district that might be able to fill in for a while. Do you have any idea how long you'd need them?"

"No. I'm not even sure we need them now if I am around. As well as I know Amos I don't know the state of his physical or emotional condition especially at his advanced age." Thinking a bit more, he added, "I guess I don't know Amos at all beyond the professional level."

"Well let me see what I can do," Ava said. "How soon do you need them?"

"I suppose we could look into it as a contingency plan, but let's put it off a couple of days and see if it's something worth exploring further." He was quiet for a while. Then he said, "You know I know it sounds foolish for a businessman but our entire operation depends on Amos and if he gets overworked when I leave and something would happen to put him out of action for a while, where would we be?"

Ava shrugged.

He thought about it for a moment. "We would essentially have to cease operations until I could find a replacement."

"Sounds like it."

"Then there is the expense of having to pay for another staff person if I leave. I'm trying to figure out at the moment how to finance a new roof and deal with your house. I know it sounds cold and insensitive but this couldn't have happened at a worse time."

She adopted a very serious demeanor and said, "Colin, you haven't really thought this out. In your zeal to keep Madsen's alive you've given little thought to the future and the future is here."

He looked at her said, "You're right."

He slowed down the car as he turned onto I-93 North from Massachusetts 3. They had completed around four miles of the thirty mile trip.

Colin said, "I can't stand the thought of giving up everything my father put his whole life into. Maybe I'm just being overly sentimental and a bit unreasonable in thinking that way. But I can't help it."

'I can understand that, Colin, but you chose another profession when you were younger. Once you did that Madsen's had a limited future. And that was the length of your dad's life or Amos's ability to keep working. All you've been doing these past few weeks is putting out fires here to keep things going. And you did a great job of it but now one of the last vestiges of Madsen's seems to be leaving and things look bleak."

He knew everything she had said was absolutely true. Yet, he somehow resented it. It was an irrational feeling. He knew that, yet he resented it.

The following weeks would likely be rough. Although Colin told Amos of his plans to possibly walk away from the funeral home, he did not tell him the entire truth about the deed or the deadline that would be coming up in forty-five days. The thoughts of another meeting with Amos to discuss the matter filled Colin with anxiety. Was he going to quit completely? Was he coming back? Would he sell?

Colin watched Ava lean into the passenger side door and rest her cheek against the window. The constant dancing light and shadow patterns from the interstate's lights cast Ava's striking features in inky blackness at times. Colin found himself losing focus on the road ahead. Passing cars from the left lane to the right lane frequently didn't help his focus.

Ava sat up and leaned over to Colin. "Have you found a way out of this dilemma?"

Colin grew somber. "Sure. But I've got to face the facts. Amos can't run the place forever and I may not be around to help."

"Did you ever think of the obvious?"

Colin cocked his head and, puzzled, he asked, "Obvious?"

"Go to mortuary school and take over yourself."

His answer was quick. "No. I wouldn't. I couldn't. It's just not in me. I'd not only never be happy at it, I don't think I could do it."

"What, not enough motivation?"

"No. Not really. I'm not the right temperament. No. I simply couldn't do it."

Ava leveled her eyes at him. "Then it's something you're going to have to come to grips with. You can only honor your father's legacy for so long and that is looking pretty limited. Hiring a new guy would be like starting all over again and with Will Newsome going corporate, I'm afraid you won't last too long."

Colin let the words resonate before his mind snapped. "Will Newsome has gone corporate?"

Ava nodded.

Colin cut her a sharp glance and then gripped the steering wheel tighter.

Trying to avoid sounding accusatory, Colin purposely lowered his voice. "How long have you known about Newsome's?"

Ava settled back into her seat. "It's been discussed in our sales meetings.

I'm not sure of the specifics or the timeline. But you can see my point about Madsen's and weighing tradition versus a fresh start."

Again everything she said was true yet he resented every word. He was almost angry when he took her home, departing with a quick, casual peck on the cheek. She tried to speak to him but he was already out the door. He didn't say it, probably didn't even think it, but the idea of a guy like Will Newsome besting him was so irritating it was hard to bear.

But then he got rational again.

As he drove onto Concord Turnpike, he realized how unreasonable he had been and was being. What was there to say? Ava was right. He had to somehow face up to the long-term problem of preserving the business and his father's memory.

He was behaving very immaturely. The problem had been the same since the day his father had died. Sure, he and Amos could keep things going for a while and they had been, but what about the long run? This problem with Amos. Amos might want to help but his effectiveness someday will be gone. The way he interacts with people might be changed. He lived for the business and for Luke. And now Luke was gone and Colin might be as well. And the business, though Amos loved the funeral home, it wasn't really his and it didn't bear his name.

Colin now knew that he'd come to a major crossroads in his life. Even he admitted that he could not and never would become a mortician, so how then could he realistically hope to keep alive all of the good work that his father had done? He kept thinking that this funeral home was more of a monument to his father than the ornate statue that stood over his grave at the cemetery.

Yet no matter how much he reasoned with himself he still tended to blame Ava for representing interests diametrically opposed to him and his feelings. Childish? Perhaps. Nonetheless...raw and intractable emotions? No doubt.

25

Just when Colin and Ava were at a pause in their new relationship she was called to New York for yet another crisis. She told him she had no idea how long she would be gone and their parting lacked the usual sweetness and longing. He couldn't put his finger on it but it was definitely different.

Since his return, Colin had begun feeling more comfortable in the small town than he did in the big city. He began to wonder why and decided that maybe it was the good times he'd had with Ava.

At the moment he and Amos were trying to figure out the financing on the new roof. The roofer had told them that if there were heavy snow this winter it would surely develop problems. So not only was their small cash reserve wiped out, they now had to secure credit to pay for the whole job.

This meant that if just one more, even semi-significant, problem developed then Colin would have real trouble on his hands. The struggle was constant and ongoing. He knew his father had handled it all but he now realized that when his father was alive business had been much better.

Colin had planned the last Saturday afternoon in January. He had planned an early lunch at the Concord Inn and then a leisurely afternoon at home or strolling through town.

Lunch was lonely and he read the newspaper in order to occupy himself.

At The Concord Bookshop, he tried without much success to get into the book about the relationship between Franklin Roosevelt and Winston Churchill during World War II. Colin picked it up off the discounted books bin after lunch. Colin liked the bookstore, mainly because the staff included former school librarians, editors, educators, and writers who could always offer stimulating conversation on a variety of topics. The room inside the bookstore was intimate and Colin loved how you could explore every crevice of the store and not be too far away from the books.

Gathered at the back of the bookstore were several people at a small bench and he couldn't help notice a woman about his age sitting nearby who kept sneaking glances at him. He was more curious than flattered and eventually he realized who it was. Debbie Pickett from high school. She had been his best buddy Dick Carlson's girlfriend. They had always been friendly but had never dated each other. He wondered if he should go over and introduce himself. But he didn't have to. She came over to him. She took off her sunglasses and flashed a big smile. She was a pretty blonde and had the same curvy figure he had remembered. She said, "I thought it was impolite to keep staring but I feel that I know you from somewhere. I haven't been in town in years."

He said, "I'm Colin Madsen and I think I remember you too. You're..."

She answered for him," Debbie Carlson. How are you?"

"It's been a long time," she said. "Have you ever heard from Dick?"

"Not in years. Last I heard of him he was running a company out in L.A. I always thought you two would get together. I take it that you..."

"No. Never happened. We went our separate ways as soon as we went to college. He was at UMass in Amherst and I was in upstate New York. We just kind of drifted apart."

"So did you ever get married?"

"Yes."

Before he could say anything else she said, "And divorced." She paused, then the inevitable. "And you?"

Somehow he didn't feel like telling her about Ava so he didn't.

She asked, "Do you mind if I drag my lounge chair over here? Maybe we could do some catching up."

"No. I'd like it very much. Here, let me get it for you."

They spent the afternoon talking about the old days and before they knew it was getting chilly and the sun was setting.

She said, "Can you believe we have been blabbing for over four hours?"

He looked at his watch. "Yeah you're right."

As they packed up their belongings he was tempted to ask her what she was doing that night as he was dreading the lonely evening ahead. He found that he absolutely hated eating alone, but his culinary skills didn't extend far enough to create a real meal. He thought he might just fix himself a sandwich. He was about to ask but she spoke first, "I'm staying with my sister. Do you have dinner plans?"

"Well actually no, I don't."

"Do you think you could stand my chattering through dinner?"

Boy, Colin thought, *Women have gotten so much bolder these days.* "I usually eat at the Concord Inn when I'm in town. Would that be okay?"

"Great. Let me give you my address."

She wrote it on a piece of paper then handed it to him. He said, "Would eight be okay?"

"Great."

He remembered now. She said 'great' to everything.

He had no sense of cheating on Ava. None at all. He was just going to have dinner with an old friend, albeit of the opposite sex, and it was just a way to fill his evening.

Over dinner Colin listened politely to Debbie further fill in the years since they had last seen each other. He didn't have much to say about himself as that was his way. He didn't realize he was giving the impression that he was a bachelor with no attachments. Her story was bittersweet but typical in so many ways. She had no children because her husband had not wanted any. Or he wasn't ready as he put it. Eventually that attitude split them up. It seemed she was careful not to get too inquisitive or nosy about his own situation.

"I've been hitting the singles' scene," she lamented, with her brows furrowed. She frowned and said, "and I'm here to tell you it's the worst."

When they got to her sister's home after dinner she said, "My sister is away for the weekend. Would you like to come in for a cup of coffee or a nightcap or something?" Before he could answer she quickly added, "Or have you had enough of me for one day?"

He said chuckling, "No of course not. Yes, I'd like to come in."

The nightcap turned into several and before long they were both feeling the effects. When she leaned into him and kissed him on the lips he was not really shocked and took her into his arms. Soon the passion was rising and both could not resist it. She took him by the hand and led him into the bedroom.

❀

Colin got up early and quietly dressed. He left her no note and softly walked out of the house.

Later that afternoon he realized that he had behaved badly by not leaving a note or talking to her. So he phoned her. When she answered he said, "I hope I wasn't rude but I'm an early riser and I didn't want to disturb you. I hope you don't think anything else."

He could almost see her grin over the phone. "No, don't worry. I'm not sure if you would leave a note or what."

He got tongue-tied. After a pause she said, "I had a wonderful time." She then added, "Just wonderful."

They chatted a while until she said, "I'm leaving right after lunch. I've got commitments to keep."

He chimed in, "Would you like to have lunch then?"

She quickly agreed.

"I know I nice little place over in Lexington. Do you like French food?"

"Great. I love it," she replied. "Would one be okay?"

Colin said, "Sure."

"Great. Give me the address because I'm going to bring my own car since I have to leave right after lunch."

Seeing a woman for the first time after sex was always awkward but it wasn't with Debbie. She was so bubbly. And she didn't mention the sex, so it was very comfortable. They had a nice lunch and he pecked her on the lips when they parted outside the restaurant.

She made him promise to call her during the week, which he agreed to but had second thoughts later.

He wondered later how and why it had happened. Wasn't he in love with Ava? Was it simply an impulse borne of loneliness? Whatever it was he felt guilty and struggled all week with the promise he made to call Debbie. Not to mention his sense of betrayal regarding Ava.

In the end he felt it would be impolite not to call Debbie since he'd promised, so he did. Before he knew it they had made another date. This time in Boston where she had a home in the suburbs.

Again they slept together. It was almost a ritualistic part of the date. The sex was more intense this time and afterwards she mentioned it in a most flattering way.

It didn't matter. Colin now felt worse than ever and began thinking about dropping in on Ava in New York City and surprising her. The more he thought about Debbie the more he felt he had to see Ava. It was a feeling of not only guilt but a need to recommit. He had already resolved not to see Debbie again.

He knew if he wasn't feeling so insecure about Ava that it wouldn't have happened. At least that's what he told himself. He wasn't used to casual affairs and this thing with Debbie couldn't be more. Could it? After all, he hardly knew her. Their conversations, like most first conversations, weren't particularly revealing. He knew that people told each other the best of themselves and naturally left out the worst. It is human nature to keep any negatives, insecurities or bad habits from a person you are trying to impress.

Colin sighed heavily and stared up at the ceiling as he struggled to fall asleep that night. "How do I get myself into these things?" he mumbled into the quiet night.

26

Guilt continued to gnaw at Colin like a hungry squirrel. Not only because of the episodes with Debbie but because he felt that whatever was now between himself and Ava was his fault. She was just doing her job yet he considered it a personal vendetta against him and Madsen's and for him that was almost sacrilegious.

He badly needed to see her and somehow overcome this rift, unspoken as it was, between them. And he did not want to call her first to see if an impromptu visit would be appropriate. He needed to see her no matter how she felt about it.

So he booked the afternoon Amtrak to Grand Central Station. The Marriott Hotel where she was having her meetings was within walking distance and rather than the hassle of air travel he could use the time to think. He had a lot of thinking to do. Whatever his feelings and the outcome of this thing with Ava he had to decide the future of Madsen's and his part, if any, in it.

As the train click clacked its way through southern New England he thought about things. How could he maintain his father's legacy without being an active part of Madsen's? How could he be an active part of Madsen's since he had no interest in the profession? For a moment he contemplated doing it whether he had an interest or not but he quickly realized one did not do well at something they simply *endured* and did not really like. He had no doubt that he would soon grow to resent the very thing he was trying to preserve. Moreover, no matter how hard he tried to rationalize it he could not come to terms with Ava being his competitor. In the deepest part of his soul it felt like a betrayal or at the very least a disinterest in him.

By the time Colin arrived at Grand Central he had resolved little. With no luggage it was an easy matter to step out onto East 45th Street and make the short walk to Park Street and down three blocks to her hotel.

At the counter he asked, "May I please have Ms. Ava Hewitt's room number?"

"Sorry sir, I can put you on her telephone line but I'm not allowed to give you her room number."

"Okay, would you do that?"

The clerk phoned Ava's room but there was no answer.

"I'm sorry, sir. No answer."

"Could you tell me if there is a meeting of the American Mortuary LTD in the hotel?"

"There are so many conferences here, sir, I wouldn't know. Check the signs in the lobby. They list everything that's going on in the hotel."

He did and sure enough there it was scheduled from six to nine. *Must be a dinner conference.*

He had to kill three hours somehow and he was much too anxious for that. He walked over to the bar and ordered a beer and a sandwich. He grimaced at the prices though he found the fifteen-dollar New York priced sandwich very enjoyable.

His dinner went by way too quickly. He tried to eat slowly and watch the Celtics game on TV but when he looked at his watch it was only twenty minutes to seven. He began to wander about the lobby until he found a conference room with a sign out front announcing the American Mortuary meeting. The door was half open so he peeked in but couldn't see much without looking like he was spying or intruding. So he basically hung around the door.

Colin was feeling so edgy now it was unbearable. When he spotted the unattended registration table out front with some stickers still not picked up he thoughtlessly picked one up and pasted it to his jacket, remembering to pick a male name. He went inside the room and hurried to the bar where he thought he would be most unnoticed. She might be in meetings. He wondered, *What in God's name am I doing?*

Evidently it was still the dinner hour and couples were sitting at tables for two and four. The dining room was a world of brass and potted palms so it wasn't hard for Colin to get himself a drink and stand behind a giant palm and scan the room. That's when he spotted her. She was wearing one of his favorite little black dresses. She wasn't alone. Instinct more than anything else told him who the man she was sitting with was. It was...it had to be. Yes, it was *Will Newsome.*

He watched them carefully. They seemed to be enjoying themselves, sharing laughs and drinks and (whether it was his imagination or not) appeared to be deep into each other. That was the image branded into his mind. It was as far as he could see or as far as his jealousy allowed him to see.

Should he approach them? It was only an instantaneous thought because he could now see how embarrassing it would be. Him wearing a phony nametag and why was he here? Checking up on his girlfriend? How embarrassing! How childish! He was still thinking about it when Will approached the bar a few patrons down from him and ordered what he recognized was Ava's favorite martini. Colin turned away, prepared to dash if he had to but it didn't come to that. He felt an irresistible impulse to flee the place, humiliated and ripping with anger.

And he did just that. He walked back to Grand Central and sat waiting for the eleven o'clock train back to Boston. What he had hoped would be some sort of reconciliation had turned into an embarrassing discovery to which he was attaching all kinds of unfounded motives.

He thought about the situation all the way home. By the time he reached Hartford he had calmed down considerably and had come to a couple of conclusions. The first was that he knew American Mortuary had been courting Will to buy his place and Ava being the district manager would be his account executive. That was the rational part of his thinking. Yet all he saw was them socializing and seeming to have such a good time at dinner. Still, he told himself, that is how business is conducted. He himself was a businessman. He knew how it worked. Although he wasn't in the sales end he knew that it carried a heck of a lot more socializing than his own job. He realized that her job required that she not only socialize but schmooze with her clients and try to convince them that to franchise was the best option for them. That took not only rhetorical skill but a good deal of charm as well. But he wasn't looking at her good qualifications as a district sales manager, he was looking at her as the woman he loved. Yet the unreasonable part of him lurking in the darkest corners of his psyche still angered him. Was it that she was enjoying herself with someone else? Hadn't he too been guilty of that? To a lot further extreme! Was this proof that they weren't meant for each other?

In the fairest, most honest part of his heart he realized that he was the one who betrayed Ava in sleeping with another woman. He had no real explanation beyond loneliness for it either, and the fact that he was feeling odd about Ava's role in Concord. He didn't really care what she did in the rest of the district but what she was doing in Concord definitely irked him.

Were they both wasting their time? Or was it all because of the mortuary business? She was actively working to weaken Madsen's while strengthening a worthless individual like Will. A person who had to resort to stealing from colleagues. A person who should be in jail but not for his and Amos's good will. Not only wasn't he in jail, he was positioning himself to compete, and compete with, all the resources of a major corporation backing him against Madsen's.

Colin had noticed on the hotel lobby board that the conference would be over tomorrow. Which means she might be home the next day or the day after that. Unless they sent her somewhere else.

It didn't much matter as he had no idea how to confront her about all this. Reason and logic told him that it was probably just his male ego at risk. Then again, maybe not.

Debbie was on his voice mail when he got home. He was caught off guard by her bubbly attitude when he called her back. "Hey there, Mr. Bachelor. How would you like a homemade dinner concocted from some secret family recipes?"

"Well, uuhh. That sounds just great, Debbie. But as it turns out I've got to get back to my office in Boston within the next half hour. Some crisis or another. I'm really sorry and I appreciate the offer. Could I have a rain check?"

She was no less bubbly. "Sure you can." Before she hung up she added, "And don't forget to redeem it."

He promised her that he would be calling her soon.

He was starting to feel like the kind of guy he disliked: dishonest, hypocritical, unable to make decisions and unable to find his way to the right path. Everything he hated in a man.

Now he had a new problem. It involved his own infidelity and what he considered Ava's betrayal of Madsen's. What had started out as an effort to continue his father's legacy had turned into a love triangle at best and a betrayal at worst.

27

It was the next morning and Ava was sitting in her boss's office a few blocks down from the hotel conference of the previous evening. It was the corporate office of American Mortuary in downtown Manhattan, located on the forty-first floor. Her boss John Luger was a tall, balding man in his fifties with a military bearing and a no nonsense demeanor. He asked, "What did you think of the conference last night? Was it helpful to you?"

Leaning forward slightly in the plush visitor's chair Ava said, "I thought it covered a lot of topics. Maybe there could be more emphasis on the marginal accounts."

"You mean how to handle them?" he said. "We have an evaluation sheet on that."

"Yes, I know. I'm aware of it. But there are some things that are not covered in it."

"What for example?" her boss asked.

"Well, situations that might be okay business-wise but are marginal morally."

Luger looked at her as though she had just said something really dumb. "I don't think I'm following you."

"Well, for example I have a situation in my own hometown where I have a decent prospect but a person who is uh, let's say, does not possess the most upstanding moral character."

He sat staring at her for a while. "Can you elaborate?"

"Okay. We have a chance at the Newsome Funeral Home and I have to be honest. The owner Will Newsome is dishonest but he has not been involved in any felonies."

Looking her straight in the eye, her boss explained, "I remember reading about that incident with the temporarily stolen money at Madsen's from your last weekly report. This Will Newsome could be a risk, but as you know, Ava, we need the Northeast and we are putting a good deal of effort and money into it. And I have to add that you are doing a great job there. I predict great things for you with this company."

When she didn't say anything, he continued.

"Our contract pretty much covers us from any liability. We don't have to worry about things like that. We just need to tie up all the available business in the area. Is your friend, I mean the other company, who is it?"

" Madsen's."

"Does Madsen's have any interest in franchising?"

"No. Definitely not. It's an old family business and that's the last thing in the world he'd consider."

"Well then, all the more reason we should go after this other guy. Or we won't have any presence in that town. What is it?"

"Concord, Massachusetts."

He repeated it. "Concord, Mass. How is our exposure in that area? Do we have anything in the surrounding area? Last time I looked we didn't. Seems we did better in southern Massachusetts where the economy is worse. The greater Boston area is filled with high tech and professional medical people and is relatively well off."

"That's true, sir."

Luger got up and went over to his window with the panoramic view of New York City. He stared out for a while thinking. He said, almost absently, "Lousy day, I can usually see the Hudson." Then he turned back to Ava who was ready for whatever he had to say. "As you know, Ava, our contracts are written so that in case there are any financial problems we simply take over the franchise." He paused and lit a cigar. "In that case we can do whatever we want. Run the business ourselves and keep all the profits or sell it to someone else. Either way we come out on top. The only way we can lose money is if the businessman is so bad that he winds up with a lot of lawsuits which we are to some degree protected from."

Ava shifted restlessly in her leather chair. "I understand that but as you can see, sir, I'm in a kind of delicate situation."

Her boss said, "Ava, my advice is try to work it out. If you have any real problem tell me and we'll assign someone else to the account."

No salesperson, especially someone on the rise like Ava, wants to hear that if she can't handle her own district someone else will be assigned to it. So it was implied that it was up to her to handle the account.

"Mr. Luger, the account in question, Will Newsome, presents another problem. He doesn't have enough money to pay for a franchise."

"You know, Ava, in certain accounts if it's strategic enough we sometimes loan them the money. That's also a good deal for us. If they default we can take over the business and still put a lien on any property or assets he owns. He has to jump through all kinds of hoops to get his business back."

Ava didn't like the way the conversation was going. "Well, sir, I think I can handle it to our advantage."

"Good enough," Luger said abruptly, indicating the conversation was over. "If you run into problems come and see me." He got a buzz on his intercom and punched the button. "Be right with you, Rita." He turned back to Ava. "Got your flight home all set?"

She nodded.

He said, "Well it's been great seeing you as usual. Next time we should have a drink together."

She smiled and said, "I'd like that."

On her way out she thought, *Fighting off wolves is bad enough. But an old wolf who is your boss is the worst.*

He smiled at her before she left.

On the way home Ava had time to think over the situation and by the time she landed at Logan Airport in Boston she was still a long way from any kind of solution.

She had never liked Will Newsome but she knew business didn't have too much to do with liking people, especially the franchising business. With Newsome Funeral Home needing financial capital, the firm was perfectly positioned for American Mortuary. Sure it was up to her to keep up good relations between the company and the franchisees, but if she recommended against Newsome they couldn't blame her if things didn't work out. On the other hand, she knew her boss was hungry for new outlets in the Northeast and no matter how inappropriate Newsome was, if they could finance him they probably would. It wasn't a complete answer but it gave her at least the outline of a decision.

28

Ava took Amtrak home because she wanted time to think things out. It seemed to be one of those times in life when one needed to discover what was important. She'd really hated teaching. As she'd told Colin, the kids today were too unruly. Or when she had kids tell her, "My dad's a lawyer." *In other words you will be subject to a lawsuit if you punish me in any way.* Did she really fear that challenge or was it just too frustrating? No, she had to admit that the threat of some sixteen-year-old delinquent didn't frighten her at all. But the gall of it aggravated her.

She had to agree that the corporate world brought challenges too but also rewards in terms of income, prestige and authority or power. Yet she could see that the corporate world in some cases lacked integrity. Morality was not a big issue. Profit was. She had seen cases where all moral values were overlooked in the pursuit of profit. And now she had this problem in Concord. It was obvious her boss was willing to go further with Will Newsome in order to corner the market and she knew where she stood. But if she made her feelings known it could possibly mean the end of her career. And she certainly didn't want that. In her heart of hearts she loved her job and everything that went with it. In teaching she was just one of hundreds. But in this corporation she shined.

Then there was the matter of travel and being away from Colin. She knew he hated it and she did too yet she had been so caught up in her career that she had to take her chances with it. Actually, she was so busy that she didn't really miss him that much. Only because she had no time to think about him.

Yet Colin had not even said he loved her yet. She knew he was shy, but maybe he was just one of those guys who was never going to make a serious commitment. She wasn't sure but she did know that she should have a serious talk with Colin regarding both their futures. In some ways she saw it as unfair. Colin was in the corporate accounting world and although he wasn't required to travel much he did mention that if he got a promotion he might be off around the country auditing large companies. How would she then feel with the shoe on the other foot? It was a dilemma no doubt about that, but she intended to broach it with Colin as soon as she could.

She knew that she was doing well enough with the company to ask her boss to let someone else handle the Will Newsome account. Yet she was competitive and didn't like the idea of some other hotshot getting a foothold in her territory doing things she couldn't or didn't want to do. Sure, she flirted with Will the other night but it's not like she would go any further with him. She even wondered why she did that much. Was it mostly to please her boss or to prove herself?

She got into Boston much too late to call Colin so she put it off to the next day.

❁

The next day Colin was happy to hear Ava's voice on the phone yet he was filled with anxiety. He hadn't had enough relationships in his life to know whether it would be best to confess his indiscretion or not. He knew it was possible that Ava could be forgiving yet on the other hand what if she wasn't? He didn't love Debbie. It had been a distraction he knew was wrong. He did have a commitment of sorts with Ava even though they had never discussed it. He stopped to think. Maybe they should be discussing these things. After all, neither knew where they really stood regarding the future. Debbie had just been something that he had been too weak to fend off. Then he rationalized that maybe he and Ava hadn't made their commitment to each other well known enough to be certain just where they did stand. They never talked about seeing other people.

During the phone conversation they agreed to get together at Main Street Market and Café for coffee.

It was an awkward reunion. While he was thrilled to see her he was torn about what to do or even how to talk about their future relationship.

So at first it was all small talk about her trip. He asked, "What did you do?"

"Well it was a meeting to razzle dazzle the holdouts and romance them into coming aboard the corporate train."

"What incentives did you offer?"

She sipped her drink. "Oh the usual, a pot of gold at the end of the rainbow. I had to work on, ugh, of all people Will Newsome."

Colin could not admit he had seen her with him. It would be the same as saying he was a weak, needy person who needed to stalk his girlfriend to keep track of her and what she was doing. Of course it was only a business meeting but Colin wasn't thinking rationally these days.

Colin could not help getting bitter at the sound of Newsome's name and the fact that he might become a big name in town in the funeral home business. So what scared him most? That Will might become the biggest funeral home in town or that Will would win out over him?

Was it that the community would eventually forget his father and his contribution to the town? Well of course, eventually as the old generation shuffled off this mortal coil they would forget him. But at the moment Colin was inwardly angry. He lapsed into silence. Ava said, "I know it's all pretty seedy. I don't like it either."

Colin lowered his eyes and repeated the name, "Will Newsome. If I didn't want to make a major scandal of it he would be sitting in jail right now. I gave him a break and now he is in a position to challenge us in Concord. There's something unfair about that."

After a minute Ava finally said, "I could ask my boss to take me off the account."

"Would that threaten your position in the corporation?"

She hesitated. "Well, yes. It doesn't look good that I'd let personal issues come before business. It also gives some other hotshot salesperson a chance to come into my territory and do what the company sees that I wouldn't do."

Somehow there was enough hesitation in her voice to tell him that doing that was something she really didn't want to do. Colin could have looked on the bright side; the very fact that Ava would even be willing to talk about it was to admit that the only reason she would be doing it was for him. Yet his bitterness let that fact slip by. "Then don't do it," he said with a little more bite than he'd intended. "We'll just have to take our chances with Mr. Newsome."

Now both became silent. Something serious had come between them and for the first time since they had met and had been apart they did not spend the night together. She feigned exhaustion and he was happy to go along with the excuse.

At the doorway of the Main Street Market and Café, Colin was holding the door open for Ava when Debbie Carlson was coming in. Colin's jaw dropped and he could think of nothing to say.

Debbie was all smiles until she realized that Colin was with Ava. Debbie was first to talk. "Ava. Ava, it's me Debbie. You remember me. Miss 'Bull' Collins Physical Education class?"

Ava, surprised said, "Why Debbie Carlson! Of course I remember you."

Colin stood, dumfounded. If anyone was paying attention to him they would see him looking as guilty as sin as his face turned bright red. He shuffled his feet but the women were too busy talking to notice. Until finally Debbie looked at Colin and said, "Are you two, uh...together?"

"Yes." Ava looked at Colin and asked, "What has it been? A month now?" Colin nodded.

"And Colin," Debbie said. "Must be time to see old friends again."

"Uh yuh. I guess it is."

❀

When they parted, Ava noted, "She looked at us kind of funny, don't you think?" she asked.

Colin lowered his eyes and mumbled, "No, I didn't notice anything."

"Do you remember her from high school?"

"Uh, no, I don't think so."

"Yeah. She was one of the prettiest cheerleaders on the squad. Most boys were gaga for her."

Colin let it drop and said nothing else.

❀

When he got home Colin sat in his favorite chair and continued to mull over the situation. In his own mind he dismissed his infidelity with Debbie and concentrated on the fact that Ava of all people was working against Madsen's. Her offer to get off the account seemed only semi sincere. He saw it as a concession. Then he thought, *Well isn't that a pretty good concession for her to make. To jeopardize her career because of my sensitivities.* Yet she didn't come right out and agree in any kind of enthusiastic way to drop the idea of a Newsome franchise in Concord.

By the time it was time to go to bed he realized that Ava had not done anything physical with anyone else. If he wanted to think that she had it was only to assuage his own guilt about Debbie. But deep down in his gut he knew she didn't do anything. No, the guilt was all his. Whether or not it was a deal breaker depended on how he handled the situation.

When he began to think about the night he and Debbie went to bed it was about a very pretty lady offering herself to him at a time when he was extremely lonely and feeling down. Not that that was an excuse. But all of this made him realize that he and Ava had to discuss their true feelings and their ideas about the future.

Come to think about it, what were his true feelings about Ava? .

Well, he said to himself, *Would I hop on a train and travel to New York because I was feeling guilty? Or because I wanted to see what she was up to? Maybe it was one. Maybe the other.* Then he decided. Either one meant that he felt very strongly about Ava and he didn't want to lose her. Now that that was settled he had to figure out what to do next.

He couldn't see how admitting a bad mistake could possibly strengthen any bond between them. On the other hand he hated lying. Despised it really. But he also knew that women took these things quite seriously and it might scar their relationship or kill it altogether. And he didn't want to risk that. So he decided that discretion was the best course. Again, they were not engaged. They were not exclusive. They never even said they loved one another. He thought that was maybe because he was too shy. He knew by now how he felt about her and at this point he had to find out how she felt about him. He wasn't sure how to do it. Does one ask a woman, "Do you love me? And if so, enough to marry me? Or are we just having a casual relationship? What do they call it these days, 'friends with benefits'?"

Maybe some people do, but it just wasn't his style.

29

February 1st. Thirty-five days have passed since Colin returned to Concord and Madsen Funeral Home. Now, only ten days remained of the 45-day deadline imposed on him by the state. It was going to be a long weekend and neither Ava or Colin had work so Colin decided to plan a wonderful Saturday. His intention was to mend what was some kind of unspoken rift between them.

He invited her to the Main Street Market and Café the next day. He asked, "Are you feeling rested up?"

"Yeah. New York can be a madhouse. It takes a day or two to get my equilibrium back."

"Yeah I hear you. I'm finding more and more that I'm enjoying my time here in the country than in Boston, as low key and provincial as it is. This long weekend how about taking in a new play over on the Maine seacoast? It's at the Ogunquit Playhouse. It's *South Pacific*."

"Oh great! One of my favorites."

"Then we can visit the Cliff House. Ever been there?"

"No."

"Beautiful place. High up on a natural cliff with outstanding views of the ocean. And the food is wonderful."

Colin felt his stomach quiver with excitement. "And before you ask, I did check with Amos and Paula before planning the day."

"Sounds even better."

"Then on Sunday we could go to that new auction in up country in New Hampshire."

"Sounds wonderful." Tongue-in-cheek she added, "What have I done to deserve such a wonderful weekend?"

"I uh..."

Still being playful, she added, "Or should I say, what have you done?"

He must have looked like a deer in the headlights because his astonishment got her laughing. "What did I say, silly? Let's face it, maybe I'm not such a great jokester."

Somehow this teasing wasn't taken as she had obviously intended. Colin felt guilty. As if the comment was a crack that he had done something wrong. He had a hard time shaking that feeling.

❧

On Saturday the weather was clear and sunny, only a late afternoon buildup of late winter gray clouds piling on one another till it was a magnificent formation tinted at the edges with pink. Viewed with the ocean backdrop from the Cliff House veranda it was spectacular.

The food was wonderful, the ambience too. But something special and powerful was missing. They seemed to go through the motions, and the feelings that they usually had were missing. Something was wrong. Colin hoped that on the long drive up to New Hampshire he might find out more.

Trouble was he had no idea where to start, so they began chatting about antiques. It got to what they liked about the antique business.

Colin asked, "What do you like best about antiques?"

Ava had to think about it. "I think the mystery of what the piece had been to somebody. Somebody long ago. Sometimes somebody famous."

The tires hummed on the pavement. "I see what you mean. That's intriguing for me too. I love to touch the piece and try to guess where it's been and under what circumstances. For instance, my Civil War Navy Colt that I bought a while ago. Just looking at it and handling it stirs my imagination. I like to imagine things."

"Like what?" Ava asked.

"Like maybe an officer fired it to save General Grant's life. Things that might change history. It might have happened or I may just like to dramatize things in the past. I like old firearms. I think if I could afford it I would love to collect them."

"Furniture is my passion. I love things that have survived the ages. Things with a unique beauty."

Finally he got the courage up to ask. "What else do you want from life, Ava?"

She thought a moment. "I guess I want what everyone wants. Family, home and happiness. But I find myself growing older every day. I hear the proverbial biological clock ticking away. None of these things seem to be coming my way."

They were silent as the scenery passed. Colin asked, "What do you see as your future with the company you're with now?"

"Well, I'm told I made district manager in record time. I don't know when my next promotion will be, if there is one," she added. "But the next step is regional manager."

"Is that something you want?"

She gave it considerable thought. "I...I guess so." There was more silence. Then she said, "You know, I think it's something in our culture that says you must aspire to achieve. You must get ahead. You must climb the corporate ladder. I have to agree I like the accolades I get. I like the prestige. But I'm not entirely sure it's my life's dream. In other words I'm not certain I would prefer it over the simple domestic life of the average person my age."

The road hummed under the tires for another ten minutes. Ava said, "How about you? I know you didn't want the mortuary business."

"That's true and the more I think about it I don't know what propelled me to accounting other than I have a facility with figures and math." He hesitated. "And I guess as a young person I saw it as a dignified profession that most people respected."

"No other reason?"

"I don't think so."

"So at this age you still don't know what you want to be when you grow up?"

They both chuckled, but that seemed to be the last good feeling of the ride. At least until they arrived at the auction site in Lancaster.

The ambience of the auction and the fascinating pieces offered for sale temporarily lifted their spirits. Ava fell in love with an authentic nineteenth century Shaker spinning wheel. Colin smiled. "What in the world would you do with this?"

"Other than admire it I bet I could sell it for more than I'd pay for it here."

They had a wonderful afternoon. Ava bought the spinning wheel and fearing it would be damaged transporting it in the car, arranged for it to be delivered to Colin's house in Concord.

As for Colin he found a seventeenth century blunderbuss associated with warfare at sea. He was thrilled with this blunderbuss, bought it and carefully wrapped it for the ride home in his trunk.

At lunch they talked about their antiques and everything they saw. Both were somewhat limited on what they could spend and they talked about their second choice items.

On the way back to their hotel in Ogunquit, Ava seemed deep in thought. "Ya know. One of the things that I think makes the corporate world so exciting for me is," he mentally winced at her use of the word exciting, "is that I come from the teaching profession. Which I feel isn't a profession at all. It's more a matter of babysitting a bunch of spoiled brats who appreciate nothing you do for them."

Colin shot a glance at her as he drove. "That's a pretty depressing commentary on today's youth. Surely they can't all be spoiled brats."

"No, you're right. But you're talking to a frustrated teacher who really wanted to teach and make a difference but who wound up, as I said, babysitting a bunch of spoiled rich kids."

She frowned. "I know. I sound bitter. You're right, they're not all like that. But," she added quickly, "enough of them are to make you feel like you're fighting a losing battle."

Colin said, "And in the corporate world you are quickly appreciated and applauded for your efforts. You are the hero of the sales meetings. You win trips to Las Vegas and Acapulco. You're somebody."

She cocked her head and looked at Colin. She leveled her gaze at him although his eyes were on the road. "Some of that sounds pretty cynical, but I guess you're right. You are a hero. Especially in sales. The company lives or dies according to the quality of its salespeople."

"Speaking of sales, how are you handling the Will Newsome thing in Concord?"

"Colin, I told my boss that Newsome is not of good character but as you might guess he didn't care much about that. I didn't get a chance to say more about it."

"Are you comfortable with that?"

"No. I don't like other people tramping in my vineyard, so to speak."

The remark upset Colin and his reticence made it a concern for Ava who looked over at him and asked, "Do you think there is a better way to handle it?"

"No. No, it's not that. I just hate to have you make sacrifices in your career that make you uncomfortable as a favor to me. I guess I shouldn't care if Will Newsome gets ahead in Concord. I can't protect my father's legacy by keeping him down. My father made his legacy through honesty and compassion and there's nothing Will Newsome can do to lessen that. I guess I am just...I don't know, confused about it."

"What you just said doesn't sound confusing. Sounds like you thought it out and know how you feel."

"You're right. I do know that nothing Will can do will dim Dad's contribution to the town and his neighbors."

Ava chewed on that for a while before saying, "Then you don't mind if I tell my boss I can handle every account in my territory and there's no need to send in any substitute?"

Colin was trapped. *That's not what I wanted to hear. If I'm honest with myself I would prefer that she stuck with her original decision to recuse herself from the handling of the account. But it seems her career is more important to her than even she realized.*

The lack of conversation between them at dinner that night was telling. Here they hadn't seen each other for a while, they were in one of the most romantic places around and their ardor somehow, with the conversation of the afternoon, had cooled.

Ava was the first to approach it. "I have the feeling that my decision has disappointed you."

"I didn't say that."

"You didn't have to. I could cut the tension in the car with a knife. As soon as I said I was going to go back on the account you got distant."

"That's not true."

"Colin," she said, her teeth slightly clenched, "let's not lie to each other. One of the best things about our relationship is the honesty that has always been between us. I have the same feeling right now as I had when I saw your face upon meeting Debbie Carlson the other day."

Now he got red and tight-lipped. He sipped his martini as if he really needed it.

Women's instinct. Somehow she knows or is guessing about Debbie.

She said, "I'm not very hungry. Why don't we take our drinks with us and take a stroll along the beach."

By now the sun was a giant orange ball on the horizon as they walked barefoot along the sand, the cold Maine water lapping at their feet. She said, "I'm not quite sure what it is but there's some thing or things that have come between us. We don't feel the same about each other as we did."

He said nothing.

She said, "Your silence tells me I'm right."

"What do you want to do about it?"

"I don't know," she replied. "I have strong feelings for you but at the moment they are in limbo or at least somewhere else."

"Do you want to take a break?" he asked.

"Yes," she answered, perhaps a bit cautiously. "I think we both need some breathing space to figure out what is happening between us."

With that, he knew they had broken up.

30

These feelings of dismay were new to Colin. He'd never had a serious relationship that had gone awry. He found himself completely unprepared to handle it. He was sluggish and moody at work and found himself listening carefully to the lyrics of sad songs about love gone wrong. Songs about unrequited love, false love, distorted love. He found that he could empathize with lots of the feelings of loneliness, emptiness and the general feeling that his world was not right.

Still he wasn't sure how things really stood between him and Ava. In fact, he didn't even understand what the problem was. All during their weekend neither committed to the other by declaring their love. They seemed to be just two happy people who enjoyed each other's company.

His thinking got heavy for the first time in his life. *I haven't spent enough time thinking about the important things in life and without me realizing it my life is going by. I'm already thirty five. Most people are well into having a family by now. Is it my indecisive nature or is it that I just haven't found the right woman yet? Am I in love with Ava? Is she in love with me? I really don't know.* Colin realized that he needed a sign from God to tell him. He was completely confused.

Now he hated being in Concord on the weekends because he was close to Ava and that made him feel even worse.

On Monday morning Amos presented him with yet another big problem for the funeral home. The roof that they were hoping would hold up a little longer had started to leak and in the worst place. It was dripping into one of the viewing rooms so it had to be closed. Amos's voice was full of worry as he told Colin, "We have one funeral going on but I am expecting another shortly and we simply can't do a viewing with water leaking from the ceiling. When we got an estimate for the cost of a new roof I checked the books and found that we don't have nearly enough to meet current operating expenses. Let alone a new roof."

Colin folded both hands behind his head and let out a low groan.

Amos continued. "While you were gone on Saturday, Will Newsome came by looking for you. American Mortuary was testing the waters to see if Newsome's was a good potential investment."

Colin flashed Amos a puzzled look. "A good investment?"

Amos nodded. "They want to see if Will wants to franchise the business with American Mortuary. Will told them that we might be interested in it as well. That information got back to Ava's boss and somebody in New York now thinks both our funeral homes might be interested in franchising. Now it appears American Mortuary is putting operating capital into the business knowing that we are the only other competition in town."

Amos stepped closer to Colin and stared coldly into his eyes. "What this means lad is that Newsome's, with American Mortuary's backing, will have the money to advertise and promote their business, plus have the capital to buy new equipment and make improvements to the facility. This will cut into our business."

Colin paced the halls for the rest of the morning. Amos had to excuse Colin when Daniel Jackson came to make arrangements for his mother. Colin, lost in thought, did not notice either men coming down the hallway to the arrangement office.

Paula appeared and offered Colin a cup of coffee, which he gladly accepted. After a few minutes had passed, Amos asked Colin to join them in the arrangement office. Colin shook hands with Daniel Jackson, a large, burly man with a square jaw and sandy hair. Colin noticed that Daniel did not sit down in the seat behind him, but hovered above it as he braced himself against the desk with both hands.

Amos, eyes wide, pointed at the seat. Several droplets of water had splashed on the seat behind him.

"Evidently the leak has now spread to the east side of the building."

Amos cleared his throat and sat back in his seat.

"Mr. Jackson's mother has died and his family has been using Madsen's for a couple of generations."

Daniel ignored what Amos was saying and instead kept peering behind him and studying the pooling water. He looked up at the ceiling and said, "Uh oh. Looks like you folks have a roofing problem."

Amos said, "I know, Daniel, and that's one of the reason why I was going to tell you that we can't handle your mother's funeral. I wanted to make sure Colin heard this as well."

Daniel looked stunned. "You can't handle Mom's funeral? We've been using you people for years. What will I do? You buried both my uncles and my cousin Tom."

Colin stepped in. "I hate to admit it, Daniel, but we're in a bit of financial trouble. It's been a slow summer and we don't have enough to get the roof repaired. In fact, we may have to close till we do. I'm afraid you may have to go somewhere else. I hate to have to tell you that."

Amos shook his head. He was very intimate with the customers in town and their families.

Daniel said, "I know and that's why I feel so bad about going some-place else. Your Dad helped us through some of the worst times in our lives. I can't imagine Madsen's not there for us now."

Colin was thinking, *If we close down we can't generate any income to be able to repair the roof.*

Daniel said, "Look folks. I'm a builder. Roofing isn't my specialty but I have done a few in my time. I hate to see this happening to you people and I would be willing to help as much as I can." He stopped to think a bit. "If you can supply the material I can supply some of the labor. My crew is busy but I can help myself and maybe get another worker to donate some time. But I can't afford to buy the materials too. If you can do that I think I can help."

Colin said, "That's very generous of you, Daniel. Could I call you this afternoon and let you know? If we can do it maybe we will only have to delay your mother's funeral a couple of days."

Colin had a hard time getting through to anybody at his company to try to find out the status of his 401k. He called his friend, Dick Adams who was his accounting firm's treasurer and told him his problem.

Dick was sympathetic and said, "I'll tell you what, Colin. I'll go on into the office and get to my computer and tell you the status of your 401k, but I have to warn you, the last time I looked, everybody in the firm was in bad shape because of the economy."

"I'd appreciate your finding out for me, Dick."

"Okay, I'll call you back in a few hours just as soon as I'm able to check it out."

When he called back Colin could tell by the tone of his voice that it wasn't good. "You, like everyone else in the firm is down by a significant amount. Your pulling your money out recently has something to do with it but your losses are mostly due to the economy."

"Thanks, Dick. I appreciate your effort."

Colin called Daniel Jackson and told him, "From the figure you quoted me I think we might just be able to scrape up enough to buy the material."

Daniel said, "Okay, that's a start but we're going to have a labor problem. I can't get the person I was thinking of to donate his time. He's working two jobs because of the economy."

Every time Colin thought that he might be nearing a solution another problem cropped up. He said, "Daniel, please be patient. Give me another hour or so and I'll call you back."

When Colin called back he said, "What type of work is it that your man was going to do?"

"Well, I can do the actual roofing with one helper that I'm able to provide but we need someone to bring the materials up to the roof when we need them."

Colin went silent for a moment. He knew he had a phobia about heights but he didn't say that to Daniel. Instead he said, "What if I help out? If it's not technical work of any kind, I'll be able to do the physical work of bringing up the supplies."

Daniel said, "Great. Can you start tomorrow morning?"

"You bet. I'll be there."

Colin couldn't sleep that night just thinking about his ability to help. Would he panic when he got up on the roof? The building was an old Victorian, full of turrets and extensions and worst of all it was high.

The next morning, Colin's first job was to bring some material up to the roof. Daniel and his assistant were already up there tearing off the old roof. Colin took a deep breath and started up the ladder. He hadn't gone three steps when he realized he had a problem. Daniel saw him hesitating from his rooftop perch. He called down, "Colin, use one of those backpacks we have. Pack the backpack and you'll be able to use both hands on the ladder."

Colin called back, "Okay, good idea." But he took his time in loading the backpack and mustering up his courage to climb the ladder to the roof of the old building.

He was finally ready. He knew the best thing to do was to not look down at any time. Slowly he made his way up the ladder sensing rather than seeing the height he was at. The aluminum ladder tended to bend at the joint where it held the extension and the little bit of swaying that it caused sent Colin's heart leaping to his throat. He still didn't look down. When he got to the top, he unslung the pack and unloaded it, horrified to actually tote the materials to the two men working on the far side of the roof. He hoped they didn't think badly of him because he quickly started back down the ladder to get another load of material.

He had brought up three loads before he had the courage to call out to Daniel and ask, "Do you need me to bring the material over to you?"

Daniel seemed to sense the fear in his voice and said, "No, that's fine, Colin. We're wearing safety harnesses and you're not. So we'll come over there and pick it up. Don't worry about it. You're doing fine."

It was a heart stopping day for Colin. Each time he started up the ladder his fear gripped him like a bear trap but he forced himself to conquer it and to continue climbing the ladder.

By nightfall they had accomplished a decent amount of work. Daniel came down and told Colin, "Too dangerous to work up there at night. We'll go at it again in the morning."

His assistant piped in, "They're talking about rain tomorrow." That sent a chill down Colin's spine.

Daniel said, "We've worked in the rain before, we'll just have to be careful."

❀

If Colin had no sleep the night before he got much less that night. The thought of climbing that ladder in the rain terrified him. But he knew he had to go on. He had to do his bit.

While the morning threatened rain it was only cloudy. Seeing and probably sensing Colin's fear having known him all his life, Amos came out when he could and held the ladder steady for Colin. This gave him some confidence that the ladder wasn't going to slip while he was halfway up it.

By afternoon it was drizzling and the decision was made to keep working. At least until or if it came down harder. It did come down hard by two o'clock and the crew had to knock off work for safety reasons. They threw a tarp over the exposed roof keeping the inside of the building relatively dry.

Daniel and his assistant left and Colin lay down on the couch in the office and immediately fell asleep.

The streetlights were on when he awoke, and he felt much more rested. When he looked at the clock he realized that he had been sleeping for six hours. Sleep he badly needed.

He went home and ordered a pizza and had it delivered. He ate most of it with a beer. The physical work and his phobia had kept his mind off Ava and their dilemma. He resisted the temptation to call her because he had nothing new to say. He hadn't yet figured anything out and he didn't want a useless conversation that would confuse them both even more. They needed time away from each other to enable them to explore their own feelings and try to determine how they really felt about things.

The morning was cloudy but they went right to work extra early. Daniel had said that with any luck they may be near finished by nightfall. If not there wouldn't be too much work to do in the morning. In the meantime with the tarp over the bad part of the roof there was no more leaking inside the building.

By eleven o'clock the next morning they were finished and Colin ordered Chinese food and beer for a minor celebration. It seemed that Madsen's had stumbled through yet another crisis and was still operating. But Colin felt best about being able to do Daniel's mother's funeral. The long tradition of Madsen's service to Daniel's family remained unblemished.

31

Ava was heading for a meeting with her boss at the New York office. She had requested the meeting and her boss welcomed the subject of the meeting, namely how to handle Newsome Funeral Home. After she was comfortable and settled in his visitor's chair she said, "I've decided that I don't think it's necessary to have anyone else work the Newsome account. It's in my territory and I know the area best."

John Luger leaned back in his big leather chair, his gaze leveled on her. "Ava, I'm glad to hear that. I was a salesman once and I know I wouldn't like anyone else messing around in my territory. If that's your decision, I'm all for it." But then he hesitated and added, "Are you sure now that you are going to be able to compete against a friend? I don't want you to promise something you can't do. I know that you have a promising career with this company and others higher up feel the same way."

Ava had no way of knowing if this was true or not. Her boss was prone to exaggerations or anything else that would produce results for him. By heaping praise on her and hinting that higher ups in the company had their eye on her he was doing what he had to do to get her to perform.

When she left his office she was convinced that her job had been in jeopardy. It was more what was not said than what was.

But they were both smiling before she left his office. She had assured him that she would stay on the Newsome account and do everything she could to bring him into the fold.

The truth was that Newsome didn't have the money or assets to qualify for a franchise but he was being courted because American Mortuary needed to thwart Madsen's business. Ava had been worried about someone else moving into her territory. She knew it was a selfish motive but she felt she didn't want to lose the progress she had made in the company. She had been considered an up and coming executive but this Newsome thing might show her to be weak and unwilling to compete with friends.

She spent the next two days working in Boston, mostly from her downtown condo. She made it a point to stay away from Concord.

She had to push her relationship, or lack of relationship at this point to the back of her mind. American Mortuary was her new career now and she had to be very careful with every move she made. Colin didn't make his living from Madsen's but was involved only for the sake of his father's memory. She had a feeling that this wasn't a good enough reason to ruin her new business career. Ava convinced herself that if Colin really cared for her he wouldn't put her in an awkward position.

Now she had to go to Concord and dreaded running into Colin. She was so confused about her life and her relationship with him that she was in no position to see him. So she arranged to meet Will Newsome at La Boniche Restaurant and Café in nearby Lexington.

Newsome was in a good mood. He knew he was lucky that American Mortuary was courting him since he had nowhere near what was required for a franchise. And he knew they wanted to cut into Madsen's business.

When they were seated and sipping cocktails, Will said, "I'm surprised to see you back on the account. I know you got something going with Colin Madsen." He was wearing a leering grin when he asked, "Trouble in paradise?"

Ava's gaze was steely. "Will, business is business and has nothing to do with personal relationships."

"I'm glad to hear that. I know Madsen's is having trouble. I actually saw Colin up on the roof the other day helping the roofers fix it."

Ava's eyes dilated. "What? Colin up on the roof? He has a phobia about heights."

Newsome grinned. "I guess he had no choice. That's why now is the time to advertise heavy and put him out of business."

Ava said, "Look, Will. I know I work for a company that is competing with Madsen's but I have no intention of putting Colin out of business. There's enough in the territory for both."

"Are you sure your boss feels the same way?"

Ava's contempt showed on her face and he let her quickly change the subject knowing he was in no position to leverage anybody. He'd be lucky if American went along with him and franchised him without the required financing. But still he was enjoying what he perceived to be his advantage for the first time in his life over Madsen's, the darling of Concord.

His grin was as close to evil as he could get it and that look on her face ticked him off and skewed his better judgment. His bravado got the better of him and he had to say, "Yeah. Well my intention is to put them out of business. They've hogged the business in town long enough. Time for new blood."

Ava didn't want to get into an argument with him as she knew this was no way to handle a client. So she settled the matter by simply saying, "There's no reason why we can't compete fairly. We're not out to destroy anybody. We don't want that kind of an image in an industry that is based on sensitivity and compassion. So let's get on to the advertising budget and what we're going to do for the fall campaign."

Ava skillfully steered the conversation away from personal issues but when she left the meeting she was feeling worse than ever about things. Now her mind was filled with, *What do I really want out of life? Is it worth losing a wonderful man like Colin over business?* Then she got a bit paranoid and thought, *But then again isn't he risking our relationship for the very same reason?*

She headed home to Boston feeling worse than ever. *Colin up on a roof? Things must be really tight for that to happen. Yet my job is to see that this loathsome character Will Newsome gets as much of the available business in town as possible.* She made it a point to aim the advertising and marketing efforts for the out of town business. The new yuppie population now invading the suburbs of Boston. Of course, there were only a limited number of these new types in town. Most were the old established families so the business wasn't nearly as good as in a town like Concord with an elderly population.

While she didn't want to run into Colin she had a yearning to head to Boston and hang out by the harbor. She bought herself a tuna melt and a cup of coffee and took it down to a deserted bench on the harbor near a big rock by the shore. She was sure that she had a lot more thinking to do before she wanted to see him again.

The Boston Harbor was always a good spot to think. Ava looked out over the expansive water, bisected by docks, ships, and warehouses. The harbor seems intimidating, mainly because there are always ports with ships, tugs, barges, and commercial finishing boats plying the waters at all times—even in winter. Ahead, Ava could make out the silhouettes of the Boston skyline shrouded by thin gray clouds. The air was cool, but not overly nippy, and the water in the harbor churned as several ships passed by each other entering and exiting the Port of Boston.

Ava took a generous sip of coffee and swallowed it forcefully. She didn't want to make up with Colin simply for the sake of making up. She wanted them to understand each other. She remembered all their great times together, including antiques and the esteemed nineteenth century writer Henry David Thoreau.

She remembered the lively discussions about Thoreau's ideas about wanting to live life to the fullest and being independent. Isn't that what her and Colin's problem was? Colin could not balance her independence as a woman and as a businessperson and how that dichotomy interfered with his business. Wasn't it about whose life goals and dreams should be satisfied and whose shouldn't? Put that way there was no fair solution, but she knew she wasn't really sure what she wanted out of life. Sure, this corporate job was exciting and challenging but maybe that was only because she was comparing it to the only other job she'd ever had, which was teaching. And teaching in an environment where it was hard to be appreciated. Yet, why should she give it up? Would he give up his beloved Madsen's for her? She sipped her coffee and thought, *Maybe I'm being immature and overly sensitive. We never really discussed anything so serious. We have never even made a serious commitment to one another yet.*

She remembered something Colin had said about Thoreau that she didn't really know. He had said, 'I want to front only the essential facts of life and see if I could not learn what it had to teach, and not when I came to die discover that I had not lived.'

That suggested something deeper than what she had thought Thoreau was all about. She associated him with independence and that was what she hoped she was doing. Living an independent life. A life doing exactly what she wanted to do.

Did it actually boil down to she couldn't do what she wanted to do and that was this sales job without hurting Colin? After all, somebody, if not her was going to do the job and whether they did it as well as her or not, it would compete with him and therefore hurt Madsen's. Of course, they had never talked about it in those terms but she knew him well enough to know that she seemed to be a traitor in his eyes, though she believed he would never say that. Maybe it was even worse because he would feel it and not really tell her he was hurt about it.

So would the one who gave in be the martyr and give up what they wanted for the other? But wasn't that the essence of love? She thought about it. *Was love about giving up something you want for someone else?*

All she really knew was she wasn't a kid anymore and she hadn't found the love of her life until Colin came along. And she was thinking that Colin might very well be the lifelong quest. He might be the real thing. Her soul mate.

But if she went back and told her boss she was going back to her original decision and to give Newsome's to someone else she would be jeopardizing her career.

In a lucid moment she said to herself, *So what? There are other jobs.*

But then her thinking came full circle and she thought, *But why should I be the one to give up what I want? Would jeopardizing my career show my love for Colin as much as simply quitting the job? Why shouldn't he give up Madsen's for me? Wouldn't that show his love for me? Or was there any real fair and solid middle ground where neither of us will end up feeling like we had been taken advantage of?* Ava knew that wasn't a good basis for a relationship.

She truly missed Colin. She missed their relationship, their fun together, their genuine feelings for each other. But she couldn't get together with him today and tell him what she would like to do. Or for that matter what she would like him to do.

But she knew that Thoreau was about a lot more than independent thinking. She knew that he believed an ideal spiritual state goes beyond the physical or what a person knows through experience and what is most important is personal insight.

Hmmm, she thought. *So the solution is supposed to come to me naturally. Whatever feels best? But I don't know what feels best. If I give up my job will I be bitter and therefore blow the whole relationship? I just don't know. If I can convince him or if he decides to give up Madsen's for me will that make me feel good? I hardly think so.*

She finished her lunch, threw the empty bag into a trash can in the parking lot and headed back to Boston.

There was a message on her answering machine. It was Will Newsome.

When she returned his call he said, "I need to see you. It's important."

"Well ok. I'll be by on...uh Thursday."

"No good. Can I come to Boston tonight?"

She winced. Ugh. He went on. "We need to meet somewhere. How about the bar at the Ritz. Say seven?"

"Well, uh. Okay. I guess so."

After she hung up she regretted agreeing to the meeting. What could be so urgent? She would never want to meet with him anywhere but in a business environment but it was too late to change plans.

32

Ava didn't want to meet a guy like Will Newsome in any other place but a business setting with other people around. Yet she couldn't insult him and say no. He claimed what he had to talk about was important so she agreed for a meeting at the Ritz in Boston.

She was ten minutes late only because up till the last minute she was looking for ways to cancel the meeting.

The Ritz was old Boston. Rather than the sleek world of glass and stainless steel like the new Four Seasons, Westin and others the Ritz was more subdued in nature although ultra-modern in amenities. It was more brass, potted palm and polished mahogany which still maintained an almost Victorian elegance and charm. When a Bostonian said "meet you at the Ritz" there was no question about the location as everyone knew this Boston icon which was across from the Public Gardens and on the corner of Boston's equivalent of Fifth Avenue, Newbury Street.

Newsome rose from his barstool when he spotted her. She was dressed for business. Nothing like an evening out, but strictly business, a pinstripe black two piece suit with white silk blouse. Her makeup if anything was understated.

Newsome said, "I've reserved us a seat in the corner. You can order a drink or anything you like from there."

Ava opted for a drink as she was always nervous at first when meeting with someone. The expression "undressing with the eyes" seemed to have sprung from his leering gaze.

When he ordered a whiskey rocks she decided on a light white wine she liked, Riesling.

Newsome decided to wait for the drinks before he launched into the reason for the meeting. Meanwhile, they made light and awkward small talk.

When the drinks came he got down to business. He said, "I think you might be especially useful in this idea because I know you're tight with Madsen." She raised a brow, which asked, *how would you know that*, which he countered with, "I've seen you guys around town. My staff has seen you around town. It's obvious."

"I know your boss is eager to bring me under the American Mortuary banner and I have to admit it's tempting. But as you already know, I don't have the financing so you guys, wanting me so bad, are willing to give me the franchise on credit. Of course, I have some healthy monthly payments with interest to make but I think it'll be worth it in the end."

Her answer couldn't have been more non-committal. "I agree," she said.

"Now here's the problem. It's going to be tough for me to make those payments even though I know that being hooked up with you guys will be far better for me in the end. So I need some kind of....uh, shall we say, guarantee that I'm going to make it. If I don't make it with American Mortuary, I'll be closing my doors within two months. And I hate working for other people." This last remark came with a grin that Ava answered with only a polite half smile.

Ava sipped her wine and waited for the proposition. "Now I know Madsen's ain't doing so hot either. Remember, I did see Colin up on the roof helping a local roofer fix it."

"Believe me, he's struggling. He might even be in worse shape than me," Newsome said, not trying to hide the grin. "Imagine being so broke he has to do manual labor to help fix his roof." There was an awkward silence. Ava sipped more wine. "Anyway, here's what I'm proposing. Me and Madsen, through you, raise our prices together."

Ava quickly interrupted. "But that wouldn't be legal. Not only with us but that's a form of price fixing. Some people might even call it gouging."

He grinned. "Only in a technical sense. As I see it this way we both survive and when I, or both of us, is over the hump we can do what we like. Now of course there would be nothing on paper so both me and Madsen can back out of the deal at any time. I just think that Colin would be more interested in seeing his family business survive. In fact, more than me. With me it's only a business. With him it's a kind of...I dunno a kind of family heritage or something like that. Isn't that right?"

She looked away. "Probably."

She wanted to reject his sleazy proposition out of hand but she also realized that this might be one way for Colin to save his business. She knew how important it was to him.

"How would American not know how much you are charging?" she asked. "You know we have monthly financial sheets to be filled out."

"If you're handling the account who are you, or anyone else, to know, what we really charged for a funeral. American will still get their regular cut and I will be guaranteed survival. Colin and Amos may have all the in-town business, but I should get a lot of the outskirts and the towns along the industrial beltway."

"I could never do anything like that."

He ordered another Jack Daniels. After a quick sip he spoke earnestly. "Look, I kind of knew you'd react this way but you should be thinking about Colin and his plight. Besides, like I said, once we're over the hump we could do business any way we want. Meanwhile, I need American Mortuary's advertising clout to get me the business I need."

Again there was a prolonged silence. Both were thinking. He said, "I know it probably goes against your grain but it doesn't have to involve you really. As I see it you're not the person who reviews the monthly reports."

"I get a copy of them."

"Yeah, only to see how we're doing, but nobody has to know what we're charging for a funeral and that includes you."

"Price fixing is illegal."

"So what? You're not doing it. Who could ever prove you knew anything about it?"

When she said nothing, he said, "Right. Nobody. You should at least put it to Madsen. Let him decide."

"I know what he'll say."

"You think you know him that well, huh? But what you don't really know—not really – is what he'd be willing to do to save the family business and his father's legacy."

Ava's silence suggested that he was right.

He studied her as she gazed into her drink. "You have to suggest it to him. What do you have to lose? Who knows, you might not know him as well as you think and this would be a chance for him to save himself."

All the time he was talking, she was shaking her head.

Finally he said, "Well, I guess I'll have to put it to him myself. I really do think you'd be helping him more than you know if you proposed it to him."

"I don't see how. It's wrong. It's blatantly dishonest. And it's illegal."

"Baloney. When's the last time the Commonwealth of Massachusetts has investigated price fixing? They're so short-handed and over budget they can't afford to do anything like that. This is the time to do it."

As Ava wavered, Will waited. Then he said, "You've got to at least tell him about it. What he does is not your decision. Let him make the choice that might save his business."

'I suppose I can do that. But I can tell you right now what the answer's going to be."

"Maybe that's true. But then again maybe it isn't."

Ava spent the rest of the evening at home deep in thought. Here she wasn't even speaking to Colin and she was supposed to put this proposition up to him. *What would he think of me then?*

Yet on the other hand she realized that she was only the messenger. Whatever Colin decided to do it wouldn't be her decision. It would be his. But she couldn't imagine him going for it. Then she was beginning to think that she was understanding the depth of Colin's commitment to Madsen's. Who knows what he might do to save it. Is it the son's fault if he doesn't wish to follow *in* his father's *footsteps*? Of course not. But that was the practical side of it. There was an emotional side too. That's the side she wasn't able, at least not at this point, to figure out.

Ava got very little sleep that night. Newsome said he would call her by the weekend to see what she had decided. She was hesitant to approach Colin only to give him this idea of Newsome's. She wanted to reconcile with him on their own terms.

She then got into an argument with herself. *Is this business, this corporate rat race what I really want anyway? Is it worth pursuing if it comes between Colin and me? Now that I think about it, it actually has already come between us! And now this. Getting involved with an immoral sleazy businessmen.*

Most mortuary people she had met while in the business were decent but occasionally like every other field you will find a Will Newsome. Colin's father, though, was outstanding for his devotion to his profession and for the good he brought to his community.

Now the only question was, what about Colin?

33

Colin had enough. He missed Ava and he wanted to try to mend things, so he called her at home on Saturday. There was no answer. After calling three or four more times during the weekend he decided she must not be home. *Hmmm. Where could she be?* It was one of the longest weekends of his life. He hung around mostly thinking. But nothing came to mind. Finally, Monday morning came and he got on the phone to her office in New York.

He was anxious as he dialed her office number. His heart was pounding and he had no idea what he was going to say to her other than he wanted to see her. She never answered. Only her voice mail, so he contacted the receptionist. "Could I speak to Ava Hewitt please? When I ring her, the phone goes right to voice mail."

"Oh," the receptionist said, "I have to check the computer." A minute later she said, "I see that she's on some kind of leave."

"What kind?"

"I'm afraid I can't tell you that, sir. If you want to come in and talk to her boss he might be able to help you."

Colin had no intention of talking to her boss, that she had evidently gone on leave was enough for him. He went over to her house. The door was locked, there was mail in the mailbox, newspapers on the porch and her car was gone. Baffled, he drove over to her sister's house.

She might or might not have known about her sister's problem but she was honest. "She was very mysterious, Colin, she didn't tell me or anyone else as far as I can tell, where she was going. She just said, not to worry. She had things to think about and she'd be in touch."

All kinds of things went through Colin's mind. *Did she quit her job? Did she find out about Debbie?* He couldn't go to work as upset as he was so he called in for his remaining vacation time balance.

Without thinking he found himself at Madsen's. He didn't want to tell Amos his problem but he did need someone to talk to.

Seeing Colin was down, Amos took him to the arrangement office.

At one point Colin could see the old man had something on his mind. "Colin, I know you're in a dilemma but if you are not going to be a mortician I don't see how you can protect the future of Madsen's. Eventually it will pass on to a stranger and your dad's memory will fade. Not with everyone mind you but only a few remaining old folks will remember him. That will not make your father's legacy any less noble in this town."

Colin didn't answer for a while. "I...I haven't made up my mind yet, Amos. But don't worry about anything right now. You're going to be here as long as you want. That I can assure you."

"It's not me I'm thinking about, my boy. You can't carry on a legacy you have no natural inclination for."

"I know, Amos. I know."

After their conversation, thinking the unthinkable, Colin decided to call Will Newsome on some pretense, only to find out that he was out of town and his employees didn't know or wouldn't tell where he was. Colin did a mental double take at that information and decided he needed someplace peaceful to think.

Later, sitting alone at home he wondered, *It couldn't possibly be. Could it?* He could think of nothing else but finding her. He thought of the lake and the conversations they'd had there. He remembered once when they were talking about their heritage and how they had been affected by growing up and coming from Concord, Massachusetts. Ava had said, "After all, this is the home of Thoreau, Emerson and Hawthorne." She went on, "Louisa May Alcott and a lot of other great thinkers, all the great transcendentalists. In those days Concord was the Mecca of philosophers, especially those who thought outside the box. Those who in modern times would be considered radical and dissenters."

He jokingly remarked, "Yeah, the hippies of the nineteenth century."

"No," she said, "they were much different. They thought more about human values and man's place in the universe. Let's face it. We have dissension in our blood. We march to a different tune."

He remembered chuckling at the image and reckoned it was only Ava acting out what she perceived as her heritage as a native of Concord in some mystical way.

Is Ava dissenting now? Has she gone to seek some deeper inner truth? He slammed his hand onto his knee in frustration. Where in blazes was she?

That's when her mailbox came to mind. Maybe there was a clue there. He knew this was serious business, a Federal offense actually but he didn't plan on telling anyone who caught him that he was taking a friend's mail.

He drove to her condo complex. The townhouses had mailboxes on poles in one place.

By now the mailbox had more mail. He quickly grabbed it and hopped in his car and took off. In a mall parking lot he went through it. Nothing but bills. He was sinking lower by the minute. Then his eye caught a logo on one of the envelopes. It was the blue and red of MasterCard. On impulse he opened it and scanned the billing. Sure enough, there were gasoline charges in New York, Delaware and Virginia. There was also a hotel bill in Richmond, Virginia. Did she know anybody down in Virginia? He didn't recall her ever talking about friends or relatives in Virginia. Now he was more baffled than ever. But one thing was clear. *She drove down South. But why? Was she alone? Did he have any right to try to track her down?* The Richmond charge was a week old. What would be the chances that she would still be there? Nonetheless, he telephoned the hotel only to find that they gave out no information whatsoever about their guests. For all he knew she might still be there. He noticed his knee pumping in anxiety. His impulse, as foolish and hopeless as it might be was telling him to drive to that hotel in Richmond.

He went home, packed an overnight bag, and telling nobody headed his car south for the Massachusetts Turnpike.

At two in the morning he checked into the Old Southern Hotel in Richmond. He was still wound up and couldn't sleep. But going downstairs to question the night clerk might him seem odd and he wanted their cooperation so he decided to wait till morning.

He hadn't realized how tired he was and he slept till ten the next morning. He went downstairs and ordered breakfast, scanning the dining room for her. But there was no sign. Knowing they wouldn't give him any information he went to the desk clerk and said, "Would you ring Miss Ava Hewitt's room for me?"

The clerk went to his computer and made an entry. He gazed at the screen and turned to Colin. "I'm afraid she checked out more than ten days ago, sir."

Colin's jaw dropped. He simply said, "Oh, I see," and ambled off.

There was no point in staying, so he checked out. A half hour later he found himself sitting in his car staring blankly at the windshield. Well, it was a dumb idea anyway. His gaze fell on the pile of mail and he sorted through it again. Nothing. He sat gazing blankly. Once more he sifted absently through the letters. Only one wasn't a bill with her name looking at him through a cellophane section of the envelope. It was written by hand and had no return address although he did see the postmark was Florida. It was a letter from a real estate agent in Naples, Florida. It said she was sending available listings over the Internet.

Bingo!

She was in Naples, Florida and looking for a place to live. He started his car and picked up US 95 for Jacksonville. There he would turn southwest and head for Naples.

He arrived late that night and found himself a motel room. In the morning he got directions for Seacoast Real Estate in nearby Marco Island, an upscale community on Florida's west coast. But he knew he was going to have trouble getting any information on Ava's whereabouts. So he didn't set out for the real estate office. He had to devise a plan first. He had to sit and think up some way to do this. Parking his car by a nearby beach he sat on a bench watching the rollers wash ashore. An hour later, nothing had come to mind. He could stake out the real estate office but that seemed hopeless. No, he had to think of something.

By twilight he had found himself hungry. He had wasted half the day deep in lethargy produced by his exhaustion and despair.
He went to the closest restaurant he could find which turned out to be an American Pancake House. Pancakes, eggs and bacon seemed to hit the spot better than a steak and the meal along with two cups of coffee renewed his energy. He decided to book another night at the motel and try to find some answers in the morning.

But like most days in his life morning only brought another sunrise.

He sat on his bench at the beach and kept gazing out to sea, tired of trying to find a solution. It was only at this point that a realization came to him. *What if she doesn't want to be found? Especially by me. That would be very awkward.* And worse, he was not ready for any bad news like she was leaving him for good.

He was about as deep into the abyss as he could sink when an idea came to mind. It wasn't perfect but it was an idea. And it just might work. He went back to the motel, his spirits ratcheted up a notch or two.

34

It wasn't until Colin got to the post office did he realize that he hadn't thought his plan out very well. He asked the clerk, "Can I have an Overnight envelope and a Priority Mail envelope until I figure which one I want to use?"

The clerk gave him a frustrated look and said, "I can give you the Priority envelope which is guaranteed three-day delivery, but for the overnight you have to fill out a form and with that you are guaranteed delivery before noon next day. That's ten dollars and fifty cents. The Priority Mail is four fifty."

"Okay well then give me the Priority, please."

He planned to go to a Staples and buy a rubber stamp kit in which he could make up the return address. U.S. Treasury. And they could type her address on a piece of paper which would fit into the cellophane portion of the Priority envelope. He was too paranoid to go in and do an overnight with a U.S. Treasury return address. He was sure it would get him into trouble. So although he would like to have it delivered the next day he had to opt for the three day Priority.

At Staples he made up the U.S. Treasury return address and had a single sheet of paper addressed to Ava Hewitt c/o Seacoast Realty 1330 Ocean Blvd, Marco Island, Florida. His hope was that the realty people would consider this an important document and either call Ava to come get it or deliver it to her. Either way he had a good chance of finding out where Ava was living. Of course, there was no correspondence beyond the note from Seacoast Realty. He had to understand that she might not have done business with them and had gone to another Realtor. If that was the case his only hope was to drive the streets aimlessly like Don Quixote on an impossible quest of trying to spot her car and license plate. This was a heavily populated area. Not likely.

He wrote a note on the reverse side of the sheet of paper. "Ava . I'm here in Naples. Please talk to me." He included the name and address of the motel where he was staying.

He went to a different post office, bought the proper amount of stamps and put it in the Priority Mail slot.

Now his only choice was to stake out Seacoast for three days and see if Ava showed up. It was going to be impossible to determine if they either forwarded it on to her or called her to pick it up. He might have some chance if someone from Seacoast delivered it to her. He'd follow them or Ava. He didn't want to confront her in a parking lot of a strip mall, so instead he would try to follow her home where they could talk. That is if she would talk to him.

Next morning he bought a breakfast sandwich and coffee at McDonald's, parked in the strip mall parking lot making sure he was amongst other cars and settled in for what could be a three day wait.

As he sat there munching on his sandwich and sipping his coffee he wondered, *How nuts am I? I'm actually a stalker now. I can't handle an adult problem without becoming a stalker.* He was getting down on himself so he concentrated on the life of the strip mall and waited.

He knew he hadn't known the meaning of boredom before until he had spent a full day at the mall and saw the Seacoast people lock up and go home at five-thirty.

When he had to find a men's room he panicked, fearing he might miss her. So for the first day he held it in until after five-thirty. But the second day he knew he couldn't do that again. It was too painful. So he found a restaurant four doors down from Seacoast and parked in front of it. He would go in and buy a sandwich when he needed to use the restroom. Even in that brief period of time he worried he might miss the mail delivery.

As he sat there he wondered, *Does the regular mail carrier deliver the Priority Mail too or is that a separate carrier? More things to feed my paranoia.*

On the third day of the wait Colin was ambivalent. On the one hand he knew if he hadn't missed the mail carrier, it had to be today. On the other hand, he feared he was going mad waiting in this parking lot for three days.

It was afternoon and he was hungry but didn't dare eat. It would be just his luck that the mail would come. Colin sat up straighter when he spotted the mail truck. He kept his eyes glued to the Seacoast office. He would have used his binoculars except he was afraid of attracting attention. About a half hour later a young woman with blonde hair wearing Bermuda shorts emerged from the office. She had something in her hand. It was a piece of mail. He couldn't tell if it was or was not his. He had to take a chance. Besides, if he had any more waiting he'd go mad. He fell in behind her car, a Ford Escort. He followed her until they got to the bridge connecting Naples with Marco Island and he nearly lost her there at a red light. He took a chance and ran the light and managed to keep two cars behind her. It wasn't too long before she turned off the main thoroughfare and headed up a beach road filled with cottages and condos. In a while she stopped in front of a cottage and walked up to the door and rang the bell. He sat across the street. His heart was thumping. When nobody answered the bell the young woman slipped the letter under the door and left.

This was a crucial point. Should he assume this was Ava's place or go back to the real estate office? He decided to wait.

Around seven, with the sun beginning to sink into the sea, Ava showed up. She was carrying something that looked like a large framed picture. She leaned it against the wall while she fished out her key.

Colin wondered, *Should he just go up to the door? That was bound to frighten her. Or should I try for her phone number and call her? Come to think of it why hadn't I tried for a phone number before?* He slapped his forehead with his palm. *Well, Dick Tracy, looks like you learn the hard way.*

Colin decided to wait until she had a chance to read his note and simply knock on the door. And that's what he did.

She was dressed in black shorts and a white halter. Her hair was kind of wild. Not like her usual well coifed look. She stood there in bare feet and gazed at him. Tentatively he asked, "Can I come in?"

Ava said, "Of course." She motioned him to a veranda that overlooked the ocean. He sat down. She sat opposite and gazed at him. "How in the world did you find me?"

"It took some detective work and well, you know," he said, trying to be light. "Us Concord people come from a long line of folks who think outside the box."

She looked like she wanted to grin but she veiled it.

Colin said, "I just have to straighten things out between us. One way or the other."

"You mean there is one way or another?"

He guessed he did make it sound kind of final. He quickly said, "No. That's not what I meant. I know how I want it to come out and, Ava...well, I've missed you."

"I missed you too."

He wanted to say, *But I'm the one who came looking* but decided against it.

She cocked her head and kept looking at him. "It's just so damn amazing. You found me. I don't know if I should be miffed because you're invading my privacy or be thrilled that a man cares so much that he would go to these lengths to find me."

Colin was beginning to get hold of himself. "I know it's taught me one thing."

"What's that?"

"I know I really love you, and that there should be nothing so powerful that it can come between us."

She started to say something but hesitated. "I was going to grill myself a steak tonight, but I have more than one. Would you like to join me?"

He simply nodded.

"Okay, I'll fetch them and the potatoes. I'll get the wine and set the table on the veranda. It's cool enough to eat outside, but the bugs can get pesty."

"Whatever you think."

"Okay, on the veranda it is."

He was thrilled. At least she hadn't screamed and thrown him out!

They had grilled steak, baked potatoes, green beans and a bottle of local wine.

They simply ate and didn't talk about anything serious. Colin said, "I see you brought in a picture."

"Yeah, I've been going to the local auctions and following ads on the 'net for some interesting stuff. If you look over in my bedroom you'll see a lot of stuff already piled up."

He almost didn't want to ask but did. "What do you plan to do with it all? Ship it home?"

"No," she said.

"I plan to open a store down here and be an antiques dealer."

"So you're giving up your corporate job. They said you were just on leave."

"That was my boss' idea. I actually quit but he said he was going to leave the door open if I wanted to come back so he officially said I was on leave."

"I know what your questions are, Colin. I'm trying to find my own way. Not that I planned to abandon you. I just wanted to find out what I really wanted to do with my life. I thought I had a great reason for leaving teaching, but I also found out that the corporate world is full of deceit and overly large egos."

"So you are doing this so you can find out where you fit in life."

"Exactly. I was going to see how it goes, make some kind of decision about it and then get in touch with you. Of course, I was hoping you'd still be around and wouldn't dump me for someone like Debbie. And of course, I still have no idea what you have planned for the rest of your life. If you want to stay at your corporate job and I want to stay here I guess life will have made the decision for us. So while I'm trying to find my way I think you should, not only for my sake, but for your own decide what you want to do with your life."

His heart plunged. He wondered if she knew about Debbie and whether or not he should tell her.

"Debbie?" he said, losing eye contact.

"Yeah, I saw how you two looked at each other. I understand that I have competition."

"I wouldn't have gone through this to find you if I wanted to be with someone else."

"I see what you've done. And I'm impressed. But that still leaves us with our same old problems. What do you do about Madsen's and what do I do about a career?"

"Why should those things separate us? Most spouses don't care too much where their husbands or wives go to work. As long as they go and bring home a paycheck."

She thought about that for a moment. "So you're talking marriage? When did you plan to propose?"

Colin was adamant. "Hell, I'm ready to propose now. I love you, Ava. I don't want to go through my life without you. Or live wondering what I did wrong."

Ava dropped her head. Tears welled. He went to her and took her in his arms. Her tears were salty. "What...what are we going to do?"

"Let's talk about that tomorrow. Tonight I just want to be with you."

35

Colin parked his car in downtown Concord, near Lexington Road and decided to walk to the funeral home. Too excited to sit, he needed to walk and expel some energy. Everything with Ava had been resolved. She made him feel like nobody else had before.

The weather had become colder after a couple of weeks in the mid and upper 50s. A light snow had fallen overnight. Passing through Concord, the chill forced Colin to breathe into his hands, making them clammy and cold, only to repeat the process a few times because the cold had taken over again. As he kept walking, he did love the way in which the snow on the ground and the smell of the air made him want to lock down his senses in a jar.

A vibration from his pocket startled his thoughts. He opened the cell phone only to hear Paula start talking.

"Colin, it's me Paula. You need to come to the funeral home fast. There's a man from a real estate company from Cape Cod here with Owen and he has a paper in his hand saying that he now owns the funeral home."

Paula sounded like she was garbling her words as she spoke.

"Paula take a deep breath."

"Just get here Colin, and fast."

Coming down the alley behind the funeral home on Thoreau Street, Colin decided to walk around the funeral home and the adjoining property. He blinked twice at a large shadow that disappeared. In the parking lot of the funeral home, a dumpster stood in the middle of the parking lot filled with debris. Folded scaffolding and tools were strewn throughout the lot. Colin stepped over the sidewalk curb and noticed that the Hewitt home had been demolished.

A large, burly man with a pointed nose and wide face dragged a hose to the rear of the house, where the back porch once stood. He sprayed a wide, thin stream of water on the ground as large puffs of disturbed debris dust rose around him. Another man, tall and sinewy with a narrow waist pointed to the other side of land for the man to move to another corner on the lot and keep spraying.

The ground, dark and soft, and devoid of a structure, looked like a scar. Colin didn't realize how much space the Hewitt house occupied until he stepped back into the alley. The amount of space would allow the funeral home to greatly expand their parking lot, if and when the money became available. Colin ran through the soggy ground covering the bottom of his shoes in a ring of mud.

He raced around the side of the funeral home to the front door. He stopped after passing the front door. Looking through the window, he saw Owen and another man facing Paula and Amos holding a long sheet of paper in the air. The paper swayed back and forth as the man jabbed it with a pencil.

Colin walked in, nearly out of breath. "What's going on here?"

"Ah, you must be Colin Madsen. I'm Anthony Phillips from Bayview Real Estate in Cape Cod. I'm going to be the new owner of Madsen Funeral Home."

Colin locked eyes with Anthony Phillips. He was tall and broad-shouldered, with a mop of dark hair with heavy, solemn brows that were offset by a boyish grin. A pair of eyes the color of sea glass gleamed behind square-framed glasses that kept slipping down his long nose.

Colin looked over at Paula, and she flashed a pained expression. Amos sat in the chair, hands folded and resting on his lap. His pious demeanor made Colin nervous.

"I don't understand," Colin said. "I own this funeral home. Amos and Paula are the staff that operates it. I have no plans to sell the funeral home."

"I'm afraid it's too late for that," Owen said. He looked at Anthony briefly then swiped the yellow paper from his hand. "Remember when you did your little disappearing act and you came back to apologize to Paula? Something you said caught my attention. You mentioned that you did not want me as a partner in the funeral home because Dad's will had you listed as the majority shareholder of the funeral home. Then, it hit me. I've never seen Dad's will. You never let me look at it before. So, I went to the probate office in the Concord courthouse and got a copy of the will. I wanted to make sure that you were not bluffing me on the shareholder percentages as a way to run me off. Well, I was surprised to see that you had one year to take ownership of the funeral home or the state would take the property to settle the estate."

Anthony cut in. "I believe the deed said you had until February fourteenth of this year to make a decision. And guess what day it is?"

Colin bent forward and placed his hands on his thighs, balancing himself. Colin cut a quick look at Amos, whose face twitched as he spoke. Owen picked up where Anthony left off. "It's February 13th and it's the last day the Madsen family will own the funeral home."

Amos stared at the floor as a tear trickled down his cheek. Paula stood alongside Amos, coiled her arm around his neck and rubbed his shoulder. Her eyes were wide and hard and her lips trembled as the anger and hurt of the situation rested in the wrinkles of her face.

Colin felt his hands cringe and a chill ran down his spine.

"Your brother Owen has been a friend of mine for a while," Anthony continued, his voice higher and more playful than before. "He showed me the deed. That's when I decided to hire him to work for Bayview Real Estate and assign this as his first real estate transaction."

Colin looked at Owen and flared his nostrils, taking several deep breaths. Seething, he spoke through gritted teeth. "So, this is a business arrangement to you, Owen? Damn you! This is our business! The business that our father built, our legacy!"

Colin pointed a finger directly at Anthony. "And you know nothing about funeral service or how to run a funeral home and neither does Owen. Who is going to be responsible for making removals, and making arrangements with families, and embalming, and leading processions to the cemetery? Not you two, that's for sure. I may not know everything about running this place, but I sure know more about it than you two do."

Owen smacked his lips and looked away. "Yeah, well, a few weeks ago you made it clear to me that the funeral home was *your* legacy and I didn't have much to do with it. Colin, you didn't want to go into business with me so I found someone who did."

Anthony nodded and slapped Owen on the back. "I'm prepared to make a generous offer for the property, Colin, and as a gesture of good faith, my company tore down the Hewitt home and absorbed the costs of demolition. Mr. Boggs here said that removing the building was a pressing need of the funeral home."

Colin didn't look at Amos this time, but heard him softly add, "I'm sorry Colin. When he presented me the deed and explained to me what had happened, I told him everything about our financial challenges and the Hewitt home."

"And," Anthony added, "I plan on offering Mr. Boggs and Ms. Matthews here an opportunity to stay with the funeral home as long as they would like. The community of Concord needs their talents and expertise and experience."

The words stung. Colin had assumed he would have time to rectify the situation. Instead, he pursued Ava and never set a specific deadline for doing something about the funeral home. Now it may be too late.

Colin looked at the smug grin Anthony gave Owen as Owen looked at Colin with a glare of pity. Colin thought about Ava, thought about Will Newsome and American Mortuary and what he had witnessed and observed over the last several weeks. He watched as Amos and Paula, no matter what, delivered compassionate service to the families they served, and delivered it in a meaningful and professional manner that exceeded expectations. Madsen Funeral Home had offered service with dignity and respect, delivered without distinction of social, cultural, or economic background. He thought about Daniel Jackson who had to be turned away because of the leaking roof and how much hurt was on his face. Service second to none. That's what his father always noted about the funeral business. What Owen and Anthony were proposing was not an extension of service, but a takeover.

As soon as the word 'corporate' crossed Colin's mind, Owen got another jab at his brother. "Oh, and another thing. American Mortuary has also expressed interest in taking over the funeral home. I also understand they are closing soon on the purchase of Newsome Funeral Home across town. I can assure you that we have the option of selling to American Mortuary for a large sum of money and everyone will benefit."

"No! No! I won't allow that to happen," Amos said, standing and shaking with anger. "American Mortuary is a large corporation that has a board of directors. The pressure is on the funeral home to grow profits year after year. Families in Concord will end up paying more money and receiving less value for their funeral services."

Owen regarded him for a moment then looked back at Colin. "Amos tells me Colin that you have put some of your own retirement money into the business." Owen slipped his fingers under Colin's chin and searched him with his eyes. "If we sell to American Mortuary, you get that money back and more. Then, you can be an accountant in Boston or retire, or run away with Ava Hewitt. Your life will be worry free."

Amos scoffed. "This funeral home has a long, proud history of personal service provided by a local family with deep roots in this community. I will not stand for it becoming a place run by a corporate chain. If that's what happens, if you two take this place and sell it to American Mortuary, then I'll leave and I'll make sure nobody else darkens the door to Madsen's. Word of mouth is still powerful."

"Me too," Paula interjected, chest extended and head cocked. "If Amos leaves, so will I."

Owen dropped his head and his face grew darker. "Then so be it. We will have our money and what happens to the funeral home after that will be American Mortuary's problem."

Colin took a deep breath and felt his resolve stiffen. "No. This is not going to happen. You two have no intention of keeping Madsen's. You want to buy it and sell it to American Mortuary for a big profit. I know what's going on here. It's the same thing that will happen to Newsome's. American Mortuary will keep the Newsome Funeral Home name on their business because they know that at a family's greatest time of need they are more likely to turn to a local name they recognize. But the place will be different. Neither you nor American Mortuary can guarantee that Amos or Paula will be employed here if the place is sold. That's unacceptable. Luke Madsen would not stand for it and I won't either."

Owen raised a hand. "Colin, I don't think you are thinking this through completely and objectively."

Colin crinkled his face and clenched his fists. "The hell I'm not." His eyes darted back and forth like a fluttering breeze at Anthony and Colin. When his eyes crossed the paper in his arms, Colin went for it."

"Give me that deed!"

"No," Owen replied. Colin grabbed for it and began tugging at the paper.

"I want it Owen, now give it to me!"

Owen clenched the paper tighter in his hand as Colin pulled in the other edge of the deed. Paula gasped and Anthony pleaded for them to stop. "Quit! You two are going to tear it."

Colin clenched his fist again and reared back with one hand and swung. He hit Owen hard on the jaw. Owen yelped and winced in pain. His momentum carried him backwards and Anthony caught Owen as he slid onto the ground. The deed hovered in the air for a moment before landing, crinkled but not torn, between the men.

"Oh my," Paula said.

As Owen moaned on the ground in pain, Anthony lightly slapped his cheek. "Owen, Owen, are you all right?" He looked up at Colin. "I can't believe you punched him!"

Colin scoffed as he scooped up the deed. "I know. The nerve of some people." Colin knelt down in front of Owen as he massaged his jaw. Garish purple splotches, roughly the size of a fist, spread across his jaw and neck. Owen froze and looked at Colin from the corner of one eye, expecting another punch.

"Dad would be ashamed of you," Colin said ruefully. "I still own sixty percent controlling interest in the funeral home and I still have one day left to settle with the state and that is exactly what I plan to do."

Colin glanced at Anthony, whose mouth gaped. "Mr. Phillips, please bill us for the cost of the demolition of the Hewitt property."

He rose up and looked back at Amos and Paula. "Please escort these two people off of our property and if they do not leave, call the police." Colin winked at them. "I need to get to the courthouse before they close. Madsen Funeral Home is staying just as it is."

36

Ava walked into the bedroom with a sandwich bag loaded with ice. She looked at Colin lovingly as she lifted his right hand. His eyes became slits as a he sucked air through his teeth and bit down on his lip. "Be easy."

She rested the ice on his swollen knuckles and hand. "This is going to hurt for a while, but you need to reduce the swelling. I can't believe you punched Owen, but it sounds like he deserved it." Ava held the bag on his hand and tenderly stroked his fingers.

Colin laid back on the pillow and stared at the ceiling while the cold ice began to numb the pain in the hand. Ava said to him, "So now do you know what you want to be when you grow up?"

He smiled. "I don't know. I haven't lived long enough."

"But God only gives us so much time on this earth. We can't take a lifetime to decide."

"You're right. Okay, I won't be coy about it. I kind of know what I don't want to be anymore."

"Me too."

"So why don't we start living our lives."

"Uh," Ava said somewhat cautiously. "It seems to me that I remember something about marriage? Something about you making an honest woman of me so that I can take you home and sleep over in my old room."

"Ohh yes that," he said. "Wait here a minute." He pulled himself up from the bed and dashed off into the living room. The bag of ice tumbled to the floor. Ava picked it up and held it overhead, counting the number of ice cubes that remained solid. She was impatient, not knowing if he was purposely making her wait.

He was. He waited, grinning,, peeking around the bedroom door as she kept looking up at the ice bag. Finally he jogged in.

He had his hand behind his back and he didn't immediately show her what it was hiding. He kept up the pretense, asking her questions that needed no answers. She was squirming with anticipation. "What is it you silly goof?"

"I hope you like it." Looking a bit worried, he handed her the Tiffany box. "I want you to be my wife if you'll have me."

Looking at the box, her jaw slack, she opened it. The diamond sparkled in the sunlight.

She gasped. "How did you?" He slipped it on her finger. Holding her hand at a distance she admired the ring. A single solitaire diamond set on a gold band, it was exceptional by any standard.

"Where's my notebook?" she murmured.

"What, you're going to put in another characteristic?"

"Yes. Great taste. How in the world did you manage..."

"When I told my boss I was ending my leave and leaving the firm, he suggested that I do something with my retirement account, so I cashed out my company 401k . I know what I want to be when I grow up."

She smiled. "I think I know what it is."

Becoming serious he said, "I have come to realize that I'm not my father. And he wasn't his father. I can still honor his memory and love him and carry on in his footsteps. I never really realized that before. I was sure that I had an obligation to carry on his life's work *exactly* as he did. He is remembered and loved all over town. If I could do that I would consider myself a success. But I can't do it by being him. I have to be my own person and do things my own way."

Ava said, "I'm finding too that one has to be happy in their work or it becomes drudgery. I don't think I can ever get bored hunting down pieces of Americana and the antiquities. There's always such an interesting story behind each piece and a world of imagination too. One could only wonder what that particular piece has been to someone, someone who was influential in this world. It's just a fascinating profession. And I only recently rekindled my attraction to it. How about you?"

Colin seemed to already have a reply right on the tip of his tongue. "Until now, I never really gave it too much thought. I just gravitated to the thing I seemed to do best in school, which was math, and decided it would be my life's work. And when I think about it at the end of the day what have I done? I've successfully added and analyzed some numbers to some higher up's satisfaction. That's on a good day. On a bad day I can't make the numbers add up. And all I get out of it is frustration. I know life can't be a bowl of cherries but it should be as close to something fun or interesting as possible. And I've learned that helping others during a difficult time of need is quite rewarding."

"Life's too short, Colin. We should try to be as happy as we can while we can. I'd love to open up an antiques store. It doesn't have to make a fortune. But I don't think there will be a boring day in it."

"I couldn't agree more. But now I have to explain things to the community about Madsen's. I've been trying to keep the place above water for all the wrong reasons, none of them valid, but all based on the false premise that my father won't be respected unless I keep his business going just as he did. Well, he is respected in his own right. He doesn't need me to make people remember and respect him. Instead, I need to make sure the principles of business and people that he stood for continue."

Colin added, "Legacies are funny things. We make them and hope they follow us through life. But if they don't you're in another life and that legacy is no longer necessary."

Ava agreed. "That's true—and you can't be responsible for others or their life choices. Amos understands that you are not a mortician in the conventional sense. I'm sure he does. In a way he looks at you as the son he never had and you joining him in the business has him thrilled. People are different and we all can't follow the dreams of other people. You know the old song if a man has one good friend in life he is blessed. Well the same goes for your life's work. It isn't something to be thrown away on things like legacies. Each person has or should have their own ambitions and life dreams and they shouldn't have to worry about when dreams change. Even if it is your beloved dad. He'd be the first person to want you to be happy in what you do."

Colin kissed her and said, "Are you sure you want to give up the glamour of the corporate world?"

"More than sure. I was just comparing it with teaching. Yeah it's different from teaching yet the only satisfaction is racking up good sales numbers. Other than that you are doing nothing useful. At least in teaching, as bad as it was, every once in a while you come across a kid that you are able to help and that's a turn on. One of the biggest thrills I had in teaching was seeing one or two of my pupils succeed. And I don't mean just academically. I mean as a person. Leave the pack of adolescents who live only for their next thrill and do something useful. Reach out and help someone. That's what I consider a success. Not bringing someone from a C average to a B average although that miracle is welcome too."

Colin was thoughtful. "Why do we have to do things we're not crazy about before we find what we'd like to do?"

"It takes courage to start something new," Ava said. "Start all over. I know people who spend their whole lives trying to figure out what they want to do and never do. They just stick with what they have because they have responsibilities and need to make a living. You have to be blessed to truly find what you want to do and actually do it."

Colin was deep in thought again. "I think it's never too late and you have to consider this. What if you fail at the thing you love?"

Ava said, "I don't consider that a tragedy. How many people even get a crack at doing what they'd like to do? If you fail, start over again. Don't give up. That's the way I'm looking at it."

"If you put your heart and soul into something you like to do, how can you fail?" Colin asked rhetorically. "I'm not going to let Dad's lifetime work just fade away. It employs good people. I'm going to carry on the tradition of caring and compassion and be a true service to the community. As a matter of fact, Amos and I are going to be looking for an apprentice; someone that he can take under his wing that is interested in the funeral business. We can sure use the help when we get busy. I'll do my best to find that person."

It had been an emotional outburst by the two of them and they knew that a new threshold had been reached and that life was going to change for the better. They also knew that they now had a direction. No more wondering and no more feeling guilty.

Energized by the talk of a new future they felt a burst of energy so they walked hand in hand into the living room, Ava careful of her new ring, holding it high and making sure it was safe.

The next day, Ava went home and gathered her laptop and printer and began researching business property for rent in Concord as well as looking at interesting antiques that might be good items to sell in her store.

She found a spinning wheel in Georgia and a set of silver plates supposedly done by Paul Revere in New Jersey. A Connecticut man had one of Benedict Arnold's childhood toys for sale. Or so it was purported. Ava emailed him, negotiating such a good price that it would be profitable whether authentic or not, just as a period piece.

The ideas kept coming all their way and each time a new one popped up they were like kids with the new concept, as if no one else had ever thought of it.

Ava talked nonstop about the antiques business and her goals for her own store. Ways you could authenticate things, places to look for items. Participating in auctions. Holding auctions. Their minds were percolating with ideas that kept on coming.

With her education background Ava had some ideas on involving students at every level on archeological digs like the one now going on in Virginia where they were trying to locate the exact and authentic location of the first Jamestown settlement. Imagine the thrill of digging up pieces of American history. Finding a piece of pottery from the first English settlement in America. It was all fascinating for them.

37

On Monday, Ava and Colin each called their relatives and friends and announced their marriage, which would be at the end of April.

Colin had been the actual owner of the funeral home for just a few days. He had Amos and others from the community of Concord, including Daniel Jackson, and some other families gather in the front office of the funeral home. He had pizza and soft drinks served and everyone was expecting something. Colin had already talked to Amos and told him of his plans to keep Madsen's. Even though there would be increased competition from Newsome Funeral Home now that American Mortuary owned the business, Colin assured Amos and Paula that attitude and reputation, and service would guide the funeral home into the future.

Ava had been right. You can't control the choices of others, but you can make sure that you do your best in all situations in life.

Colin and Ava had decided to live in his father's house and they would rent a shop for their antiques business right down the street from Madsen's.

"So," Colin said, "I want the community of Concord to know that I'll always be around for that broken plumbing or anything else I'm needed for." A tear formed in his eyes as he said, "Not to mention be near the dearest friends and family a man could have."

As the applause grew and Paula began distributing refreshments, Colin looked for Ava. Down the hall, Colin heard her voice coming from one of the parlor rooms. Colin went down the hallway and stood behind Ava as she held her phone to her ear and covered the other ear with her hand. His stomach sank. Colin thought she had changed her mind.

He sobered up when she began speaking. "I just have something to tell you about one of the franchisees that you might not know."

A pause ensued. "I warned you about Will Newsome. Yes, he'll be a pain in your butt. But you need to know John that he's got a scheme, one you would never agree to but Will wanted to price fix. American Mortuary would be in a world of trouble if the Attorney General's office found out."

Ava covered her mouth. Colin could hear muffled words through the phone, but couldn't make out the words.

"Well I think that's best for all," Ava said. "I don't like to betray a confidence but when it comes to illegal stuff I follow my conscience."

She turned around and saw Colin watching her. She smirked. "And John, thank you for the opportunity."

Ava closed the phone and tossed it on the chair. Colin went for Ava and wrapped his arms tightly around her waist and nuzzled her neck for a moment before pulling away. "What was that about? Everything okay?"

Ava kissed Colin lightly on the lips. Her eyes searched his face and she stroked his hair. "Seems that Will Newsome went on a bender for the past two weeks and nobody at American Mortuary knows where he is. My old boss says American Mortuary is reviewing their purchase agreement of the funeral home."

Colin let out a quick chuckle. "Serves him right. But enough about Will and American Mortuary. We have only a brief period of time to prepare for the wedding."

Ava leaned back for a moment, taking him in. "Then there is furnishing the new store, stocking it and as always the requirements of Madsen's."

His voice grew low. "I like the way you think Mrs. soon-to-be Colin Madsen." With that he kissed Ava again. "I think we need to get back up front. We have plenty of things to celebrate."

As the party continued and Colin moved through the crowd like a seasoned politician, Ava pulled Amos aside. She had something on her mind. She said, "Amos, I don't want you to ever think that I talked Colin out of Madsen's because I didn't."

Amos immediately put up a protest. "No. I never."

"I just don't want you to ever think anything like that. Colin was as lost as I was about the future. Neither of us were doing what we wanted and he felt guilty at first because he had no calling for the mortuary business."

Amos smiled. "I knew that, Ava. I didn't want to push him one way or the other. But I did try to keep things going which I could not have done without his help. He pitched in wherever he was needed. He's a stand up kind of guy that way."

She smiled back. "Yes I know. We've learned more about each other in the past month and a half than we had known since we were kids."

Amos said, "Aye, I never wanted Colin to feel he had to take over. But I did need him to keep the building together and the operation going at times. Owen would never step in the way Colin did. In fact, nobody would have done what Colin did. He bought out Owen's share of the funeral home and found money to take care of all the problems with the building and the equipment. For that I am grateful. This place has been the best part of my working life and I would feel terrible if it went out of business because of these problems. If it weren't for him Madsen's would have had some blemishes on our record. We all feel those blemishes would dishonor Luke, God rest his soul."

With a wide smile, Amos said, "I'm just glad the time was right for him and for us."

Ava said, "I'm glad you feel that way, Amos."

Amos cocked his head. "Are you sure you're ready to be the wife of a funeral director? You can ask my wife, it's not always easy."

Ava smiled and tapped his cheek. "I'm ready for all of it."

Amos nodded. "The best way to preserve Luke Madsen's legacy in this town is for you two to make sure Madsen's goes on under the same name with the same level of service and compassion as always. I'm not going to be around forever, but I will rest easier knowing that you two are here."

Ava took the old man's hand. "I'm so glad you feel that way Amos. Colin wouldn't want it any other way."

"One more thing, Amos. I came across something that is not only valuable, it is a part of Concord as well as American history."

Amos cocked his head in curiosity. Ava reached in her bag and pulled out a piece of tissue paper. She handed it to Amos. Inside was a musket ball with some markings on it. "I found this in my antiques search. It was in an old barn in Lincoln, down the road. I had it checked every way possible. Carbon dating, everything. See the two nicks in the middle? I have authenticated that this musket ball was taken from the body of one Daniel Cooley at the battle at the North Bridge. It is a piece of history and I would like it to have a place of honor in the chapel. People can come and see it and read the inscription.

Where it was fired and who it was taken out of. I think it will give Madsen's another special place in the hearts of the locals."

Amos was stunned. A tear welled in his eye. "This must be worth a fortune on the market," he said.

"Yes, it is valuable but I think it will be more valuable at Madsen's, which is as much a part of Concord history as anything."

Just then Colin came in. He knew nothing about the musket ball, and when Amos told him, Colin said, "I knew I picked a winner. I don't see how I can fail."

Acknowledgements

The process of writing a novel is often solitary, but I'm grateful for the support and encouragement of many people who supported the idea to write this book and coaxed me forward when I became distracted.

I want to thank my editors Mike Valentino and Kristine Reardon of Arizona Edit for their guidance and for reading through several versions of the manuscript and always offering constructive criticism. I also want to thank Sandy Tritt for reminding me of the power of words and the strength of a strong narrative.

Several fellow writers were also generous in supplying advice and encouragement, including: John Herrick, Amanda Eyre Ward, John Patrick Grace, Marie Manilla, Laura Tracey Bentley, and Carter Taylor Seaton. These talented writers are also dear friends, and their friendships mean more to me than words can express.

I want to thank the Concord, Massachusetts Visitor's Bureau for helping me with the research of the local shops, cemeteries, and places located inside their beautiful town. Also, the staff of the Massachusetts Department of Tourism and the staff of the Massachusetts Department of Transportation provided with me help regarding roads, distances, and locations between places.

To my former classmates and the faculty in the Bluegrass Writers Studio at Eastern Kentucky University, I give you my praise. All of you have shaped and impacted me as a writer and teacher, and I thank you for always believing in me, even in those moments when I don't always believe in myself.

I also want to thank my Dad, Brent Parker, who will always be my hero and was the best funeral director I've ever seen. His warmth and compassion for grieving families coupled with his business acumen made him the perfect funeral director. To my Mom, Tonya, and my brother, Evan, thanks for supporting me and carrying on Dad's legacy.

A special thank you goes out to all of the funeral directors and their employees who work tirelessly to help families get through the death of a loved one. Much of what they do is not visible to the public, but their kindness and love for other people is what makes the funeral business a strong, dignified, and necessary profession that helps so many people each day.

To the staff of Cunningham-Parker and Johnson Funeral Home, I want to say thanks to all of you for all you do for the families you serve and for being a part of my extended family.

Finally, I want to thank you, the reader, for reading this book. With spare time being such an important commodity today, I thank you for spending some of that time reading my book. Your time and devotion is very much appreciated and not taken for granted.

Readers Guide

1. One of the key goals for Colin Madsen is to ensure that Luke's pristine legacy as a funeral director in the community is maintained. How are Luke and Colin alike? How are they different?

2. Despite the fact that Colin works in the accounting profession where deadlines are important, he ignores the threat of having the funeral home taken by the state of Massachusetts. Knowing the risks of the decision, why do you think Colin ignores the deadline for so long?

3. When Colin returns to Concord and the funeral home, everything appears to be going well. Colin soon discovers that the funeral home is in financial trouble, leading to a crumbling building and faulty equipment. Why do you suppose that Amos and Paula never contacted Colin or Owen sooner regarding the problems the funeral home was facing?

4. Describe Colin and Amos's relationship throughout the novel. Is Amos justified in being upset with Colin when he heads to Florida to find Ava? Why does Amos ultimately forgive Colin?

5. Despite the fragile financial conditions plaguing Madsen Funeral Home, Amos helps out Will Newsome by providing funeral home supplies to Newsome Funeral Home. What does this say about Amos? Why does Will jeopardize that relationship by stealing money from the funeral home safe?

6. Discuss the role of Paula Matthews in the novel. How does her terse demeanor influence the events that take place in the novel?

7. Colin and Ava have a complicated relationship throughout the novel. Even when Colin learns that Ava has taken an acquisitions position with American Mortuary, he doesn't end the relationship. Discuss the influence that Ava has over Colin in the story and why, despite her behavior and actions, does Colin continue to pursue a relationship with her.

8. Throughout the story, Colin excludes Owen from many of the decisions concerning the funeral home, even though Owen is part-owner. Is Colin doing this to punish Owen in some way, or do Owen's actions and behavior justify Colin's behavior?

9. During one scene in the novel, Colin refuses to provide funeral services for Mary Stover and her family, despite insistence from Amos. Discuss the importance of that scene. How does this influence Colin's behavior through the rest of the novel? Does this give some insight into how he might operate the funeral home as an active owner?

10. How is Ava able to manipulate Colin throughout the novel? What do you suppose are her ultimate goals for doing so?

11. Discuss the importance of Madsen Funeral Home in the novel. As a primary setting for the story, is the funeral home a symbol for something more than just a business? Why or why not?

12. The theme of secrets is an important one in the novel. Several characters keep secrets from one another, which often cause problems for others. Which secret do you find the most problematic? Why?

13. How do you think Amos's relationship with Luke impact his relationship with Colin throughout the story?

14. Discuss the role Will Newsome plays in the novel. Is he in anyway a sympathetic character? Why or why not?

15. Did you have a favorite character in the novel? Which character did you find the most surprising and why?

www.ingramcontent.com/pod-product-compliance
Lightning Source LLC
Chambersburg PA
CBHW031952010726
47493CB00007B/2171